Pickin' Tomatoes

Pickin' Tomatoes

a novel with recipes

J. W. Bull

To Mom—
Maggie's co-creator and my inspiration.

To Curtis—
"Mister Right" and my best friend.

Acknowledgments

Many thanks to Linda Chung and Ken Barton for believing in me, Linda Hines for being the best editor in the world, Mike Bailey for providing wonderful graphic art, and 52 Novels for formatting and designing *Pickin' Tomatoes*.

Chapter One

"Seize the moment. Remember all those women on the Titanic who waved off the dessert cart."
—*Erma Bombeck*

BECOME A COLUMNIST!

Cooking and Women is holding its annual writing competition
Submission Guidelines: Write an article of 200 words or less comparing finding Mister Right to cooking. Include an original recipe.
Qualifications: You must be single and have experience as a chef.
Published writing is a plus.
Deadline: 5:00 p.m. ET, July 1, 2011
Grand Prize: $2,500 cash award and the chance to have your own monthly column, "Cooking and Men."
First Prize: $500 cash award and two-year subscription to *Cooking and Women* magazine.
Second Prize: Autographed wooden spoon from Martha Stewart and a one-year subscription to *Cooking and Women* magazine.

Finding Mister Right is…

I pause to consider this and come to an immediate conclusion.

Downright impossible.

What am I doing? I can't type that. I crack my knuckles, hit the backspace key, and begin again.

Finding Mister Right is...

I glance around the kitchen for culinary inspiration and a pile of dirty dishes in the sink sparks my imagination. Hmm. Finding Mister Right is like washing dishes. Just when you think he's squeaky clean—bam! You find dried up, crusty old egg on him. Somehow, I don't think that's what *Cooking and Women* wants. A culinary muse, a culinary muse...*Aha!* My eyes fall to an empty Stouffer's frozen dinner box lying on the counter. Okay. Finding Mister Right is like cooking a frozen dinner. You've got to nuke him to warm him up.

I groan. It's no good. I can't focus. The problem is I need a recipe and I don't cook. *Cooking and Women* is not a magazine I would normally buy. There I was, standing in the grocery store checkout line yesterday, when my eyes were drawn to the cover. The magazine stood alone on a rack, a smiling, middle-aged woman embracing a large basket of handpicked greens on its cover. But that wasn't what caught my eye. It was the three little words printed to the left of her: *Become A Columnist!* They seemed to be beckoning to me, Maggie Malone. *Become a columnist and you'll make lots of money. Become a columnist and your life will change.* I was mesmerized.

A moment of clarity burns off my brain fog and I see the solution to my problem. Of course, *The Atlanta Journal*. They'll have a recipe. I toss aside *Cooking and Women*, grab a few pages of the morning paper, and thumb through them. Business. Arts. Want ads. No thank you, I am sick and tired of looking for a job. Food. Recipes. Salsa. Perfect! I'll just insert this recipe for salsa—with a few changes, of course, to avoid plagiarism—and voila, I'll have it, the winning entry. I scan the recipe, and make an interesting discovery—it calls for canned, not fresh tomatoes. Fresh tomatoes, it explains, are more watery in consistency and weaker in flavor.

Finding Mister Right is like choosing the right tomato for your homemade salsa. Yes, ladies, you may think you want a firm, ripe, fresh tomato that will give your salsa zest...

Zesty zest, like the kind you'd have with Brad Pitt. Now that man has some tomatoes!

What is wrong with me?! Concentrate!

```
...that will give your salsa zest and new life.
But that same young, firm-fleshed tomato might
get bored with your salsa and run off with
someone else's onion.
```

I lean back in my chair and study my daughter, sleeping soundly in her bassinet, her red hair spiked out like porcupine quills and her tiny porcelain hands snuggled close to her heart. It amazes me she can sleep with her thumbs tucked in. Oh, Catherine, my very own "Kitty Cat." I am so blessed to have given birth to you. Yes, you poop every hour and yes, you seem to want to permanently attach yourself to my breast, but don't all newborn babies? And what of your perpetual crying? It's just indicative of your sensitive and artistic nature, I'm sure. I plunk my forehead down on the keyboard and big crocodile tears spill from my eyes over being so blessed. An alarm on the computer sounds and I raise my head to gaze at the blurry screen.

```
someone else's onionnnn
```

I sniffle and strike the backspace key repeatedly, my middle finger beginning to cramp. *You can do this. You have just as much chance of winning as anyone else.* Forget the chef part. Forget the published writing part. Forget the damned credentials. I am highly motivated! Hello, money!

```
Fresh tomatoes, although pleasing to the eye,
can give you watery salsa. Ladies, when it
comes down to tomatoes and men, the everyday,
canned variety is better. Mister Right might
be a little boring. He might even be slightly
lumpy. But he has potential if you spice him
up. And chances are, he won't run away with
someone else's onion!
```

```
Mr. Right Salsa
Ingredients:
```

```
1 (16-ounce) can diced tomatoes with basil and
oregano
1/2 bunch cilantro, chopped
1 small Vidalia onion, chopped
1/2 jalapeno pepper, seeded and chopped
2 teaspoons lime juice
garlic salt, to taste

Combine and serve with chips.

Happy hunting for Mister Right!
-The Chef of Hearts
```

I start giggling. The Chef of Hearts. That's good. I like it. I scroll on down to the "About You" section.

```
Name: Maggie Thompson
```

Wait! I'm not Maggie Thompson anymore. I'm Maggie Malone from now on. Well, sort of...

```
Date: July 1
```

I glance at my watch. 4:50 p.m. *Whoops.* Cutting it close to the deadline.

```
Chef at...
```

A name. A name. I stare at the pastel purple walls. Not a very kitcheny color. The purple paint magnifies the seventies avocado-colored countertops and the peeling veneer of the dark cabinets. What can I say? Surrounding myself with a soothing color during those last tough weeks of my pregnancy seemed like a good idea at the time. Besides, painting was therapeutic.

Lavender...lavender...laven...My best friend, Justy, lives in France. She and her husband have a restaurant. Why not take advantage of that?

She'll back me up for a reference. A speedy google search of Paris restaurants reveals the perfect name: Lavande Restaurant!

```
Chef at Lavande Restaurant, located in Paris,
France
```

Now for my age.

```
Age: 35
```

Give or take five years.

```
Marital status: Single
```

I'm getting a divorce soon. That means I'm single, doesn't it? *Yeah, definitely single. My stinkin', rotten tomato ran off with my neighbor's onion.* Snap out of it! My life wasn't bad. Disappointing maybe, but not bad. If only someone had given me a recipe for a successful life with an ingredient list for happiness and detailed instructions on how to achieve it.

My daughter certainly deserves the perfect recipe for success. Then she wouldn't have to worry about turning into a version of me. Who aspires to be a forty year-old, about to be divorced, jobless woman with a baby?

```
About You

Name: Maggie Malone

Date: July 1

Previous cooking experience: Chef of Lavande
Restaurant, located in Paris, France

Age: 35

Marital status: Single
```

I quickly scroll over to the purple square near the bottom of the page. Submit article. Click and done. Exit window. No chance to chicken out.

Chapter Two

"In the end, your creativity—perhaps even your outrageousness—will determine the final result."
—Bobby Flay, chef of Food Network

10:08: Check Microsoft Outlook. No mail.

10:10: Check Microsoft Outlook. Empty.

10:11: Check Microsoft Outlook. Nope.

I have got to stop this obsession with checking my e-mails. I'm like an e-mail junkie. Have a sip of coffee, check my e-mails. Walk across the kitchen for more sugar, run back and check my e-mails. It's sick. But in my defense, it's been three weeks since I sent off my submission to *Cooking and Women*. Three whole weeks and zippo. Nada. Nothing.

Gnawing away on the lone, ragged wisp of cuticle remaining on my thumb, I entertain the idea of logging off my computer. Who needs e-mails anyway? Certainly not me. It's not like I don't have self control or discipline. Maybe just one more peek…*No!* I log off and shut my laptop cover.

See? I'm fine. I am not an e-mail junkie.

Yes, I am. Somehow the screen is open again.

Some people say patience is a virtue. Why that's just fine and dandy. I'm not one of those people. Hello, my name is Maggie Malone, and I'm proud to be an impatient member of the frequent cuticle chewer and e-mail checker club.

• • •

An hour later, after smelling a pungent odor in the air and figuring it has to be me, I take a shower. A long shower. An uninterrupted shower, with the exception of popping my head out from behind the glass door every couple of minutes to monitor Cat's activities. But she's had her morning mommy latte and seems content to snuggle in her bassinet, staring at the black and white thingamabob swinging above her head. Wouldn't that be nice. I can't remember the last time I did just one thing at a time. Women are just natural born multitaskers. Shampooing hair while simultaneously scouring prehistoric mildew from wall tiles. Or ironing, painting fingernails, watching a soap opera, and rocking a baby carrier with a foot while talking on the phone.

Have you ever asked your husband to multitask? And watching the Golf channel while throwing darts doesn't count. It could be something simple like taking out the trash while drinking a beer. Toss in doing the bills or mowing the yard and good Lord, he's over the edge.

I remember one time asking my husband Richard to help me with a fundraiser. My mom died of breast cancer when I was six, and I was eager to do my part to find a cure. I was really excited because if I got enough people interested, I could host a *Passionately Pink for the Cure* event.

"Okay, Richard, you take this stack of fliers and put them in the neighbors' mailboxes. I'll take the rest and hit the neighborhood across the street, plus I'll go around Lake Norman and get some of those houses too."

"I'm on it." Richard lifted a stack of fliers off the desk and walked towards the front door.

"Oh! I almost forgot. Can you take a couple of these posters and put them on the clubhouse bulletin board? And maybe tape some to a couple of stop signs too. People would see them there." I rolled up a few posters and put them on top of his stack. "You know, what about a couple down by the tennis courts too?" I handed him a few more. "And here's some tape. Got to have the tape."

Richard sighed. "Posters. Right."

"And if you don't mind, put one of these magnetic bumper stickers on your car too, okay?" I draped a sticker over his shoulder. "I really appreciate this, honey. You know how much this means to me."

"Uh-huh," he grunted, struggling not to drop anything.

"And remember to get gas. You mentioned you need to fill up. I'll run by China Wall and get takeout…actually, now that I think of it, if you're out and about, can you copy off some more…"

"Margaret!" Richard exploded.

"Okay, okay. Just put the fliers in the mailboxes. That's good." I took back the posters and tape and propelled him towards the door, but not before I tucked one poster under the crook of his arm.

A woman could always hope.

Nope, Richard definitely wasn't a multitasker. Dad wasn't either. Always the professor, even at home. Never involved with the little details of life. But when mom died, he did try to step up to the plate. Sure, there were lots of wrinkled clothes, frozen dinners, and missed dance recitals, but I never once doubted his love for me. He'd drop everything for his little Mag-pie and I knew it.

Men. Go figure. They are what they are. I guess it's up to us ladies to pick 'em. I just wish I'd picked an Heirloom tomato like Dad instead of Richard the roaming Roma.

I'm shaving my legs when Cat cries out, startling me. Forget one leg is shaved and the other isn't. Forget the little river of blood trickling down my shin and swirling into the drain. Motherhood calls. Perfectly shaved legs are overrated anyway. I step out of the shower, grab a long stream of toilet paper, and plug up the flow of blood just as the phone rings. Wrapping a pink, threadbare towel around me, I rock Cat's bassinet with my toe and answer the phone with my free hand.

"Hello?" I bend over Cat and pull up her doggie tee shirt.

"Yes, is this Maggie Malone?" a woman inquires.

"You're my little girl. Boo booboo." I blow on Cat's tummy with a juicy mouth.

"Hello? Hello? Are you there?" the woman persists, her voice chopping each syllable.

"Oh, sorry. Yes, I'm here. This is Maggie Malone." I lift Cat into my arms and sniff her tush.

"My name is Peg Winthrop, special pub…"

"Oh, Cat!" I explode. "I just changed your dia…excuse me, I didn't get that. You're who?" I quickly put Cat back into her bassinet.

"Peg Winthrop, special publications editor from *Cooking and Women* magazine," she clarifies, drawing out each syllable. "You submitted an entry in our annual writing competition. I'm calling to inform you your 'Mister Right' salsa recipe has won the grand prize. It will be featured in our September issue."

Catherine scrunches up her mouth in a jack-o'-lantern expression. Red streaks across her face. I know what's coming next, and I rock her bassinet back and forth, faster and faster with my foot.

"My article? No! I can't believe it! I mean yes, I can believe it, but… oh, that's wonderful!" Hello, prize money! Hello job! I dance a little victory dance. *I won, I won, I won.*

"However, before we hire you as a columnist, we would like to see an expanded sample column based on a fictional reader's letter. If it meets the board's approval, you can then begin work on a monthly column called *Cooking and Men.* We pay by the word for freelance work with the possibility of a salary if the column takes off."

My body halts mid-dance. What? I'm not the winner yet? At that precise moment, Catherine lets it rip. A full-fledged, blood-curdling scream. Like the kind you'd expect from Jamie Lee Curtis in the movie *Halloween.* Whatever possessed me to watch it on Netflix last week? I'm still having nightmares.

I place Cat on the dingy white bathroom rug, all the while quietly singing a nursery rhyme, *"the itsy bitsy spider…"* Cat's scream morphs into a series of sounds reminiscent of a donkey braying. "Ahhhh! Eee arhhh! Ahhhh! Eee arhhh!"

"Hello? Hello? What is that incessant noise? Is that a baby crying? An injured small animal?" Peg asks, her own voice crescendoing in sync with Cat's donkey cries.

"No, of course it's not an injured animal, it's a baby. It's my, uh, my niece." I reach for the ever-present diaper bag.

Hiccups accent Cat's donkey cries, producing an interesting beat box effect.

I giggle at the thought of a donkey singing rap. "I'm babysitting for my sister today." Diaper off.

"You're not married are you? You do realize we are looking for a single woman's approach to this column. Although both single and married women will be sending in letters, we think someone who is going through the whole dating process herself will have more appeal to our readers."

"Well, that's me! Single as can be and cooking up a storm." Wipe, wipe, wipe. I slap on another diaper. Done! I could be a world record holder in diaper changing.

"Any articles published?" Peg queries.

Cat's cries dwindle. She expels a theatrical, quivering sigh worthy of Violetta's last dying breath from *La Traviata* and she is reborn, oohing and aahing.

"Articles? Uh, no but I've always…"

"No articles. Books?"

"Well, not exactly but…"

"No books. I see."

There is a dramatic pause that leaves me wondering just what this woman sees. Why must people do that? Leave you hanging in anticipation? The silence, taunting you with possibilities, like a cluster of grapes dangling just out of a starving person's reach. I hate it when someone does that. Let me tell you how I really feel. I hate it.

"Yes, well perhaps it won't matter," the woman concludes, magnanimously offering me one measly grape of hope. But then she blows it by adding, "Or maybe it will. We shall see. Regardless, write the expanded column and e-mail it to us when it's ready. A sample reader's letter with some sort of a relationship issue, and a response comparing cooking to men. Be sure to include an original recipe. If your column is up to par, we will notify you and you would begin work immediately."

"Wow. Peg, it all sounds so wonderful. Thank you so much for consider…"

"Yes, yes. Now, my e-mail address."

My mind is overwhelmed. I feel like I'm drowning in reality. A fan letter. A response. A recipe. Peg's e-mail address? My brain kicks in and I swim to the surface. "Your eee-mail address. Just a minute, let me grab a pen." My eyes dart around the room. I jump up from the floor, grab my lipstick, and begin writing on the countertop. "Peg at cooking and women dot com. Got it. And thank you so much for…"

"What's the number for the restaurant you worked at in Paris?" Peg demands out of the blue. "I googled it and couldn't find it anywhere on the internet."

"Um, that's because…" I think quickly. "It's not…It's a small restaurant. You know, a favorite of the locals." A number…a number…*Justy's number!* "The phone number is 33-1-43-28-88-98. And thank you…"

The sound of a dial tone interrupts and I stand there, stunned by the turn of events. *How am I going to pull this off?* I snap out of it and begin to dial. "Justy? It's me…Yeah, great thanks…No, Catherine's wonderful. She's lying right beside me, sucking her thumb…I was thinking around her birthday in July…Yeah, a nice time for a baptism. She'll be a year old by then. I'll let you know the date…Just, I have a favor to ask you. Someone from a magazine called *Cooking and Women* is going to call you…you read it too? Yeah, I saw that article. I never knew a bowl of chili could prevent PMS. And did you read about—oh, never mind, just listen. Someone's going to be calling you about the chef who used to work for your restaurant, Lavande…I know your restaurant's not called Lavande! Focus! We don't have much time."

• • •

The fabrication of a lie is like a cough. It can be a one-time cough like the clearing of the throat, or it can be a chronic condition that haunts you. The kind that tickles your throat every few minutes and if you don't cough, you feel like you're going to die. The kind that comes more and more frequently until all you're doing is coughing.

I hope I'm not going to have to get into that kind of lying. I am, by nature, a semi-honest person who tells white lies only when backed into a corner, so to speak. Like the time my friend, Cheryl bought a new winter coat. Rather than tell her she looked like a woolly sheep at Disco Dynamite, I lied to protect her feelings. "That curly white furry stuff gives you a kind of foreign flair." Or when, after seventeen years of marriage, my husband had an affair with our next-door neighbor's wife. And God knows who else. Maybe that perky blond teller from Sunshine bank on the corner of Fifth and Main. So rather than tell him I loved him—and that I always would—I lied to protect my feelings. "I stopped loving you long ago Richard. It's over. Get out of my life. Oh, and the baby we tried so hard to conceive? The reason for all those fertility drugs? I guess it wasn't meant to be. End of story, Richard."

Okay. Maybe I do have a chronic condition. The lies are hacking away now like the croup. And to top it off, I have just lied to the editor of *Cooking and Women* about being a chef, being single, and not having a baby. I look down at Cat, asleep in my arms, and I realize that none of it matters. I need this job. No, it's more than that. I need a new life.

"*And the itsy bitsy spider went up the spout again*," I whisper.

Chapter Three

"Let books be your dining table,
And you shall be full of delights.
Let them be your mattress
And you shall sleep restful nights."
—Author Unknown

Dear Chef of Hearts,

My boyfriend snores horribly. The doctor says
it's from his allergies. The more I gently remind him to stop snoring, the more he says I'm
harping. Now all we do is fight over it. I'm
tired and my boyfriend's annoyed with me. How
do I find my way back to his heart and stop him
from snoring?

Girlfriend of a Snorer
Atlanta, Georgia

    Snoring. A universal problem affecting millions of women. Whose boyfriend or husband doesn't snore? Man, I write good stuff. No wonder my article piqued the attention of *Cooking and Women*. All I need now is an analogy to cooking and a recipe. I've done the salsa comparison. I certainly can't compare snoring to making a frozen dinner. *Think, Maggie, think*. No, not Maggie, The Chef of Hearts. I am The Chef of Hearts.

Able to dissect problems with a single paring knife. What the heck is a paring knife any way? You always hear about cooks using a paring knife. Do they cut pears with it?

Snoring…snoring…Definitely something I know about. Richard snored like a banshee. I thought I'd get used to it at some point. But after three months of interrupted sleep, it all came to a head one night when we were on our honeymoon.

"ZZZ-Zzz-ZZzzz-hckGGuggh-Ppbhwoo-zZZzzzZZZ…"

"Richard, sweetheart, you're snoring," I attempted to mumble as I smacked my dry lips together. It was 3:15 in the morning and we'd been drinking all night at the casino while we played slots and Blackjack. I felt like my body had been stuck in one of those food dehydrators you see on the Shopping Network.

"Wwhhhooeeeoooooheeeoooh…"

A train whistle. How creative. I lifted my hand and patted his shoulder. "Richard, darling, turn over on your side. You're snoring."

Richard flopped over, facing me, and the sleep rumblings began again. Only this time, it was the train whistle and a gale force breath of rancid gin. "Wooshhhhh…"

I lifted my hand and wacked him in the shoulder. "Richard!"

The train came to a stop, the wind died down, and there was silence. Blessed silence.

Then a solitary, phlegm-y, pig like snuffle. "Harumphhh…"

I waited. And waited. I knew it was coming again. Maybe not. My eyes began to close, then flew open. What the hell was that?

"Click. Click. Clickety click. Om nom nom…"

What was he doing? I forced myself up on my elbow and stared down at him. He was chewing and biting in his sleep. Who does that?

And the rumbling cadences began again. "ZZZ-Zzz-ZZzzz-hckGGuggh-Ppbhwoo-zZZzzzZZZ…Wwhhhooeeeoooooheeeoooh…Harumphhh…Om nom nom."

Oh my God. I had just acquired a lawn mowing, whistle blowing, pig snuffling, night chewing husband.

I glared at him. A newlywed should not feel this way. Where was the lovey-dovey-ness, the passion? If I couldn't sleep, he shouldn't be able to sleep. An idea began to form. I reached down, grasped a curly chest hair and jerked it.

"Argh!" Richard yelped.

I threw myself back on the pillows and closed my eyes, trying not to giggle. Hello, sleep.

A warning whimper drifts out of the baby monitor and I glance at my watch. Cat's nap is almost up. I have maybe two minutes if I'm lucky.

```
Dear Girlfriend of a Snorer,


Have no fear. The remedy for snoring is a sim-
ple, nonmedical cure known secretly to women
for generations and generations. Please do
not divulge this remedy to the male sex as it
would affect the sleep of women worldwide. The
remedy for snoring is...
```

Never sleep with a man. True but not feasible. Sometimes you've got to sleep in the same bed.

```
The remedy for snoring is...
```

Pinch a man's nostrils together and cover his mouth. Okay, not a good idea to suggest murder. This is no good. My creative juices have dried up. I need guidance. A recipe. A cookbook. I need a brain transplant. Just the other day, I was looking at a book from Barnes and Noble about a woman who wanted the government to pay for a lobotomy for her. She claimed…wait, Barnes and Noble!. They'll have loads of cookbooks. Maybe even a French cookbook. I am a chef from a French restaurant after all. I'll just buy a cookbook tomorrow, try out a few recipes, pick my favorite, and I'll be good to go. A bona fide chef.

Cat fires up her hunger squall and I bound up the stairs. I wish I could submit the recipe for breast milk to *Cooking and Women*. Now there's something I know how to make, and I don't have to know how to cook to do it.

• • •

Barnes and Noble—a veritable literary maze. Winding my way through the aisles, sidestepping fellow lost customers, all I can think is how much I miss small bookstores. Like the kind in the movie, *You've Got Mail*. I think the bookstore was called The Shop Around the Corner. You could share a cup of coffee with Meg Ryan while she picks out the perfect book for you, cuddles your baby, and asks how you're doing. Of course, in that movie, the big bookstore also put the quaint, personable bookstore out of business. But still. It's the principle. With big bookstores, the customer is lost geographically and emotionally. Yes, there's quantity and variety, but it's hard to find the book you want and there's no one to bond with over the whole book buying experience.

I guess I should just be grateful to be in any bookstore today. Bookstores are disappearing like peppermints in a candy bowl. Pretty soon there won't be any more left, and all the browsers and readers will have is an empty bowl. The Internet may be like a giant candy dish full of temptation, but it's not refreshing like bookstores.

I take a hard left in the maze and finally emerge in an aisle where rows and rows of cookbooks and reference books on cooking line the shelves. A woman wearing a gray flannel jumper over thick woolly tights strides by me in her brown Birkenstocks.

"Excuse me, ma'am? Do you work here?" I call out, placing Cat's carrier on the floor.

She pivots, tucking a used tissue into the top pocket of her jumper. "Yes, I do. Can I help you?"

I glance at her name tag and smile at her hopefully. Maybe she's like Meg Ryan. "Yes, uh, Gail. Can you recommend a good cookbook or reference book on cooking?"

"What type of a cookbook do you want?"

"Oh, just a good one,"

"I'm afraid you'll have to do better than that," Gail retorts as she whips out a pair of tortoise-rimmed glasses like a shield against my ignorance. She plants them on her nose, adjusts them a bit, and strides towards some books. "Ah, how about this?" She plucks Rachael Ray's, *30-Minute Meals* from a shelf and offers it to me.

"Oh, I've heard of her, I think. Yeah, I'll take that." I stretch out a hand for the book, but Gail has already shelved it. I'm beginning to sense she is not Meg Ryan at all.

"Or you might prefer Giada De Laurentiis's, *Everyday Italian*," she comments, as she partially slides out another book.

"Sure, why not." Once again I reach forward but the book is gone—back on the shelf. The woman's hair-sprayed bob is like a silver helmet, impenetrable, as she defends her stash of literary treasure.

"Or, perhaps you want the basics, like Irma Rombauer's, *Joy of Cooking*," Gail muses, deftly removing a thick white book.

This time I don't even engage. I know better than to spar with this woman. Surprise, surprise, she shelves that one, too.

"Hmm. And then, of course, there are the classics like Julia Child's, *Mastering the Art of French Cooking*," she declares, wonder of wonders, offering me the big red book.

Is it a trap? Dare I take it? I stare at the book and feel as if a golden light has appeared from above it. I hear a voice singing Handel's Hallelujah Chorus…*Hallelujah. Hallelujah. Hal-le-lu-jah!* I take the book from Gail's hands and open the creaky cover. "Wow, this is ex…"

"Perhaps not." Gail reaches for the book as if to snatch it away.

It *is* a trap. I slam it shut on her fingers. We have a small tug-of-war before she turns around, facing the shelves once more. The battle for a cookbook is not over. Gail's finger buzzes across the shelf, relentless now in its pursuit of culinary pollen. "What about Paula Deen's, *The Lady and Sons?*" Gail attacks, now personally invested in my purchases. "Or *The Silver Palate* by Rosso and Lukins?"

She is a swift and admirable foe, but no match for me. I have my cookbook. "Nope, this will be fine. Thanks for your help, Gail." I protectively clutch Julia Child's book to my chest and reach for Cat. I am about to depart for the checkout counter when I have second thoughts. *What if it's not fine? What if Gail wants me to take this cookbook because she knows I'll just have to come back for another one?*

At this point I realize I'm cracking up, but I don't care. I need a good recipe and I will do anything to get it. I feint a move for *The Silver Palate*, but just as Gail goes to grab it, I quickly seize the other fat cookbook, *Joy of Cooking*. If I can hear a voice singing *The Hallelujah Chorus* for one cookbook, a whole choir ought to sing for two.

I risk a glance at Gail, waiting for her strike, but she has wisely admitted defeat, moving on to other shelves and other victims. I smile, proud of myself. I have found them—The Chef of Hearts' textbooks. Strike that. The Chef of Hearts' love manuals. Maggie Malone may not be successful at relationships, but The Chef of Hearts will be.

Chapter Four

"Recipe: A series of step-by-step instructions for preparing ingredients you forgot to buy, in utensils you don't own, to make a dish the dog wouldn't eat."
—Author Unknown

I survey the seventy-eight-dollars-and-change worth of groceries spread out over the kitchen counter. Cat and I spent a good hour and a half at the grocery store this morning, buying all the ingredients for three recipes of coq au vin. From what I can tell, coq au vin is a staple of French cooking. Both Julia Child and Irma Rombauer have recipes for it, so it's got to be good. I'll do an Irma version, a Julia version, and of course, an original Chef of Hearts version. One of them has to work.

The phone trills a couple of times and I pick it up. "Hello?"

"Margaret?" A smooth, cultured voice articulates, rising up at the last syllable of my name.

Shit. There's only one person in the world who insists on calling me Margaret despite the fact he knows I hate it.

"Richard. What do you want?" I can't believe it. How did he find out where I was? I never told him where I was going when I left. I guess he figured I'd go home to Dad's house in Atlanta. Richard has always been smart, one of the best defense attorneys in Charlotte.

"Just checking in to see how you are faring. Can't a man check on his wi…"

"Soon to be ex-wife Richard. And no, you can't check on me. What do you want?"

I listen to him lamenting his loneliness and his problems, and all I want to do is stick my finger down my throat.

"So, Richard, screw any new women lately?" I break into his syrupy speech. "Gee, I guess I do sound a little bitter. Listen, from a woman's point of view, I'd have to give ballsy points to that chick in Charlotte. She's a keeper. What was her name? Oh, that's right…it's sweet little Celeste, our next door neighbor. Richard, don't call me again. We're almost divorced. You're out of my life."

I whack the phone on the counter a few dozen times, extra hard, in the hope it might break his eardrums, then calmly press the button and hang up.

It's time to cook.

• • •

"How ya doing, Kit Cat?" I coo as I open Irma's cookbook. Cat's in her Pack n' Play portable crib by the kitchen window. Close enough to hear me but far enough away that I can get some work accomplished. I glance over at her. She's occupied with finding her hands. That's my girl. Obviously very inquisitive. Just like her mama.

I skim my finger down the index. *Chicken*…blah, blah, blah…*Braised in fruit*…yada, yada, yada…*Cockscombs*. What the hell is that? Ah, *Coq Au Vin*.

Okay, Irma, speak to me. Tell me what you know. "In other countries, blood is often added as a thickener." Okay that's just gross, and let me tell you, it's not happening in The Chef of Hearts' kitchen. I continue reading—yada, yada, yada—"wash and disjoint the chicken." I frown at the meat I purchased—three whole roasting chickens and a package of thighs for extra measure. *I've got to wash them? Those oozy, fleshy, decrepit looking things?*

Let me just say up front, I like poultry. I like to eat poultry with a variety of sauces. But I've never had to cook it. Not with my dad, not with Richard, not by myself. There was always a takeout, restaurant, frozen dinner, or a man willing to grill.

Raw flesh of a dead bird. Why would anyone want to touch the stuff? I begin to have second thoughts about this whole cooking shenanigan. Maybe masquerading as a chef isn't such a great idea after all. *Come on Maggie, pick up the bird. Pick up the poor chicken that has been slaughtered so you can become a columnist and begin a new life. And make lots of money.*

I stare at the chickens and *voilà!* Of course. I don't have to touch the fetid fowl flesh, I can use rubber gloves. I reach under the kitchen sink and pull out a box of unopened rubber cleaning gloves. Perfect.

Then I think of cutting up one of those birds with blood and chicken juice squirting me in the eye. Germs! Bacteria! What if I get food poisoning? My breathing quickens and I feel my chest tighten as if a boa constrictor is wrapped around my body, squeezing the common sense out of me.

Good God, I've got to get a grip. I must be a card short of a full deck. Cooking is easy. It's fun. It's not life threatening.

I practice breathing in and out. Like that Lamaze breathing I tried when Cat was born. Hee hee ha. Hee hee ha. But it didn't work then and it's not working now. Wait a second, I've got it! I run down to my father's workshop and grab his old protective eye gear. Safety first, that's what Dad always said.

Armed with the gloves and protective eye gear, my confidence restored, I stick one of the birds under the faucet for wash time. There you go, my chickadee, get a nice bath. Now, what about soap? Did Irma mean wash with soap? Well, of course she did! Why else would she say "wash" the bird? I add a few squirts of Palmolive, then a few more, just to be thorough, and I suds up the bird extra good. After a nice, long rinse, I lay it on some paper towels to dry.

Done. Mission accomplished. I pull off my gloves and turn them upside down to dry, feeling very proud of myself. So this is what a traditional woman feels like slaving in front of a hot stove. Not so bad.

Now to disjoint the chicken. Hmm. Disjoint. Guess that means to cut up the thing. My heart races and my fingers get all clammy. *I can do this. Really, I can.* These birds are clean. Not a single germ in sight. A ray of sunlight bounces off the steel of my newly purchased knives and the light distracts me. What a bargain those knives were. The whole set cost twenty-nine dollars and ninety-nine cents at Walmart. Now which one shall I use? Surveying the wood block, I pull out a massive, wicked looking knife. Bigger's got to be better.

"How you doing, Kit Cat? Shall we sing a song? *Twinkle twinkle little...*" I stab the bird and saw away. "Shit!" I explode. That's my index finger I just cut! I clamp my mouth shut in horror, glancing at Cat. What kind of a mother cusses out loud around her baby? When I found out I was pregnant, I had made a pledge with myself to quit.

I thrust my finger under the faucet, grabbing a wad of paper towels with the other hand. Five paper towels and a Band-Aid later the bleeding has stopped. Someone really should invent a safety knife for cooking novices, strike that, chefs like me. Then people wouldn't need so many band-aids. Ah, Band-Aids. Who doesn't love them? They're medical fashion statements. I currently am sporting a Barbie Band-Aid. When I discovered I was pregnant with a girl, I went overboard with the girly stuff. Now I have enough sparkly powder, watermelon Chap Stick, and Dora the Explorer bath bubbles to last well into the next millennium. I even changed the ringtone on my phone so it'd play the theme song from Cinderella.

I unsheathe a different blade and resume my butchering. Maybe the last knife was defective.

"*Twinkle twinkle little star,*" I continue to sing, hacking away at my bird. "*How I wonder what you are. Up above the world so high, like a diamond in the...*" I slice right into my thumb. "Oh, fuc...I mean uh..." Rooting around in my brain for a cuss word suitable for Cat's ears, I glance at the half-eaten container of fudge on my counter. Fudge, now there's a swear word. Kind of old fashioned, maybe not as cathartic as saltier expletives but still, it could be the start of something. New life, new leaf. The Chef of Hearts will express herself as only she can, by creating a concoction of culinary cuss words for parental chefs.

"Oh, fudge!" Hmm, actually pretty cathartic.

Three paper towels and another Barbie Band-Aid later, I begin yet again. Forget germs. Forget food poisoning. I am going to disjoint this stubborn bird if it kills me. Maggie Malone does not give up. She just needs to change tactics. Maybe I need to approach this like an experiment. Experiments always yield answers. Just like tenth grade chemistry class. Justy—Justine Beignet at the time—and I found out lots of answers to important questions in class that year.

"*Justy, come on. We have to do it. The science fair project is due tomorrow and if we don't do this, we won't have a project.*"

"*But Maggie! Zis is permanent!*"

I giggle at Justy's accent. "Just, you need to veg. Listen, this is totally bangin'. Everyone's doing it on MTV and it's perfect for our project on chemical reactions. And, hello? It's not permanent—it says here it's demi-permanent. That's probably like semi-permanent. I'll just wash it out and we're good to go. Now take a before picture of me and let's get going! Hello A-plus in chemistry!"

The next day, we had our before and after pictures, graph, and data poster completed for our chemistry project. I also had Kermit the Frog green hair. Even after twenty shampoos, the demi-permanent dye would not come out. But Justy never once said I told you so. In fact, she even dyed her hair green so I would feel better.

Our experiment yielded many important answers that day: demi-permanent is not the same as semi-permanent hair dye, blondes might have more fun but greens get more attention, and Justy and I were BFFs.

Perhaps, a bit of finesse is required in this butchering. No more sawing or hacking. Just elegant carving. I face my adversary, clucking my tongue. "Come here chick, chick, chick, chick, chickadee."

Chapter Five

"The best way to execute French cooking is to get good and loaded and whack the hell out of a chicken. Bon appétit."
—Julia Child

Ah…I actually cooked something. I gaze at my simmering chicken and a wonderfully satisfying feeling of accomplishment bubbles up inside. It doesn't matter it's quite gloppy looking what with all those onion and shallot skins floating around. They're vital nutrients, I'm sure. Besides, the recipe didn't say to take the skins off. What's important here is that I cooked the bird myself. No frozen Stouffer's. No takeout from a restaurant. It's a gourmet dish, made exclusively by The Chef of Hearts.

I've got to say, though, it took me forever to disjoint the blasted fowl, and I ended up cutting every finger on my left hand. Finally, I had to resort to using a pair of large scissors from Dad's tool drawer. The bird came apart fine and I didn't cut a single finger. Why couldn't Irma just say to cut it up with some scissors? I discovered something else too. Scissors work great on everything. Onions, shallots, carrots…even bacon. The recipe called for salt pork but I couldn't find that so I used maple-flavored bacon—there was a great sale on it.

Now, the garlic clove was a pain. The recipe called for a peeled garlic clove, finely chopped. Let me tell you, that's a heck of a lot of garlic to peel and cut up with scissors. There must have been twenty-two sections to that garlic clove. But the rest of the cooking went great. I browned the chicken in butter—it was a little black, perhaps, but there is a fine line between dark brown and black, I think—added the cut up veggies, lots of herbs, brandy, and two cups of wine. *Voilà!* The bird is now simmering for one hour.

Ignoring the dirty dishes stacked in pyramids on every inch of available counter space, I stroll over to Cat. "Oh, you're such a good girl." I lift her proudly and we settle down in a big armchair to nurse. "Mommy loves you, yes she does, Mommy…ouch, Cat! Be gentle with Mommy!"

An hour later, my coq au vin is done and I plate up a large helping for lunch. I'm starved! I poke my fork into the blackened—excuse me, browned—chicken and wrestle off a bite, inhaling the aroma. Ah, garlic. Very gourmet. And it smells like Palmolive. Which is a good thing. You've got to eat clean food. I'm amazed at my prowess in the kitchen. But why should I be amazed? I am a chef, after all.

I insert the token bite into my mouth and begin to choke. *My God, the garlic!* I run to the sink and spit out the chicken. And then a gloppy bit of onion skin. And then a—what is that?

I spit it out and study the thing. It looks suspiciously like a piece of the netting from the garlic clove package. I smack my tongue against the roof of my mouth a few times. *Is that Palmolive I taste?* Surely not. My bird was washed and rinsed, thank you very much. It must be a rogue garlicky-soap bite. First bites of gourmet creations can't all be tasty. Maybe some are acquired tastes. I spit again. Bleck. Very acquired tastes.

I plunge my fork into the chicken and tear off another bite, careful not to get any onion skins this time. I put it into my mouth and almost immediately, spit that one out, too. Definitely not a rogue garlicky-soap bite. This dish should be called Coq Au Soap and Garlic. I get out a pencil and piece of paper. If I am to be a famous chef, I need to be organized and make notes to myself. A good chef is not afraid to learn from her mistakes.

```
*Note to myself: Do not use Palmolive on
chickens. Leave out onion and shallot skins.
Watch amount of garlic! Call Pizza Hut for
dinner.
```

I arm myself once more with my bright yellow rubber gloves, my protective eye gear, and, this time, Julia Child's *Mastering the Art of French Cooking*. Speak to me Julia. Speak to me.

• • •

I gaze at my second simmering chicken, trying to ignore the stinging pain on my face. Let me tell you, it was a fierce battle. I ran into some problems with the cognac.

Julia said to pour in a quarter cup cognac and, averting your face, ignite the liquid. Well, my match blew out because I had the ceiling fan on to get rid of some of the garlic smell in the house. So I turned off the fan, lit another match, and forgot to avert my face. The alcohol ignited with a whoosh! Before I knew what had happened, my eyebrows and eyelashes were singed, my face blackened.

The protective eye gear would have been quite handy at this point, but I had taken the goggles off to reapply my makeup. I mean, who wants to cook with a greasy complexion and no lipstick? Well, minor mishaps. That's why Neosporin and Band-Aids were invented, for times just like these.

An hour later, my coq au vin is done. I jab my fork into the blackened chicken—maybe watching TV while cooking isn't a good idea—and raise it to my mouth. It should be better this time. No soap, just water, and limited amount of garlic. Julia called for two mashed cloves of garlic but I thought that a bit much. That was forty-some sections of garlic. The woman must have had a garlic obsession. So I used only half the clove. Twelve sections of garlic seemed plenty. I really didn't know how to mash them, so I took out a hammer and bam-bam-bam, they were mashed in no time. The whole pounding process was quite therapeutic, actually. Got rid of a lot of built-up stress and anxiety, too. Everything else went really well—except I ran out of wine and had to substitute a different alcohol, the only one Dad had hanging around.

As I plunge the bite of chicken into my mouth, a horrible taste accosts me. Like bitter licorice with tinges of garlic. Darting to the sink, I spit it out, rinsing my mouth over and over with the sink sprayer. Has The Chef of Hearts been defeated by birds and booze? Is this as good as it gets? I don't know and don't care. There are far more pressing matters at hand. Drying my mouth off with my shirt, I reach for the phone and dial. "Yes, I'd like to order a large pepperoni pizza, please."

Cooking works up an appetite.

*Note to myself: Always wear safety gear. Watch amount of garlic! Never use Jagermeister as a substitute for wine.

• • •

The final bird battle. The ultimate showdown.

This time I have taken my recipe from the Internet. All I had to do was type in "easy chicken coq au vin" and out came a recipe. So simple. I don't know why I didn't think about it before. It even called for chicken thighs, which is good because there's no way I'm going to attempt to cook that third bird. I'll just use the recipe as a guide, add a little Julia this, a little Irma that, and I'm good to go. One original Chef of Hearts recipe.

Before starting, I walk up to Cat's crib. She's fast asleep, drooling on one of Richard's favorite silk ties. How convenient it was to find it mixed in with my clothes. I only wish that I had more of Richard's things. Oh, the uses I could find for them. His power toothbrush with dual speed control would definitely make a great toilet bowl brush. Ooh, ooh! And how stylish his Armani brushed Egyptian cotton shirts would be lining the inside of Cat's diaper pail! Giggles bubble out of me. Those stupid expensive shirts. He must have had one in every color. I could cut them up and make…but the thought of ruining Richard's hydrangea blue Armani button-down puts a damper on my mirth. *Okay, maybe not that shirt. I loved that shirt on Richard.*

I shake my head in denial, scattering the handsome images of my husband to the furthest corners of my mind. Time to move on. Time to cook.

Coat chicken with flour, put aside. Easy enough. I dump a handful of flour on the chicken thighs, roll them around a bit, and set them aside. *Heat frying pan.* I am careful to turn the burner to medium and turn off the TV. *Add some bacon.* I've already cut it up into little pieces using my handy scissors. No maple-flavored bacon this time, thank you very much. *Cook until golden-colored.* Done. I sample a little of the bacon, feeling smug. Quite tasty, if I do say so myself.

Drain the fat off the bacon and set bacon aside. Why not dump it down the sink? That's what sinks are for. *Melt some butter.* A hunk of butter plops into the frying pan. *Cook chicken for a few minutes, turning once. Remove chicken, add mushrooms, carrots, onions, garlic.* How handy it was to find precut garlic and veggies at the grocery store. Why would anyone want to cut their own? *Cook until everything is tender.* I swirl the veggies around in the butter, making patterns for a few minutes, then poke a carrot with a fork to see if it's done. Seems tender to me. *Put everything, including chicken, into a slow cooker.* Good thing it's a slow cooker. That's the one appliance in Dad's pantry. *Add some wine.* A little Burgundy and maybe a little Cognac too. The Jagermeister has retired. *Add chicken broth.* Hmm. Why not some beef broth as well? And how about a little tomato paste? My creative juices are sizzling now. *Toss in some herbs, salt, and pepper.* A few shakes of this, a few shakes of that. *Cover and cook on low six to seven hours. Season with salt and pepper to taste.*

And now, The Chef of Hearts is taking a commercial break to watch a movie. Do all chefs have this much in-between time? I could get used to this job.

· · ·

At midnight, I taste my final coq au vin and heave a weary but contented sigh. The Chef of Hearts is victorious but also incredibly tired. Cooking's really hard work. Maybe that's why Richard was always pushing me to learn how to cook. He had some old-fashioned idea that a wife should slave over a hot stove for her husband. If it was good enough for his mom, it was good enough for me.

"Margaret, I think you'd really enjoy cooking. Wouldn't you like to serve your husband a homemade meal?" Richard beamed his most charming smile. "You know, there was nothing more Mom loved than preparing a big feast for Dad."

"Yeah, right." I looked away, coughing into my hand the word "bullshit."

Richard narrowed his eyes, studying me.

"Excuse me, I had something in my throat," I explained, clearing it a few times in demonstration. "That's really nice, honey, but I tried that at Christmas, remember? And look how that turned out. There's just something about cooking that kind of turns me off. Maybe it's touching all that raw meat. And those germs!"

"Come on. You're being a germophobe. So you cooked once and it was a catastrophe. I would imagine that was because you had, perhaps, just a bit too much spiked eggnog, my dear. The point is you need to get back on the horse when you fall off. Which leads to my surprise: I signed you up at Johnson and Wales Culinary School. They have a summer program for people who want to…"

"You what? You should have talked to me. If you think after a few months of marriage you can coerce me…"

"Calm down. I thought you'd enjoy it. I'm not coercing you into anything."

"I know you meant well, of course, but you should have asked me first, Richard."

"Alright, alright, Margaret, stop it for Pete's sake." Richard pulled off his tie, folded it, and stuck it in his pocket. *"Is it that time of month? Is that why you're blowing this all out of proportion?"* He pulled me into his arms. *"Let's not argue anymore."* He nuzzled my neck. *"How about a little makeup sex?"*

I snorted in disgust and pulled myself free from his embrace. *"No, I don't want to have makeup sex, Richard. We need to settle this. You know I hate cooking. Things never turn out. I either get hurt or break something in the kitchen. Besides, I thought you liked Papa Murphy's Take 'n Bake."*

He began to nibble on my earlobe and all rational thought flew out of my mind. What were we arguing about?

It's funny how we change as we go through life. Seventeen years ago—heck, one year ago—I would never have imagined I would be cooking today. And here I am trying to show other people how to cook. Go figure.

I guess desperation opens closed doors in a person's mind. And now that I have the doors open, I plan to invite *Cooking and Women* to my housewarming party. The Chef of Hearts has moved in and she's here to stay.

Chapter Six

"A mother is a person who seeing there are only four pieces of pie for five people, promptly announces she never did care for pie."
—Tenneya Jordan

It's four in the morning and I am awake. I have slept precisely two hours and thirty-seven minutes, total. I have been up four times in the past hour alone. "Shhh. Sh-sh-shhhhh…," I shush Catherine as I pat her rhythmically and rock in the glider.

Why must babies cry at night? I can understand crying. I feel like doing it all the time. A female thing, I guess. But can't babies at least wait until morning to begin their tear-fest?

"Shhh. Sh-sh-shhhhh." I thump Cat, soft pats in cadence with the shushing, my head lolling back on the glider's neck rest. My eyes close and…

"Wahhhhh, wahhhhhhhh!"

What? What does she want? I have fed her. Changed her. Walked her. What's left? Singing…A mother's ultimate sleep aid.

"Hush little baby, don't say a word, Momma's gonna cook up a tasty bird… and if that bird don't cook too well, Momma's gonna work at Taco Bell…."

• • •

From: Maggie Malone
To: Peg Winthrop
Subject: Sample letter and recipe

Hi Peg,

It was a pleasure speaking with you on the phone the other day, and I'm really excited about the possibility of writing a column for Cooking and Women. I've decided my angle for the column is humorous woman-to-woman advice with easy, time saving, and flavorful recipes. Here's my sample Cooking and Men column and recipe. Thank you for considering me to be a columnist!

Maggie

Cooking and Men

Dear Chef of Hearts,

My boyfriend snores horribly. The doctor says it's from his allergies. The more I gently remind him to stop snoring, the more he says I'm harping. Now all we do is fight over it. I'm tired and my boyfriend's annoyed with me. How do I find my way back to his heart and stop him from snoring?

Girlfriend of a Snorer
Atlanta, Georgia

Dear Girlfriend of a Snorer,

Have no fear. There is a remedy for snoring. It is a simple, nonmedical cure known secretly to women for generations. Please do not divulge this remedy to the male sex, lest it affect the sleep of women worldwide.

The remedy for snoring is similar to plucking feathers from a chicken. Irma Rombauer de-
scribes it well in *Joy of Cooking*: "It is much
easier to pluck and draw a bird that is thoroughly chilled. After plucking the bird, remove all pinfeathers. Use a pair of tweezers,
or grasp each pinfeather…then pull."

So ladies, here is the secret remedy. Pull
back the covers from your man, very carefully,
so he becomes chilled in his sleep. Then gently, ever so gently, grasp one of his chest
hairs (if he has no chest hair, just use an
arm hair instead) between your thumb and fore-
finger and quickly yank it out.

His snores will stop, I guarantee it. However, a word of caution: the key here is speed.
You must resume your sleeping pose before your
sleeping beauty of a boyfriend awakens startled, cold and with a sore spot. He will see
you slumbering peacefully and never suspect
you. By the time he is able to get back to
sleep (if he is able), you will be enjoying a
well-earned slumber.

As for finding your way back to his heart, cook
this recipe. Remember, the way to a man's
heart is through his stomach!

Sweet Dreams Chicken

Serves 4

Ingredients:

8 boneless, skinless chicken thighs
Salt and pepper to taste
2 handfuls of flour
8 slices bacon, cut into pieces
2 tablespoons butter
1 tablespoon olive oil
1 (10-ounce) package precut mushrooms
1 (10-ounce) package precut carrots
1 (10-ounce) package precut onions
2 teaspoons minced garlic
1/4 cup chicken broth
1/4 cup beef broth
2 ounces tomato paste
1 1/2 cups Burgundy wine
1/4 cup Cognac
1 teaspoon thyme
1 teaspoon marjoram
1 teaspoon parsley

Season chicken with salt and pepper, then coat
with flour and set aside. Heat frying pan over
medium heat. Add bacon and cook until gold-
en brown and crispy. Drain fat and set bacon
aside. Melt butter, add chicken, and carefully
monitor color. Ladies, you want lovely brown
chicken, not black. Cooking is all about the
details! Set chicken aside.

Pour the olive oil into the same pan then add
mushrooms, carrots, onions, and garlic, cooking until tender. Put everything, including
chicken, into a slow cooker. Add remaining in-

gredients and cook on low heat for six and a
half hours.

Bon appétit and sleep well!
—The Chef of Hearts

• • •

Sleep is overrated. Who needs it? Certainly not me. Okay, I lied. I do need sleep. Lots of it. I turn off the computer and stagger towards the couch for a little nap. Blessed sleep. I stretch out, my eyes begin to droop, and then I hear it. "Wah!"

I can't take it anymore! I've been up all night, fed her a billion times, changed her a quadrillion times, and sung every possible nursery rhyme on the planet to get her to sleep. What about me? What about my needs? My needs!

I jump off the couch and run towards the portable crib. "Be quiet!" I yell, flailing my arms and jumping up and down. "Be quiet!"

Cat is quiet for a moment, and then the crying really begins. Horrible wailing and screaming.

I cover both hands over my face and sob, big convulsing sobs. *My baby is a demon. My life is a mess. I make no money. I'm forty and about to be divorced...*

Cat's silence interrupts my crying jag. What's wrong? I peek through my fingers, hiccupping in my haste to stop crying, and I see her. Really see her. She looks so tiny and frightened. Frightened of *me*.

Is it possible? Am I the demon? Good God, motherhood is hard. How do women, especially single women, cope without cracking up?

I reach over and pick her up, gently swaying her back and forth. "Shh. Shh. It's okay. Mommy didn't mean to yell. She's just tired. You're not a demon. You're an angel," I whisper in her tiny pink ear.

• • •

Motherhood is not at all that I expected. I'd always thought it'd be easy. Bam! Perfect mom here. But it's not that way.

No matter how many books I read, I still don't know what to do. What to say. How to act. And Cat doesn't know any more than I do. And what she does know, she's pretty much incapable of sharing. It's kind of like the blind leading the blind. But we mothers learn to sleep when our babies sleep. Eat when they eat. Cry when they cry. Somehow, mother and baby grow up together.

I trudge up the stairs with my sleeping princess and pause to gaze at a picture of my mom on the wall. She's so young and beautiful. For probably the millionth time, I wish she and I could have grown up together. I bet she'd have some advice to give me now. I study Mom's smiling face and a memory of her flutters through my mind. gently nudging an awareness that maybe she did grow up with me. Even if it was just memories of her that came along for the ride.

"Momma? You don't feel so good?" I whispered as I peeked from behind Daddy's legs. The hospital was a scary place with weird smells and lots of whiteness. Where were all the colors? Momma stretched out her hand to me. I crept around Daddy and put my hand in hers. It felt dry and warm. "Sometimes even mommies get sick, Maggie," she replied in a voice that didn't sound like her.

I tucked the sheet carefully around her body like a cocoon. She was cold. That's why she was sick. Didn't doctors know anything?

"Come lie with me, Maggie," she said. I looked at Daddy to see if it was okay. He nodded his head and lifted me up onto the bed. I laid my head on Momma's pillow and she turned to face me. Her green eyes were big like a cat's.

"I like your new hair Momma," I said, gently touching a brown curl. She must be playing dress up.

"And I like your hair, too. Did you put the bow in it yourself?"

I nodded my head real fast.

"It seems like only yesterday you were in my tummy," she murmured. "Now, look at the big girl you are."

"I am a big girl, Momma," I said, trying not to cry. But it was so hard. I didn't like it when Momma was sick.

"Yes, you are sweetie. Hey, you want to know a secret?"

I got in close-real close and felt her gentle breath upon my ear.

"Smiles are like big, strong knights in shining armor," she whispered. "They protect you and keep you safe."

"Really?" I whispered back, thinking about what she'd just said. Can smiles really be that strong?

"Really," she said and then she smiled.
I smiled back. I felt safer already.

My mom was right. Smiles *are* strong. Kind of like protective brain coatings or "PBCs." When things get out of control and the stress is overwhelming, a smile cushions the mind from overload.

Maybe I needed to smile more.

Chapter Seven

"Age is something that doesn't matter, unless you are a cheese."
—Billie Burke, American actress, 1885-1970

I pour some coffee into a mug and inhale the heavenly aroma. *Ah, elixir. If only I could inject you directly into my veins.* I slurp some down, pausing momentarily to read the front of the mug. MENOPAUSE; MEN TAKE PAUSE. I choke and snort coffee down the front of my pink pajamas. I'd forgotten about this mug; Justy sent it to me last year as a gag gift. I was so sure I was going through menopause.

"How are you, Maggie?" Dr. Westinghouse commented as he stood between my legs.

"Good," I lied, smile in place, tears locked out for now.

I wasn't good at all. Richard and I had a major fight a few days ago. Out of the blue, he said he needed space and some time alone to figure things out. Maybe I should go visit my father for a while. I was flabbergasted. Who says they need space in a marriage? No one has space in a marriage. By definition, marriage means union—not separation, union. So my temper erupted, sky high like Mt. St. Helens. Horrible words were volleyed back and forth between us and I found myself on the plane to Dad. Then while I was crying out my eyes out to dad, he began to have chest pains. I had to call 911 and they took him to the hospital for tests. I'd still be there by his side, except I had this stupid OB/GYN appointment. It took me months to get the thing and Dad insisted I come back for it.

I studied the poster above me. There was a fat, rosy-cheeked baby in a huge egg shell on it. With sunflowers. And bunnies. Gag me. Why must obstetri-

cians do that? Tape baby paraphernalia to the ceiling of their offices? Almost every OB/GYN I've ever known does it. It's a plague—acute babyitis.

"Excellent," Dr. Westinghouse remarked. "Now what brings you here? I see on your paperwork we discussed in vitro at your last visit. Did you and your husband talk about it? Forty is not too old to have a baby these days."

My eyes immediately teared up. In vitro? How could I do in vitro now? "No, in vitro is not an option for me." I turned my head and wiped my eyes with the back of my hand. "Actually, Doctor, I did want to discuss something else with you. Do you think I'm going through perimenopause?" *Fatigue. Missing periods. Mood swings. I had all the symptoms. I know because I googled it.*

A nurse handed Dr. Westinghouse a set of latex gloves and he pulled them on finger by finger, culminating in the ominous snap of the latex against his wrist.

"Hmm..." Dr. Westinghouse probed and poked around. "Are you experiencing any other symptoms? Tenderness of breasts, nausea, anything like that?"

"No. Well, actually now that you mention it, my breasts have been really sore but I never did lay off the caffeine like you suggested. I guess it's due to that fibrocystic thing you mentioned."

"I see. And when was your last period?"

I thought for a moment. It was the beginning of October and I hadn't gotten it yet. And last month, no, I didn't have it then, either, I think. How would I know? Periods had never been high on my list of things to track because I couldn't get pregnant anyway.

"The beginning of August," I took a stab. *Awareness started to rear its ugly face and I sucked in my breath.* "You don't think I'm..."

What if I'm not going through perimenopause? What if it's...my heart began to pound like the timpani in the soundtrack for the movie, 2001 Space Odyssey

"Do you think I'm going through menopause?" I whisper. *Of course. My father was probably having a heart attack right now, and I was going through menopause. I knew it as surely as my name was Maggie Thompson. No, Maggie Malone. Shit. Who the hell was I these days?*

Dr. Westinghouse was silent for a moment as he concluded his exam. "Well, it's my guess you don't have to worry about menopause, Maggie."

"Oh." I said, disappointed, though I wasn't sure why.

My life was so neatly wrapped in depression that menopause seemed like the perfect red bow for a sorry excuse of a life. I thought for a moment, still choosing bows. I was dying of cancer. There. That's a good one. Ooh, ooh—no! Something really debilitating that wouldn't kill me. Something that would just torture me for years. I smiled, protective brain coating in place. Tell me the horrible news, damn it! I was ready for it. Bring it on.

Dr. Westinghouse beamed a smile that lit the room. "I think you're going to be a mother, Maggie."

So much for menopause. I take another sip of my coffee and wander over to my computer.

```
From: Peg Winthrop
To: Maggie Malone
Subject: sample letter and recipe


Maggie,


I received your letter and recipe. I think
your approach of humorous woman to woman ad-
vice with easy yet flavorful recipes is ex-
actly what we are looking for in a column. The
editorial staff will review it today at our
weekly meeting and I'll contact you later this
week.


Peg
```

• • •

```
From: Peg Winthrop
To: Maggie Malone
Subject: sample letter and recipe
```

Maggie,

Peter, the chief editor of Cooking and Women,
will be in Atlanta next week. He would like to
meet with you to discuss the possibility of
becoming our *Cooking and Men* columnist. Are
you available for lunch on Monday at the Merci
Restaurant on Maple Drive in Buckhead at 12:30
p.m.? Also, we would like to see some professional pictures of you, preferably in your
chef uniform. If you are chosen to be our columnist, your picture will be featured on the
cover of our magazines.

Peg

"Yes!" I shout, raising my arms like an Atlanta Falcons cheerleader. They want to meet with me! I bask in the glory of the e-mail for approximately ten seconds, but then the moment slips away like a melting ice cream cone, leaving a sticky residue all over my brain. My victory V crumples into a dejected upside down U as my arms fall to my side.

What am I getting myself into? Professional pictures? The last picture I had taken of me was, good grief, I don't know when. I always took the pictures when I was married to Richard. No one ever offered to take them of me. Maybe it's time for Maggie Malone to have a little primping and pampering done. If I'm going to be a columnist and a chef I need to look like one. Don't exactly know what a culinary columnist looks like but, hey, she's got to look good, right?

• • •

THE SALON DOCTOR

SPECIALIZING IN TOTAL MAKEOVERS.

LOOK TWENTY AGAIN! FEEL TWENTY AGAIN!

I peer at the larger-than-life framed poster in the storefront window. It shows a stunning, sexy woman wearing a cropped shirt and flaunting her pierced belly button, low-riding blue jeans exposing a tattoo of a thorny rose on her curvaceous hip. *Is she really a grandma like her black T-shirt says? What grandma looks like that?* Who cares? I find myself inside the front door in a split second. I want to look like her.

A woman with the name "Li" embroidered on her white beautician's jacket glides around the front desk as if walking on water. She's model slender like Heidi Klum and I can't help but be impressed. Does she diet, work out? And that beautiful complexion! I don't think she's wearing any makeup. Glossy black hair to her waist. Please tell me she has hair extensions. I raise my hand self-consciously to my face, pat it a bit, then smooth my hair. I knew I should have washed it. But who washes their hair when they're going to a salon? That's like cleaning your house before the maid comes. Seems kind of redundant.

"Yes?" she inquires, circling me like a vulture and eyeing me like I'm road kill.

"Um, I'm looking for some new clothes," I mutter. I clutch Cat, who is nestled in her Baby Bjorn, closer to my chest, and glance longingly at the door. Maybe this is a mistake, I can still leave.

Li clucks as she circles again.

I bet it's only ten steps to freedom. Eight if I take really big ones. "And maybe a new hairstyle," I mumble.

Li halts directly in front of me, reaching out a long, slightly curved, acrylic nail. I cringe, shielding Cat from the pink-lacquered weapon. What's she going to do? Impale me? She grasps a lock of my hair between her pinchers, and turns it this way and that studying it with slivered almond eyes. Without warning, she walks away.

Great. I have two days left before my lunch with Peg and the senior editor and I'm stuck in a sagging, middle-aged body with faded blond hair and out-of-style clothes. Even The Salon Doctor doesn't want me. I hang my head in dejection, my spirits drooping so low they're mopping up the floor.

"You may come in," a voice startles me. I look up and see Li holding a door open, as if granting entrance into Nirvana. I hustle myself and Cat past her as fast as I can say "Chef of Hearts."

Nirvana might just have a timer for acceptance.

• • •

"So, exactly why do you have blond hair?" Li asks as she studies my roots.

"Well, actually, I used to have red hair when I first got married. My husband, he's not really my husband now, we're separated, liked blond hair. So I've been blond for the last seventeen years."

Just then, I panic. *Where's Cat? Did I leave her outside? In the car? At home?* My God, I've turned into that woman I was reading about who left her baby in the car carrier beside her car by accident and she drove away, without the baby! My heart plummets as my eyes dart around the room, crashing abruptly as I spy her in her car carrier by the wall. What a fruit loop I am! Parenthood gobbles up brain cells like they're potato chips. Pretty soon I'll be an empty bag.

"Ah, I see. But your complexion is that of a redhead," Li comments as she snaps up the front of my plastic smock and wraps a towel around my neck.

I don't respond because I am too busy scrutinizing myself in the mirror. *When did I start looking so old?* "Do you have any of that thick, pancake makeup? I think I need it to hide these little lines I'm getting around the eyes. Richard always said more is better with makeup." I stretch the skin taut beneath my eyes and then tug on my neck flesh. Maybe a facelift would help, like one of those Lifestyle facelifts that get rid of jowls and turkey-neck skin.

Li holds up a lighted magnifying glass to my face and peers closely at my eye area. "You can barely see them. It's normal to start getting a few little lines around the eyes. Actually, your skin is quite good."

"No, it's bad, it's horrible. Lines are creeping up everywhere." I lean forward in my chair and study my reflection in the mirror. "There, look at that. Right by my mouth." I point to the offending line and then flop back in my chair with a sigh. "Can't you just give me a new me?"

Li shakes her head and swivels me away from the mirror. "Listen, you don't need a new you. You just need to find the old you. I'll help you. We'll find Maggie Malone together and you'll like her."

I roll my eyes in frustration. *Like I really want the old me.* I didn't like her then, why would I like her now?

• • •

"So what do you think?" Li inquires.

I don't know if I have the energy to think. Li's worked on my hair and makeup for two and a half hours and then we tried on clothes for another hour. During that time, Cat was fed twice, changed three times, and patted and burped ad nauseam. I never knew beauty was so exhausting.

I touch one of the glossy, auburn strands and then run my fingers through the wavy layers. It does feel soft. And my eyes, my skin, my mouth—they look different. I look different. I look like me seventeen years ago. It's been so long I almost didn't recognize me.

"You've done a wonderful job, thank you." I smile at Li and genuinely mean it. The woman is an artist, no, a makeover master chef. "There's just one more thing." I reach over to Cat's overstuffed diaper bag and pull out a camera and a set of clothes. "Would you mind taking some pictures of me in a chef's uniform?"

Chapter Eight

"…no one is born a great cook, one learns by doing."
—*Julia Child*

"Yes, I'm here to meet Peg Winthrop. I believe she has a table," I announce to the hostess. She scans her list with her finger, nods, and proceeds into the dining room.

Merci Restaurant is a trendy, popular, and very expensive French eatery in the heart of Buckhead. Dining here is definitely not in my budget. I'm more of a Waffle House girl. The food is cheap and the atmosphere is kid friendly. Cat can scream away and no one blinks an eye. Plus, Waffle House cooks fry up lots of sausage and bacon, giving the atmosphere a good dose of grease, which has to be beneficial to middle-aged, moisture-deprived skin.

I glance around the room. Soaring ceilings, pomegranate walls, and tables draped in cream-colored linens, topped with glass vials of orchids. I follow the hostess to a corner table where a woman is sitting by herself. She has short, pixie blond hair and is wearing a red ribbed turtleneck, a chunky gold necklace, a tiny black skirt, and up-to-the-knees stiletto black boots. A black leather jacket hangs from the back of her chair.

"Peg? I'm Maggie Malone." I thrust out my hand.

Peg grasps my hand in a limpid shake, the wishy-washy kind of handshake that doesn't commit to physical contact, then slips away as if it never happened. Could she have some sort of touching disorder?

This makes me self-conscious about my hands. They were sweaty in the car so I sprinkled baby powder on them to absorb the moisture and now they smell like a baby. Is Peg going to think I have a baby? Maybe I should spritz them with my purse perfume. That's so stupid, I do have a baby. Why oh why did I leave her with a babysitter? What if she doesn't like the lady? Mrs. Maroni came highly recommended by our neighborhood newsletter but still, what if they're wrong? What if Mrs. Maroni is really a man? Maybe she's like Inspector Clouseau in *The Pink Panther*. Cleverly disguised as a hunched old lady to trap unsuspecting…

"Peter called and is running slightly behind. Perhaps we should go ahead and order a drink." Peg raises a hand and gives an imperial wave to the hovering waiter. I have to bite my lip not to giggle. Who waves like that besides queens and princesses? She looks like she's unscrewing a light bulb.

Peg stares at me with an expectant look. "Well, would you like a drink?"

Uh, uh…It's hard to dispel the image of this woman unscrewing light bulbs. Drink. Drink. *I'd like a drink. A double Jack on the rocks. It's been a year in a half since I had one.* I force myself to focus. "Sweet tea, please."

"And I'll have a Brazen Martini. Light on the cubes and well-chilled vodka," Peg commands the waiter.

"I've got to say we really enjoyed your sample *Cooking and Men* column. The plucking chicken analogy was hilarious," Peg comments but doesn't crack a smile. It's as if her face is frozen stiff, void of any emotion. Then it hits me. Of course, Botox. Maybe an overdose in this case.

"Your column is very relatable with broad commercial appeal." She reaches for a nutty-looking loaf of bread. "Slice?" she offers as she saws through the loaf, crumbs hopping through the air like frogs.

"No thank you." I'd rather save my calories for sweet tea any day. But when the waiter arrives with our drinks, I compare my sweet tea in its plain tumbler with Peg's Brazen Martini in a slender V-shaped vessel with violet liquid, a few colored ice cubes, and a curled orange rind perched on the rim. I frown. Actually, I'd rather save my calories for Peg's drink. *Man that looks tasty.*

"Usually, it takes years to write comfortably with those comic overtones," Peg comments. "But you do it quite well." She nibbles on the corner of her slice of bread like a mouse.

"Thank you. I…"

"You're sure you don't want a slice of this bread? It's wonderfully nutty." Nibble, nibble.

"Uh, no, I'm good."

"Let me cut to the chase, Maggie. Can I call you Maggie or do you prefer The Chef of Hearts?" Peg chuckles, straight faced. "Your writing has a humorous yet knowledgeable slant to it, which is exactly what we're looking for in a column. And I must say you received glowing reports from Lavande. I was particularly interested to hear that you've served dinner to…" Nibble. Nibble.

I perch on the edge of my chair, my body quivering with anticipation and excitement. Exactly what they're looking for! *Did I win? Did I win?* Wait a second. Who the heck did I serve dinner to? What did Justy tell her?

"…to…ah, Peter. There you are. Come join us." Peg sweeps an arm in invitation, granting him permission to sit.

I swivel my body around and watch as a man advances to the table. He has sandy blond hair and is tall. Really tall. Taller than me, I think. Amazing. Richard always said I was a freak of nature, a cross between an Amazon and a crane. Half giant woman, half bird. We used to laugh about it when we first started dating, but the joke got old real fast. He kept bringing it up throughout our marriage. He was probably just insecure because I was five ten, and he was a measly five nine and *maybe* a half an inch.

As the tall guy approaches our table, I notice his eyes. Big baby blues, with long eyelashes he should be ashamed of. Do they make false eyelashes for men? All coherent thought flees my mind as I gaze at this tall drink of water and my mouth drops open. If I could drool, it'd be puddling around my chair by now. I clamp my mouth shut. Mouth calisthenics are not attractive. Whatever possessed me to wear this outfit? Li warned me about appearing too conservative, but I wanted to be business appropriate with a navy blue suit and white silk shirt. Now I'm wishing I were less executive-wannabe and more sexy-here-I-am.

"I'm sorry I'm late, Peg. The presentation took longer than I thought. You must be Maggie." His blue eyes settle on me, a wide, friendly smile on his face, and I notice dimples in each cheek. I start to rise from my chair, like a child drawn to a giant cuddly teddy bear. "No, no. Don't get up," he cajoles. My half-standing, half-sitting crouch melts into the chair, along with my poise. "Ladies? Refills?" Peter asks as he sits between Peg and me.

I am just about to reply affirmatively when Peg giggles like a school-girl. Peg, giggling? She doesn't seem the type. I glance at her empty glass. Wow, she sure downed that one. I stare in amazement as her face cracks a smile. The Botox must be wearing off. Or maybe she's just a one-drink girl.

"Oh, Peter. Always the gentleman. No, I'm fine, thank you. I was just telling Maggie how impressed we were with her cooking background. Imagine serving dinner to Brad Pitt and Angelina Jolie."

I sit there, stunned. *Brad Pitt and Angelina Jolie?* Good God, Justy, why'd you tell her that? Peg's words blend and bleed together like a Monet painting. My feet feel wobbly like they're balanced on a delicate cluster of lily-pad lies. One wrong step and splash! In I'll go.

"Maggie?"

My name tugs me back to reality. I focus and Peter is handing me a menu. "Have you eaten here before?" I shake my head, afraid to voice anything that might disturb my lily pads.

He opens his menu. "Well, the Vidalia onion cappuccino soup capped with foam and shaved walnuts is wonderful. And the duck sausage and linguini with collard greens and sun-dried tomatoes is always a winner. But, why am I telling you? I bet you cook dishes like these for yourself all the time." He leans forward, his face close to mine. "I've got to ask. Do you ever get tired of cooking for people?"

I smile, relieved my feet are on solid ground now. Not a single lily pad in sight. "No, I can't say that I do." And that's the truth, nothing but the truth. I don't get tired of cooking for people because I've never cooked for anyone besides myself. Honesty has never felt so satisfying.

Lies have been stacking up in my life like canned goods in a pantry. I've been shopping around for them on and off for the past seventeen years. It all started with Richard. He wanted a stay at home wife and I wanted a job. So we compromised, and I worked a few fundraisers for *Passionately Pink for the Cure*. It was fulfilling and made me feel like I was contributing to finding a cure for breast cancer. But then their local corporate office called and that's when the shopping for lies really began.

"Is this Maggie Malone?"
"This is Maggie. Maggie Thompson."
"I'm sorry, I was looking for Maggie Malone."

"Well, I'm Maggie Malone too. That's my maiden name."

"Oh, I'm sorry. It says here you're Maggie Malone. Anyway, I'm Marsha Fielding and I work for Passionately Pink for the Cure, in the local branch here in Charlotte."

"Oh, hi, Marsha. What can I do for you? If it's about the last event I hosted, I'm just finishing tallying up the donations and I should be able to…"

"Actually, Maggie, it's not about the last event. Take your time with that, we know it'll be coming in. You have a great track record. Listen, we took a look at your application and we think we might have a part-time position for you."

"Really?" I said, feeling surprised, elated, and a little freaked out all rolled in one burrito of a word. I submitted the application on a whim one day, using my maiden name, and promptly put it out of my mind. I never thought they'd call.

Marsha chuckled. "Don't sound so surprised. Come down to the office tomorrow afternoon and we'll talk salary, benefits, etc. I think you would be a great addition to the cause, if you choose to accept our offer."

I sat there, perched on the kitchen stool, for at least fifteen minutes after the phone call ended. How could I make this work? Richard tolerated my participating in the occasional fundraiser, but a part-time job? A key rattled in the door and panic started to set in. I took a deep breath and blew it out slowly. I was just going to have to come clean, that's all there was to it. Tell him everything. He'd understand once he realized how much this meant to me.

"Hello, my sweets. I picked up the pizzas, just like you asked." He deposited the boxes on the counter and walked over to me, cheek first.

"Hi, hon," I replied, rewarding him with a peck on his cheek, all the while plotting my next move. Tell him Maggie, tell him…

"Mm-mm. Nothing liked pepperoni pizza." He pulled out a plate, loaded up a few slices, and wandered over to the reclining chair.

I took a deep breath. "Well, I have some n…"

"The garage looks great, by the way," Richard mumbled between bites of pizza. He swallowed and smacked his lips together a couple of times. "Can you get me a beer?"

"Good, I'm glad. Listen, I got a call today from t. . . "

The sound of some announcer's voice on the television interrupted me. "Well Johnny, there was a lot of incentive for Roy McIllroy, the second ranked…"

Realization dawned on me. Richard would never accept my having a job. It just didn't fit into his big picture of marriage. Men worked, women stayed home. If I worked, who would roll up his socks in perfect little packets, color code his underwear, and organize his golf paraphernalia? I was definitely going to have to keep working part time a secret. I could open a bank account for my paychecks in my maiden name. It'd be fine. Besides, secrets weren't lies, were they?

Yup, lies in the pantry. And my pantry is definitely getting crowded.

Peg pulls out a stack of papers and begins to rifle through them. "Here are just a few pages about what we, the staff of *Cooking and Women,* want your column to include. It will be loosely built around the theme that the way to a man's heart is through his stomach." She leafs through a few more pages and looks up. "Did you bring those professional pictures I asked for?"

I nod my head and dig through my purse for them. "Yes, I had a few taken of me," I say, offering her the large manila envelope. "I really like the one…"

Peg snaps up the envelope and continues with her instructions about the column. "Women will send in letters about their problems in finding a man, or perhaps keeping a man happy, and so on. Your job is to relate these issues to cooking, give some advice about men, and finish it up with a recipe or two. You'll be writing your columns one month in advance." She pauses and scrutinizes me with her black marble eyes. I'm unsure whether she requires a response, so I bob my head up and down in agreement.

As if on a wrestling tag team, Peter jumps in. "We'll introduce you as The Chef of Hearts and feature your "Mister Right Salsa" in our September issue. The following month, we'll debut your column with the *Girlfriend of a Snorer* letter. Oh, and I thought we'd call the column *Pickin' Tomatoes,* instead of *Cooking and Men.* Kind of catchy, huh?"

Before I can comment, Peg springs into action. "We'll pay you fifty cents a word, with a cap of one thousand words per article for the October, November, and December columns. If the column does well, you'll be moved to a salaried position, with quarterly bonuses based on feedback and popularity of the column. Here are some representative figures…"

This is wonderful. An answer to my prayers. The inheritance money from Dad is gone and my *Passionately Pink for the Cure* bank account is dwindling away. I need this income to support Cat and me, especially since all I'm getting in the divorce is the 1985 Jeep Cherokee while Richard keeps the 2010 Lexus—for business purposes, of course. Yeah, right. Richard travels mostly by plane not car. He just wants the car because it's a status symbol. I should never have signed those prenuptials when we got married, but those papers seemed so important to Richard. I chalked it up to his being an attorney. Always dotting his I's and crossing his T's. Besides, it never occurred to me we'd someday get divorced.

"And we expect your column to be very popular," Peter continues. "Perhaps, if it goes well, we could book you a few gigs on local radio shows. It would be great publicity and would lead to…"

Good Lord, what have I missed? Radio shows? Publicity? I thought this would be just a few measly columns I'd have to write. I never thought it could lead to this. What happens if I blow it? My body starts slumping in my chair. I'm alarmed by all the awful possibilities of what could go wrong. What if they find out I'm not a chef? That The Chef of Hearts is really The Chef of Lies? I get fired and have to sell Dad's house. Cat and I live out of our car for a while but eventually it dies and we end up on the streets, sleeping on one of those mattresses I see beneath freeways and we get lice and…

"So, Maggie. What do you think?" Peg demands, looking at her watch. She taps a French manicured nail against her empty martini glass in an erratic rhythm. Tap, tap, tap, tap, tappity tap…

"Um, um…"

Tap…tap, tap, tap…

I can't think. Stop the tapping! Are you trying to communicate via Morse Code?

"We *really* would love to have you on board, Maggie." Peter encourages."You could be *Cooking and Women's* own personal Chef of Hearts. Plus there's that prize money. A little, *immediate,* added incentive." He shoots me a lopsided grin and presents me with a check for two thousand five hundred dollars.

I'd almost forgotten about the prize money. Forget the lies. Forget the pressure. Forget the Morse Code. *Hello, Chef of Hearts!*

So what if I'm just learning how to cook. You've got to start some-where. Julia Child didn't start cooking until she was in her late thirties and look what she was able to accomplish. "I'd love to, Peter." I smile, P.B.C.—Protective Brain Coating—in place. "The Chef of Hearts is on board."

Chapter Nine

"A true friend is someone who thinks you are a good egg even though he knows that you are slightly cracked."
—Bernard Meltzer

PICKIN' TOMATOES
LOOKING FOR MISTER RIGHT?
SEARCHING FOR THAT PERFECT RECIPE?
MEET THE CHEF OF HEARTS
SHE'S A DOLLOP OF THERAPY
A DASH OF ENTERTAINMENT
ALL ROLLED UP IN A RECIPE
p. 62

Yes! There I am, right on the cover of *Cooking and Women* magazine! I pump my arm in the air, and then my excitement propels me to page 62. Finding Mister Right is like choosing the right tomato for your homemade salsa…

Oh, what a rush this is! I am officially a published columnist. I can't believe it. I guess the reality never hit me until right now. I kiss the article over and over, finally forcing myself to snap out of my celebration orgy. There is work to be done.

I place the magazine on the kitchen counter, and then think twice. What if I spill something on it? I walk into the living room and display it on the coffee table—but who's going to see it there? Maybe I should start a wall collage of magazine covers. A Maggie shrine, so to speak. And why not? It's about time I tooted my own horn.

I pad back into the kitchen, walk over to my desk, and take four push pins and a pair of scissors out of my drawer. I cut off the September cover of *Cooking and Women* and skewer it right to the wall above my computer.

Ah, much better. Now back to business. Food Network. According to the checkout lady at the grocery store, their website has a plethora of culinary information and instructional videos. I log on to the site and scroll over to Cooking, then Cooking Demos, and finally Knife Skills. If I am to be a chef and culinary columnist, then I need to master the art of carving, cleaving, and chopping.

Let's see, Julienne…Brunoise…Chiffonade….Lovely sounding French words. Don't mean a thing to me, but lovely none the less. Mince…Chop…Ah, chop. A familiar word. I chopped off hunks of my fingers when I made the coq au vin. Definitely a technique I should work on.

I click and a woman materializes on my computer screen, her voice pleasant and efficient. I listen for a moment, and then walk over to the sink for my handy rubber gloves. I'm out of Barbie Band-Aids, so I need to be careful with my fingertips.

I lay out my wooden cutting board, pick out a wide, large knife the Food Network calls the Chef's Knife and hold the handle with three fingers like I am instructed. Fourth finger and thumb go on the blade, on opposite sides. Make a rocking motion, back and forth, leaving the end of the knife on the cutting board. Use your other hand to push the veggies forward, being careful to round your fingertips so you don't cut them. *Oh, that's how you do it.* I experiment with the cutting motion and am impressed with how easy it is.

I set the knife down and slide over a stalk of celery. The lady said chopping was just cutting food into pieces, bigger than minced or diced pieces. I carefully run my blade along the stalk, dividing it in half and then fourths lengthwise. Then I begin my newly learned technique.

Chop. Chop. Not bad. A little uneven, but not bad.

Chop. Chop. Chop. I'm getting faster. Cool.

Chop. Chop. Chop. Cho… "Shi…Son of a biscuit!" A rubber fingertip lies on the cutting board, severed from the glove. I inspect the tip to see if I nicked my finger and am relieved to see no blood. It's a good thing Dad had size XL rubber gloves or I'd be in trouble here. The extra half inch in the finger length saved my skin. But I need to continue practicing, and this is my last set of gloves. How to patch it up? I'm out of band-aids. Scotch tape probably won't hold the tip on. Duct tape? Why not? I saw it in Dad's workshop the other day when I was rummaging around for cooking safety gear. I retrieve the roll of gray adhesive and tape on the rubber tip.

Time for a little more of the knife video. This time I am going to learn what *brunoise* is and how to do it. And my sacrificial veggie will be the… the carrot.

Five minutes later, I am *brunoising* away. This time around, I don't go for speed like I did with the chopping. I go nice and slow. The knife lady said brunoise meant finely dicing exact cuts at right angles. So I carefully cut my carrots into long skinny strips, bunch them together, and brunoise them into tiny, exact dicings. Perfect. Especially considering how hard those carrots are to cut. They roll around everywhere.

Just as I finish duct taping the third finger of my glove, I hear pounding on my back door. Who could that be at ten o'clock on a Monday night? I pull off my gloves, walk over to the door, crack it open a sliver, and peek out. You can never be too safe. Even though Dad's house is located in historic Vinings, you still get some crime. The occasional burglary, vandalism…

I throw open the door and scream. "Justy!"

• • •

"So, here I am. Destitute," Justy declares in her throaty voice, even sexier than when she was in boarding school, "lonely," she covers her heart theatrically with her hand, "and…"

"Cut the phony baloney, Just. You're a gazillionaire and married to the last wonderful guy in the whole world. Who's also the most amazing chef in the whole world, I might add. When did you fly in from Paris? Why are you here? Besides to visit your beautiful god-daughter. Come on, you've *got* to see her." I babble as I grab her hand and tug her along behind me. We sneak into the nursery and peer down at the sleeping form in the crib.

"She's amazing, isn't she?" Cat's sound asleep on her back, her little rosebud mouth pursing ever so slightly. Five fingers, five toes, a tiny heart. How could I have given birth to such a miracle?

"Oh, *oui, cherie*," Justy whispers. "*C'est impossible* we gave birth to her."

I smile at the comment. Justy flew in from France for the last couple of weeks of my pregnancy and was in the delivery room with me. Because of this, she believes Cat's birth was a combined effort. I turn towards Justy and spy a tear rolling down her cheek. She must be thinking about the fact she and Jean Paul can't have children. They've had two miscarriages and after a couple of unsuccessful rounds of in vitro, they've given up.

I pull her away from the crib and we tiptoe out of the room. "Do you think she looks like me?" I ask as we curl up onto the couch in the family room.

Justy retrieves a compact from her Louis Vuitton purse, checks her reflection, and tidies up some smeared mascara. "*Non*," she sniffles, snapping the compact shut and turning towards me. "She looks like *moi*."

I laugh and throw a pillow at her. "That is so not fair. I got the pain and you get the accolades. Just as long as she doesn't look like Richard. God forbid."

"Ah, *oui*, Richard. So, what is happening?"

I groan. "Don't get me started. He is such slime."

"*Cheri,* he is her father. He cannot be so bad."

I start spluttering "Just! You can't be…"

"*D'accord, d'accord.* You Americans, always so touchy." She gestures towards my hair, changing the subject. "*Tres belle.* I love the color."

I shrug my shoulders, unused to compliments about my hair. My hair's never looked like I wanted it to. Personally, I've always loved Justy's black hair. The short bob is so chic.

She sits up with a start and smacks her head lightly with the palm of her hand. "*J'ai oublié!*" She roots around in one of her four Channel suitcases, pulls out a bottle of wine and sets it on the coffee table. "We have work to do. Papa and Mama need taste testing."

I lean forward and read the label on the bottle of wine."It's ready? The new batch?"

Justy grins. "*Oui.* The Port from the Beaune vineyard. And…" she rifles a bit more in a suitcase and presents me with a large, wrapped white box. "*C'est magnifique* with this."

"What's this?"

"*Mon Dieu*! Have your forgotten what day this is?"

I unwrap the box, open it, and suck in my breath. It's chocolate truffles from my favorite French chocolatier.

"*Bon anniversaire,* Maggie!"

My birthday! With everything that's been going on, I completely forgot what day it was. "You remembered."

"Of course. And Mama and Papa too. This is from everyone."

I pick out a truffle, pop it in my mouth and chew slowly, savoring the slightly bitter, powdery cocoa flavor followed by a sweet, creamy milk chocolate. "Oh, man, this is so-o-o yummy."

Justy reaches out a hand to the chocolates and I slap it away. "Wait your turn." I devour another one and force myself to relinquish the box.

"So how are your parents? Wait a second, you didn't tell them about my cooking column gig, did you?" I sigh, already knowing the answer. Justy can't keep a secret from anyone. "That's the reason you're here, isn't it? You blabbed and now Mama Beignet's worried."

Justy leans back on the couch, lining up her pedicured feet next to mine on the coffee table. Well, not quite next to mine. Her legs belong to a five-foot-nothing body. Stretched out, her feet come to my calves.

"What do you expect, Maggie? All those summers you spent with me. You are like another daughter to her. Always have been, *ma petite chou.* She's just concerned, we both are. That is why I am here. I help Jean Paul in the kitchen of Bienvenue and I can help you too.

I lean my head against Justy's shoulder, and then turn to look directly at her. "That's why I love you, Just. You're my best friend. Always have been, since boarding school. You ever think about those days? We didn't have to worry about a mortgage, a job, a husband. We could just be crazy and silly."

"*Non,*" she grunts, her eyes closing.

"Come on, you know you do. The midnight raids on the kitchen? The time we stuck the desks on the roof? What about the…"

"The Barbie triplets!" we exclaim together, erupting in laughter. There are some people you just don't forget.

"*I repeat, young ladies of Hopewell Academy do not engage in this kind of shenanigans. I will not tolerate it. Now, I want to know who's responsible for this,*" Mrs. Hopewell barked as she strode through our lines like a drill sergeant. Although it was dinnertime, she had assembled the whole student body in front of the school.

She passed by me and I felt my right hand rising as if of its own accord. I tried hard to resist, I really did, but this was just too good an opportunity. My hand rose to my forehead in a crisp salute and there was a smattering of giggling next to me. Mrs. Hopewell pivoted around just as I was about to put my hand down. Rats! Caught red-handed.

As a cover, I ran my hand through my hair and gave her a half smile. Mrs. Hopewell halted before me, flames shooting from her eyes, smoke streaming from her nose.

"Ma'am?" I enquired, dropping my smile, and plastering a void look upon my face. She knows nothing, I counseled myself. Just don't look at the flag. Don't look at the...I looked at the flag. Thirty pairs of panties, safety-pinned to the rope that hoisted the flag, flapped in the breeze. Ah, the Barbies' silky intimates in all their glory. I smiled in appreciation. Nice work, Maggie. That would teach those Allen triplets not to be so plastic, blond, and stuck-up.

"Maggie Malone!" Mrs. Hopewell thundered. "Are these your panties?" She stood with her feet apart, one hip jutted out, and pointed straight up with her finger like John Travolta in Saturday Night Fever.

Did she really think I'd wear lace-trimmed, pastel satin panties? Or even fit into what was wiggling on the flag pole? "Well, I..."

"Did you do this? This time you have crossed the line!"

That was it. I stared at her defiantly. So I crossed the line. I hated boarding school anyway, and I missed Dad. Ninth grade sucked.

"This is your third offense since the beginning of the school year!" Mrs. Hopewell continued. "I will call your father immediately and..."

"Excusé moi?" a voice interrupted. All heads, including mine, whipped around looking for the voice. It was Justine Beignet's, the foreign exchange student from France.

"I am sorry," Justine lamented. "C'est moi, I did it. I wanted to, 'comment dites'—how do you say..." her hands gestured vaguely.

What was she doing? I shook my head in denial. She didn't do it.

"To, to feet een," Justine declared.

"Feeteen? Fifteen? I know you are almost fifteen, but..."

"No, no, Mrs. Hopewell," one of the girls behind me spoke up. "She said 'fit in.'"

Mrs. Hopewell's mouth gaped open like a large-mouthed bass. She stared incredulously at Justy. I found my mouth gaping too and I shut it with a snap. I refused to appear fish-faced like Mrs. Hopewell.

"Students, dismissed!" Mrs. Hopewell commanded imperiously. "Justine, take those panties off the flag pole and come to my office immediately!"

As soon as Mrs. Hopewell's back was turned, I hustled over to Justine. "Why'd you do that?" I whispered, mistrusting her immediately. I wouldn't put it past the Barbie triplets to use her as a spy.

Justine pulled on the rope to bring the flag down. "Maybe I just want to be fiends," she whispered back.

"Fiends? Do you mean friends?"

"Yes. Fiends." And she grinned. There was a space between her front teeth and freckles all over her face. I couldn't resist grinning back at her.

Chapter Ten

"Y'all rub this wonderful blend of spices on any butt and watch everyone's eyes roll back in their heads over the flavor!"
—*Paula Deen*

"Maggie!" Justy exclaims. "*Mon dieu*! You look like an idiot!"

"What? You don't like my cooking safety gear?"

"Non. You look like Tim…Tim…" she starts muttering in French as she clumps and stomps around the kitchen in my size ten white fuzzy slippers.

I shake my head at her. She's just not a morning person, but come on, it's not morning. It's twelve o'clock in the afternoon! Granted, she might be tired but if I can do it she can. The last couple of weeks we've gotten into the habit of gabbing the night away. It's been so nice to have someone to confide in about Richard and the divorce. And all the little things that have been bothering me. Like the other day when I was at the grocery store and I smelled Richard's cologne, *Creed Tabarome*. I've always loved that musky, gingery scent. I whirled around, convinced Richard was behind me, but it was just some man in a business suit buying milk. And then there's the bed issue. All my married life I've slept on the left side of the bed. Where do I sleep now that I'm almost divorced? I can't sleep in the same spot. Do I sleep on the right? The middle? Maybe I should just sleep on the floor like Justy suggests. There's something to be said about her no-nonsense attitude towards life.

"Tim Allen!" Justy explodes out of the blue.

"Tim Allen?"

"Oui, that crazy guy from *Home Improvement*."

"Just, you gotta stop watching TV Land. Get a life."

"*Non*! It's YouTube. And I have a life. You get a life." She retrieves a cereal bowl and slams the cabinet door shut.

This is why the world has coffee—for cranky people. I stroll over to the pot, pour a cup, and hand it to Justy. Then I back up a few feet and clear my voice. "Ahem. Good morning TV Land. I'm Tim Allen. Welcome to another episode of *Home Improvement,*" I announce, smoothing out my apron and adjusting my goggles. I spy Justy's eyes tracking me over her coffee mug so I slip on my rubber gloves and flop them in the air to wave at her. She chokes on a sip of coffee and I continue, feeling empowered,

"Today we're learning about germs in raw meat." I pick up a rack of ribs with a pair of long handled tongs and hold them over the sink. "Ribs are raw meat, laden with germs and bacteria droplets hiding between those bones. The first thing you must do is sanitize your ribs. And for this, I suggest…" I drop the ribs into the sink, open the cupboard beneath, and pull out a can, holding it up for the camera. "Lysol. It kills ninety-nine percent of household germs."

Justy collapses against the sink, her throaty laughter filling the room. After a moment, she takes a couple of deep cleansing breaths. "Stop! *Arête*! I can't take it anymore! This is absurd. You do this every time you cook? Give me those ribs." She grabs the ribs out of the sink with her bare hands and heaves the bony hulk onto the counter.

I shudder. Those germs must be having a heyday on my clean counter. Good God, did she spray any droplets of disease on my bible, my *Joy of Cooking?* I rescue it, slam it shut, and clutch it to my chest.

"Look, I show you how to do it," Justy declares. "Raw meat is not something you should fear. But you must wash well after. Here is how we do it at Bienvenue. Grab the ribs like this…" She grabs my right hand, rips off the rubber glove, and forces my fingers onto the top of the baby back ribs. "…then rub a bunch of seasonings like this." She dumps a bit of the jar of seasoning we got at *Everything Grilled* and makes me rub it in. "*Voila*! Now the ribs sit, and we wash."

An hour later, the ribs are wrapped in foil and slow cooking in the oven. Justy has retired to the guest bedroom with a bottle of Advil.

*Note to myself: Can you purchase baby back ribs already rubbed with seasoning and sauce?

• • •

From: Maggie Malone
To: Peg Winthrop
Subject: *Pickin' Tomatoes* column

Peg,

Here's the next column. Let me know how you like it.

Maggie

Pickin' Tomatoes

Dear Chef of Hearts,

My boyfriend likes to give me practical, boring gifts for birthdays and Christmas. Our first anniversary, he actually came home with a subwoofer for my car! How do I gently encourage him to give me more frivolous gifts—flowers, perfume, jewelry—without coming across as a high-maintenance woman?

Girlfriend of a Practical Man
Seattle, Washington

Dear Girlfriend of a Practical Man,

A man's first instinct will always be to buy logical, useful gifts for his girlfriend or wife. This seems to be an innate impulse,

handed down from generation to generation dating back, perhaps, to Adam and Eve. Eve most
likely wanted a pretty, tasty apple for her
birthday, but Adam came up with the idea to
give her a saber tooth tiger skin for the floor
of her cave.

Ladies, there is hope. Although men are stubborn, sensitive creatures (if you tell them
you hate their gifts, they will become hurt,
resentful, and basically not inclined to give
you more gifts), they do learn. They just want
to come up with the idea on their own.

Therefore, my advice to you is this: Always
thank your man for his generous gift, such as
leather cleaner or an oil change for your car.
Then encourage him to give you more frivolous gifts by casually leaving magazines open
around the house, turned to jewelry pages. If
by chance they are circled with neon high-
lighters, all the better. Or, cut out pictures
of your favorite perfume and tape them to the
space above the toilet paper in the bathroom
(a sure place to catch a man's attention).

And on your next anniversary, send him—yes,
him—flowers to let him know that floral arrange-
ments are always an appropriate gift. Then
follow up the flowers with a large rack of ribs
for dinner. Men are not stupid, just slow. And
they are especially susceptible to hints and
food offerings.

Adam's Ribs

Preheat oven to 325° F
Serves 4

Ingredients:

2 racks pork baby back ribs
McCormick Grill Mates Barbecue seasoning
1 bottle Sweet Baby Ray's Hickory barbecue
sauce
Foil

Rub ribs liberally with Grill Mates, front
and back, and let sit on counter while oven
is Preheating. Place ribs on one long sheet
of foil, turning up the edges of the foil to
keep in juices. Add another sheet of foil to
top ribs, forming a sealed package. Be careful to roll the edges to seal well, otherwise
juices can leak out! Put package on a cookie
sheet and place in the oven. Cook for three
hours. Let rest for thirty minutes. Remove and
discard foil. Using pastry brush, add sauce to
ribs. Place ribs on hot grill for fifteen minutes to crisp them up, turning once.

The key to this recipe is the slow cooking at
a low temperature. Remember, patience is a
virtue!

Bon chance!
—The Chef of Hearts

I shake my head, disgusted by what I've just written. Patience is a virtue, my sweet pork butt! Not with cooking, not with relationships. How can I write this drivel? I bet Richard gave me hundreds of useful, stupid gifts throughout our seventeen years together. He never did learn despite all the hints I gave him.

"Oh, I almost forgot, Margaret, I have a little present for you."

I looked up from the laundry I was folding and saw Richard standing beside me with a wrapped package. "I saw these the other day and thought of you."

"Richard, you shouldn't have," I murmured, touched by the gesture. Ten years of marriage and he still wanted to give me little gifts.

Richard always gave me spontaneous gifts when we were dating—nothing big, just thinking-about-you gifts. Candy. A little jewelry. Perfume. But it'd been years since there was anything more than the obligatory cards on birthdays, appliances on Christmas. I bet I could guess what this was, though. I'd been eyeing a blue velour Victoria's Secret robe for a while now. And just last week I'd pointed it out in a catalogue to Richard. He must have listened for once.

I untied the bow with deliberation and unwrapped the flowered paper, smoothing it out so I could use it another time. I studied the cardboard box. It didn't really look like a Victoria Secret's box. It was too bulky for that. Maybe it was a big box of pralines or Godiva chocolates. Ooh, ooh, no, maybe a necklace from Tiffany's! In a bulky box to fool me!

I lifted the cardboard lid and peeled apart the delicate tissue paper, holding my breath in anticipation…

HEAVY- DUTY CUT PILE NYLON. FADE RESISTANT. POSITIVE RETENTION…

Floor mats. My husband had given me gift wrapped floor mats.

"Uh…Uh…" I couldn't speak.

Richard gave me a peck on the cheek. "I noticed the old ones in your Jeep were wearing down. I'm glad you like them, honey. Oh, don't forget to use those fresh-smelling dryer sheets I like. And I'll be late again tonight. I have a dinner meeting. Don't wait up." He breezed out the door, and I was left holding my present, surrounded by mounds of dirty clothes.

Yup, I'm done with being patient. With Richard. With my old life. It's time for it to be about Maggie now. I tack the October cover of *Cooking and Women* onto the wall next to September's and walk away.

Chapter Eleven

"Omit and substitute! That's how recipes should be written. Please don't ever get so hung up on published recipes that you forget that you can omit and substitute."
—Jeff Smith

From: Peg Winthrop
To: Maggie Malone
Subject: *Pickin' Tomatoes* column

Maggie,

We have been receiving very positive feedback about your salsa recipe.

Hallelujah!

However, in the future, please remember to submit your new columns only one month in advance, preferably the first week at the beginning of the month. Also, grilling ribs in the late fall? Remember, this is for the November issue. Substitute a different recipe and resubmit it to me in two weeks.

Nuts! I forgot this column was for November. I thumb through October's magazine and see my "Girlfriend of a Snorer" column. *What was I thinking?*

```
We've set up a web page for you — Chefof-
Hearts@CookingandWomen.com. Your fans will
send their letters directly to it so read
through them and pick one for your next col-
umn. Both Peter and I think it's important for
you to do some social networking so we'd like
you to start a Facebook page and begin Tweet-
ing on Twitter. You can register as Pickin'
Tomatoes to market your column.


Peg
```

Social networking...*of course*! What a great idea. I register on Facebook and begin my marketing campaign right away. Luckily, I came up with an icon for my *Pickin' Tomatoes* column the other day. I bought some cherry tomatoes, piled them into the shape of a heart, took a photo, played around on Photoshop, and bingo! One official icon.

Let's see. Create a Facebook page. Category: artist, band, or public figure. Subcatagory: journalist. Basic information, contact information, upload icon photo. Good Lord, Facebook is needy. There's a reason I've never joined.

Now, for Twitter. Log on and register. Edit profile. Download icon.

I have a headache. I have a backache. I have a cheese and crackers brain-ache. Who has the time to do this? Get a life, people!

Focus. Focus. I need to tweet. What does a virgin tweeter say? Something catchy, something to advertise my column in *Cooking and Women*.

Two hours later, I am done. Finished. Caput. The Chef of Hearts has gone viral.

Facebook

 The Chef of Hearts – Tasty Therapy

Hi everyone! Thanks for being a Chef of Hearts
fan! Check back daily for photos, letters, and
advice. Keep reading *Pickin' Tomatoes*!

Twitter

Chef of Hearts
@PickinTomatoes

Boyfriend snores? The Chef of Hearts explores.
Pickin' Tomatoes, Cooking and Women, Oct. issue. #Snoring.

• • •

"Good gravy! Just use the refrigerator crust, Justy!" I'm about to explode. We've been cooking for only a half hour and already my patience is beginning to splinter like cracks on a windshield. When I asked Justy to help me work on my next recipe, I never imagined we'd be making it from scratch. Who does she think I am, Paula Deen?

"*Non*. Homemade is better," Justy mumbles, a cigarette dangling from her mouth. I won't let her smoke in the house and she insists on keeping one in her mouth. "This is what Jean Paul does. Separate those eggs like I showed you. *Non*, not yet. You dropped egg shells in the bowl! *Oui, oui*. Brush the egg across the top of the crust."

"But why do we have to steam the apples? We can microwave 'em."

"Maggie, *s'il vous plaît*," Justy pleads, her unlit cigarette bouncing up and down. "Do it my way."

"And what about the piecrust on top? I bet we could make pretty little leaves in the crust for fall and…"

Justy throws up her hands and begins to curse in French. She storms outside and lights up her cigarette.

Why can't I microwave apples and use refrigerator crust? With today's hectic world, people appreciate recipes that are easy, fast, and tasty. That chef on Food Network does it all the time, what's her name…Sandra Lee. She's got that *Semi Homemade* show. That's kind of what I do too. Cut a corner here, cut a corner there, and *voila*! Cheatin' Gourmet.

Listen to me go on about cooking. Who would have believed it? Before this competition, I never once cooked a meal. Even when I was a teenager and in charge of dinners for Dad and me, I still managed to squeak by without cooking.

"Maggie! Do you want breasts or legs?" Dad bellowed from the kitchen.

I giggled as I studied my scrawny thirteen-year-old body in the hall mirror. I wanted both, thank you very much. Would I ever turn into a woman? I peered closer at my chest, hidden beneath the pink polo shirt, guarded by the shirt's green, embroidered alligator. Hello, is anything in there? And my legs! They were sticks poking out of shorts. White, pasty sticks with freckles everywhere. And the freckles weren't just confined to my legs. They had advanced all over my body like marching soldiers. The only relief I had from freckles was my flame red hair—the one bodily attribute I actually liked about myself.

"Or pot roast or turkey or ha—" Dad continued.

"Chicken legs, corn, mashed potatoes," I volleyed back.

I peeled off my white socks and stuffed them under my shirt. Did that help at all? My newly enhanced body was somewhat reminiscent of volcanoes surfacing from the pink void of my shirt. The socks immediately fell out. I tried re-stuffing my top, but it was no use. I needed a bra to hold in the socks, but that would have to be a project for another day. Dinner beckoned. And it was up to me to fix it.

I made my way to the kitchen, my feet creating little ripples in the avocado-colored shag rug. Making frozen dinners was a bit out of Dad's league. He always ended up burning them. He was more into growing food, anyway. Every inch of our deck was covered in tomato plants. He loved to have fresh, sliced tomatoes.

"I got it Dad," I said, rescuing us from starvation. He flashed a dimpled smile and relinquished the Banquet dinners. I expertly pried open the boxes, careful not to dislodge the brightly colored, evenly chopped vegetables from their compartment and the meat and potatoes from theirs. Everything had to have its place.

I couldn't cook, but I could make a tasty frozen dinner.

```
*Note to myself: Always use refrigerator
piecrust. Microwave apples. Buy Justy nicotine
patches.
```

• • •

From: Maggie Malone
To: Peg Winthrop
Subject: New recipe for November column

Peg,

I'm so sorry for the mix-up a couple of weeks ago. I have decided to go with an apple pie recipe that people can make for Thanksgiving. I think it will work well with my "Girlfriend of a Practical Man" column. If you could change the sentences at the end of the column to the ones listed below and substitute the new recipe, I'd really appreciate it.

Also, thanks so much for my web page—I love it. Very professional. And the fan letters—there were 145 today! I created a Facebook page and began Tweeting like you wanted.

Social networking, here I come!

Maggie

Then follow up the flowers with a large slice of decadent, extravagant apple pie. Men are not stupid, just slow. And they are especially susceptible to hints and food offerings. Remember ladies, regardless of his present, your man does love you. You are the apple of his eye.

Apple of My Eye Pie

Preheat oven to 425° F

Ingredients:

1/2 cup raisins
3/4 cup bourbon
6 to 7 cups or 9 medium cooking apples
3/4 cup sugar
2 tablespoons all purpose flour
1 teaspoon cinnamon
1/8 teaspoon salt
1/8 teaspoon nutmeg
1/8 teaspoon allspice
1/2 cup caramel sauce
2 tablespoons unsalted butter, cut up in pieces
2 (9-inch) refrigerated pie crusts
2 teaspoons apricot preserves melted
1 tablespoon buttermilk
Cinnamon sugar to sprinkle

Combine raisins with bourbon in a medium sized bowl and soak overnight. The next day, set out refrigerated pie dough for twenty to thirty minutes to soften. Peel apples and cut into half-inch slices. Ladies—you can cook these apples over a double boiler but why make more work for yourself? Cook them in a microwave in a dish for five to ten minutes or until tender. That's why we have a microwave. So use it!

Combine 3/4 cup sugar with flour, cinnamon,
salt, nutmeg, and allspice. Drain raisins, reserving 1/2 cup of bourbon., and add to flour
mixture. Pour caramel sauce and reserved bourbon into mixture, add apples and stir. Fit one
refrigerator piecrust into 9 inch pie pan.
Brush preserves over crust, spoon apple mixture onto crust and dot pieces of butter on
top. Here's the fun part. Roll out remaining
pie crust and using tip of knife, cut out decorative shapes. Thanksgiving is coming up, so
be creative and cut out festive leaves for the
holiday!

Arrange dough shapes over apple mixture, and
brush them with buttermilk. Sprinkle with
some cinnamon sugar. Bake at 425 F on middle
rack of oven for ten to fifteen minutes or until brown. Shield edges of pie with foil. Bake
at 350 F for thirty minutes or until bubbly .
Serve warm with vanilla ice cream.

Here's to being thankful,
The Chef of Hearts

Chapter Twelve

"What sound does a witch's cereal make? Snap, cackle, and pop!"
—*Joke*

"Give your mom and dad a hug for me, okay?" I murmur, hugging Justy.

"*Mais oui*," Justy responds, kissing me on both cheeks. "You will be alright?"

I nod my head yes, unable to speak. If I speak I might cry, and Justy hates emotional goodbyes.

"*Mon dieu*, you're not going to cry, are you?" Justy crinkles up her brow as she studies me like a foreign object under the microscope.

"No!" I exclaim. "Of course not." But she knows I'm lying because my voice is trembling and tears are streaming down my face in rivulets.

"Oh, *petite chou*." For a moment, her face softens but it vanishes quickly, leaving me to wonder if it was even there. "*D'accord*. We will see you in the spring? Okay? And don't forget, Jean Paul wants to give you cooking lessons."

A voice over the intercom booms, "Flight 5411 is now boarding. Please have your tickets ready. We will begin seating rows one through four." Justy bends over, kisses Cat on both cheeks, being careful not to wake her, and walks at a fast clip towards the gate.

She's eager to go home, I can understand that. The whole family is converging in Beaune for a reunion at the Beignet winery. Even Jean Paul is taking a few days off from the restaurant to visit.

I am so envious. Justy's family is amazing. Lots of fun, lots of love, and always lots of noise. The Beignets have six children, four girls and two boys. Silence is not a word in their vocabulary. I know because during my school years, I spent a couple of weeks every summer with them. I learned really quickly to yell in French to be heard during dinner, gesture when I spoke, and, God forbid, don't ever leave food on my plate. If people didn't finish their meals, Mama Beignet made it her mission to make sure they gained ten pounds.

"Mag-gie," Mama Beignet articulated. "Why are you not eating dinner?"
"Oh, well, I ate a late lunch and…"
"Zat is not a reason to starve, Mag-gie. You are a growing girl."
"Right. But all my friends are a size two and I'm…"
"Zat is zem and zis is you. Now eat, ma petite cherie, eat…"
"Mag-gie, have another slice of pie…
"Mag-gie, do you wish to hurt my feel-ings? Have some more cassoulet…"
"Mag-gie, have a little more boeuf bourguignon for Mama Beignet…"

Needless to say, I was a very plump but happy girl during my high school years. Although I missed Mom pretty much on a daily basis, Mama Beignet filled a void that Daddy couldn't fill. Sometimes a girl just needed a mother.

I lift Cat into my arms and cuddle her close, inhaling deeply. She smells of baby powder and innocence. "You will grow up with a mother, *ma petit fille*," I whisper. "I promise you will."

• • •

"As a rule of thumb, one pound of dry ice will create two to three minutes of fog effect. The hotter the water, the more fog but the quicker dissipation of the dry ice." Hmm, that seems easy enough. Thank you Google for providing me with valuable information. Now all I need to do is go shopping.

Tonight is going to be so much fun. Who doesn't love dressing up? Halloween is the only time of the year you get to shed your identity and become someone else. And I am going to be a witch. I've always wanted to be a witch. One of those sexy witches you see at adult Halloween parties. Richard would so disapprove if he knew what I was doing. It's about time I started acting like a single, attractive female. And I'm going to wear stilettos with fishnet hose too. Peg wears stilettos. Why not me? I giggle at the thought of Peg. Maybe she's a witch in real life disguised as an editor.

"Come along, my little pumpkin, it's time to go," I announce as I bend over Cat. Even though Cat is a bit young for trick or treating, I've dressed her in an oversized, plump pumpkin suit, complete with a bright green beanie on her head. *What a cutie pie.* Oh, the things Moms do to their kids. I ponder this for a moment, and then can't help but smile as I pull my camera from my desk drawer. This picture will definitely show up at Cat's rehearsal dinner for her wedding one day.

• • •

"Do you need something, Ma'am?" I turn around and recoil in alarm, trying to shield Cat with my body. There, standing in front of me, is the grossest, nastiest looking man I've ever seen. Blood is dripping from the corner of his mouth, scars crisscross his face, one eye is pulled down and oozing some yellow substance, and he's carrying an evil looking scimitar. Okay, that's surprising. What is a scimitar and how do I know its name? *Maggie Malone, exotic weapons connoisseur…*

"Uh…uh…no, I'm fine," I mumble as I hustle my cart down the aisle. Good God. I know this is a Halloween store, but seriously? Do you have to scare the pudding out of babies? I look at Cat and can't resist a smile. She's happily cooing away in her carrier, sucking on her fingers. Not the least bit afraid of the yucky, creepy man. Alright, so he didn't scare my baby, but he sure as heck scared the stuffing out of me.

I continue my search. *Cauldrons, cauldrons.* Ah, here they are. Witches' costumes too. And right next to the candy. How convenient. It's a one-stop shop, complete with everything needed to get into the holiday spirit. Dad's house, now my house, is in a wonderful family-oriented neighborhood, so there are bound to be loads of trick-or-treaters. I grab a large cauldron, a few industrial sized bags of candies, a cute witch's outfit, some cobwebs—got to have cobwebs—and finally dry ice.

The Chef of Hearts is ready to become The Witch of Hearts.

• • •

"Trick or treat!" a child-like voice yells, ringing my doorbell.

"Eee, eee, eeee," I cackle as I open the door. Smoke pours from the cauldron behind me, quite an amazing theatrical effect I might add, and I emerge, parting the cobwebs with my hand. "Would you like some candy?"

A little girl in a princess outfit gapes at me, eyes as big as lollipops. She slaps a hand over her mouth just as her mother claps hand over her daughter's eyes.

What is wrong with them? Is the fog machine too much? Granted, the house looks like it's on fire, but it's Halloween. You've got to have ambiance.

"Shame on you!" The mother grabs her little princess by the arm and slams the door on me.

This is just too weird. It's the third time the door was shut in my face. Was my witchy outfit too scary? No blood, no gore. Just a big, pointy black hat, a black dress. Okay, maybe a little snug but the store was out of my size and I had to…an odd draft tickles me on my chest and I look down.

Oh, sugar! At some point, my witchy outfit must have popped a button or two. I groan in mortification, buttoning up the offenders as fast as I can. The Chef of Hearts is not just a witch, she's a flasher too.

On the way to bed, I make a wobbly, painful detour to my desk, my toes aching from being pinched in my pointy black witch shoes, and tack up the November issue of *Cooking and Women*. While I'm there, I also jot down a note to myself.

```
*Note to myself: never wear a fuchsia-colored
bra under a too small witch's outfit.
```

Scratch that.

```
*Note to myself: never dress up as a witch for
Halloween. Maybe dress up as a fairy godmother
next year. Never buy stilettos from Payless
shoe store.
```

Stiletto shoes should be outlawed. I bet a man invented the first stiletto heel. People should never invent something they won't use themselves.

• • •

I feel guilty, like I'm cheating on Richard. How stupid is that? It's not like we're together anymore. We're getting a divorce, for Pete's sake. Besides, it's not like I'm going on a date. I'm just perusing the internet dating field. Kind of like grocery shopping. Checking out the items on sale, sorting through the fruits, feeling for freshness. Okay, that's just weird.

I type in match.com and begin. 1 in 5 Relationships Start Online. Good to know. I'm a…woman, thank you very much…looking for a… man, definitely a man…Between the ages of…25 and 30. Sure, why not? I'm a cougar, like Courtney Cox. No, I'm not a cougar, I'm a tigress and I like my meat fresh. Near zip/postal code…hmmm, a toughie. Do I give my zip code? Can they track me down? What if I get wackos responding to this? I type in my zip code and before I can back out of it four hundred and seventeen matches pop up. *Wow.* This isn't like grocery shopping. It's like shopping at Sam's Club. It's a bona fide warehouse of single men.

I begin scrolling through the matches. Martin80 looks too old. There's no way he's between the ages of 25 and 30, he's wearing a toupee! Yes, yes, and Yes! Who gives themselves a name like that? And he's got a silly, over-eager grin plastered on his face like a teenager. Bobby Does it Well. Okay, his name says it all. Tank 90. Looks intriguing, but then I spot a tattoo on his arm, one on his hand, one on his leg, and I bet there are more in places I just don't want to know about.

An hour and a half and three hundred deep into the list later, I give up. Is this what dating's like these days? This is torture. This is up there with wearing those stupid stilettos. I log out, determined not to resort to internet dating again. If I want to find "Mister Right," I just need to follow my advice in my salsa column. I need to find a canned tomatoes guy—an everyday, reliable nice guy. There's got to be one out there for me. Besides, if The Chef of Hearts is good enough to counsel women across America on dating, she's good enough for me.

That's just plain ironic. Here I am, taking my own advice after all these years of not listening to my needs and wants. Maybe that's why I need to be The Chef of Hearts so much. It's not just about the money or the career anymore. It's the whole persona I'm really interested in. After all these years of being Margaret Thompson, I need to be someone else.

Chapter Thirteen

"You get the chicken by hatching the egg, not by smashing it open."
—Arnold H. Glasgow

Facebook

Not that many likes, but coming along. I munch on a celery stalk as I update my page.

Hello, ladies. Does your man give you boring gifts? Does he like apple pie? Say no to useful and yes to frivolous! Read *Pickin' Tomatoes* in the November issue of *Cooking and Women*.

And now for a little Tweeting. How can you say that word seriously? I feel like a bird.

Twitter

Chef of Hearts
@PickinTomatoes

An apple for a diamond. Teaching men about presents. *Pickin' Tomatoes*, Nov. issue of *Cooking and Women*. #Food Bribery.

This is kind of fun. I can see why people spend their day doing this. Why live in a real world when you can live in a virtual one? I log onto my webpage and peruse the letters. Time for business.

Dear Chef of Hearts,

Thank you for being every woman's chef. Women across America love you!

An Alabama fan

Look at that, the fans love me. A warm and buttery feeling spreads over me. This is so cool. I love my job! Let me just tell you, I love it!

Dear Chef of Hearts,

My mother-in-law is a monster. She spies on us, she undermines me, and she belittles me. I can't take it anymore. I want to hire a hit man. Do you have any suggestions?

Persecuted Daughter in Law
Boise, Idaho.

Oh, dear God. She wants a hit man. Can I be implicated by opening her message? I rush to the next e-mail.

```
Dear Chef of Hearts,


Do you like kidneys? My husband and I argue
all the time about kidneys. How do you like to
prepare them? Do you like to soak them first in
cold or hot water?


Kidneys in Question Wife
Montgomery, Alabama
```

Weird question. Personally, I love my kidneys. My body couldn't live without them. And yes, they probably enjoy a warm soak from time to time. Would benefit from a glass of wine too, but hey, I'm breast feeding, so I've got to be good. Probably too much info though.

```
Dear Chef of Hearts,


I can't cook and my fiancé doesn't know. I'm
getting married Christmas Eve...
```

Aha! A woman after my own heart. She can't cook, just like the old Maggie. The Chef of Hearts has the perfect solution for her.

• • •

```
From: Maggie Malone
To: Peg Winthrop
Subject: Pickin' Tomatoes column
```

Peg,

Here's the column for December. This one is a
bit different, though, because of the fan's
letter. There is no original recipe because I
want to be accessible to every woman, especially the ones who don't cook. Have a great
Thanksgiving.

Thanks,
Maggie

Pickin' Tomatoes

Dear Chef of Hearts,

I can't cook and my fiancé doesn't know. I'm
getting married Christmas Eve and I'm afraid
he will dump me if he finds out I can't cook.
I've gotten this far because I am the takeout queen—buy, put on china, and heat it up.
Should I try cooking classes before I get married? What do I fix for our first meal together?

Takeout Queen
New York, New York

Dear Takeout Queen,

My advice to you is to talk to your boyfriend
before your wedding. Explain you can't cook.
Honesty is always the best policy. He'll understand and if he doesn't, he's not Mr.
Right. There's nothing wrong with takeout and

there's nothing wrong with cooking classes,
but only if you do it for the right reason.
Forcing yourself to do something you don't
want to do always results in catastrophe.

This Christmas, give yourself a present. Order
a pizza and spend quality time with your honey
in the bedroom instead of the kitchen. Merry
Christmas!

Honey Time

Serves 2

Ingredients:

1 delivery pizza
Beverage of choice
Extracurricular activities, preferably in bed-
room

Here's to giving presents!
—The Chef of Hearts

• • •

"Hello, my Kit Cat. You ready for a little food today?"

Without pretension, Cat ignores me, intent on whacking practice with an orange spotted dog toy. Maybe she's intent on becoming a women's baseball player when she grows up. Or maybe she's just practicing decking a guy if he messes up. Either way, it doesn't matter because I am on a mission.

Today, per the pediatrician's recommendation, I am starting Cat on solid food. It's not going to be just any old solid food either. No siree. I disagree with the pediatrician on that score. I taste tested twenty brands of jarred baby food last week and nineteen of them made me gag. Odd-ly enough, the jar of peas was pleasant. Go figure. Nope. The Chef of Hearts' heir to the family fortune will not dine on jar food. She will dine on gourmet, original Chef of Hearts recipes.

After my taste test experiment, I researched homemade baby food as nauseam. It took me days of baking, pureeing, and straining, but I finally have it. The perfect Chef of Hearts' baby food recipe. I made it fresh this morning after Cat's sunrise mommy latte. Granted the baby food took me two and a half hours to make today, and my kitchen now looks like a tornado hit it, but it was worth the extra work. And there's no doubt that I will embrace the extra effort daily, because I am all about healthy, homemade food for my child. Who knows? Maybe The Chef of Hearts will have a whole new audience for recipes and counseling—kids. They must be full of questions that need answering.

I open the refrigerator and pull out my crème de la crème, brown rice with apple, avocado, and butternut squash puree. True, a lot of the articles I read suggested introducing only one food group to your child at a time, but I think more is better. More nutrients. More flavor. More gourmet. It doesn't taste that bad, once you get past the pukey green-brown-orange-ish color. The consistency throws you off a bit because I over pureed it and it's kind of soupy. But no matter. It's goo-oo-ood and good for you.

I pour the concoction, which I have dubbed Riceappladoash, into a bowl and set it on the counter. I place my new pink baby spoon right next to it.

"Come here, my honey," I say to Cat, as I pull her out of her boun-cy seat. When the pediatrician gave me the go-ahead on solid food last week, I went out that very day and purchased the best high chair I could find. With an eight-position adjustable height, three-position reclining backrest, and a five-point harness, this amazing highchair "unites sophis-ticated design with technical excellence." At least that's what the com-mercial touts and it sounded impressive to me. I don't really get why the fashionable seat cushion is dry clean only, but maybe babies don't spill on it. That's probably why there's an easy-to-clean snack tray, to catch all the food.

I slide Cat in, harness her up, and recline her a bit so her head doesn't loll around. She stares at me with her big eyes, looking a bit like a lamb going to slaughter.

"You're okay, sweetie pie, you're okay," I encourage as I reach over to the counter and grasp the pink spoon. "Look at this. Momma has a pretty new spoon for you today," I announce as I show her the new utensil. Maybe she'll think it's a toy. Then I reach for the Riceappladoash, being careful not to scare the kid, insert the spoon, scoop up the soup—excuse me the baby food—and hold it up in the air. "Here's the choo choo. Woo woo! Open up."

I advance the spoon towards her and, no lie, she sniffs at it like a dog. I know it sounds crazy, but that's exactly what she does, then clamps her mouth shut and turns her head. Granted, it does smell a little iffy but, hello, gourmet baby food here. Show me the love, kiddo.

"Yummy, yummy," I coax and place the spoon in my mouth to demonstrate how to eat. I gulp it and try not to make a face. I don't remember it tasting so bad.

I scoop up another spoonful and advance again. She reaches out her fingers like she wants to take the spoon. Wow! My baby wants to feed herself! What a genius!

I give her my most encouraging smile, propel the spoon towards her, and thwack! She bats it back at me, just the way she batted that spotted dog tog earlier today, and Riceappladoash splashes all over my face. I wipe the goop off, insert the spoon, and press on once more.

The Chef of Hearts is all about patience and dedication. Those virtues have always been an integral part of my nature. Just like my senior year at Kennesaw State in Atlanta. I was majoring in English and my final paper was on Shakespeare comedies. Do you know how many comedies Shakespeare wrote? A whole jelly bean jarful, that's how many. What possessed me to take on all of them, all at once, I don't know. Even my professor tried to talk me out of it but I didn't listen.

"Maggie, be realistic. Shakespeare wrote a lot of comedies. How are you going to read the entire group in one term? Remember, this paper is forty percent of your final grade. Why don't you choose one comedy and focus on the theme, the battle of the sexes," Professor Applegate said.

"I can do it, professor. I know I can," I bragged. "It's just a little light reading. I'll be fine."

"We'll see, Maggie, we'll see."

It turned out to be more than a little light reading. Eighteen comedies to be precise. And I had to go into overdrive to pull it off. I almost failed my math course. I lost my boyfriend to a guy—okay, I wasn't really upset over that one—and I was fired from my part-time job delivering pizzas.

But hey, I received an A on that paper and that's all that matters.

• • •

Forty-five minutes later, Cat and I are in the bathroom. My new concoction is in our hair, on our clothes and bodies, and, oddly enough, up our noses. I think I even have some…well, I won't go there. Cat may be destined to become a ball player, but she definitely does not care for Riceappladoash. And I learned something else about my daughter. She's inherited the Malone stubborn streak.

```
*Note to myself: never make homemade baby
food. Buy Gerber. Order Thanksgiving meal from
Fresh Market. Take highchair seat cushion to
dry cleaner.
```

Chapter Fourteen

"Doctor, do you think it could have been the sausage?"
—*Paul Claudel, French writer*

Facebook

The Chef of Hearts – Tasty Therapy

```
344 Likes • 38 Talking about this • 141 were
here
```

Only 344? Pickles! Come on, people, like me! Going for a thousand here.

```
Check out my tips for making merry this
Christmas. Pickin' Tomatoes, Dec. issue of
Cooking and Women.
```

Twitter

```
This Christmas, order takeout so you can make
out. Pickin' Tomatoes, Dec. issue, Cooking and
Women. #Honey time.
```

I giggle at my rhyming. I'm a poet and I know it. Oh, The Chef of Hearts has so many talents.

```
Dear Chef of Hearts,


What a great column! It is so refreshing to
find a woman not afraid to give out a little
free advice. You're like the Dr. Phil of cook-
ing! Do you have a doctorate in counseling
too? You could open an office and hold group
sessions for couples.


A San Francisco fan
```

Thank you San Francisco fan. But no, there's no fruit cakin' way I'm counseling couples in real life. I can barely handle this.

```
Dear Chef of Hearts,


My husband lashed out at me in his sleep when
I plucked out his chest hair and now I have a
black eye. Where do you get off…
```

Ouch! I am sorry.

```
Dear Chef of Hearts,


Would you like to write a book about being The
Chef of Hearts? I could co-author it with you.
```

Intriguing idea. However I don't have time. I'm a columnist now.

Dear Chef of Hearts,

How do you know if you're in love?

    You don't. Even when you think you do, you still don't.

Dear Chef of Hearts,

My boyfriend is afraid to eat spinach.

    I hate spinach too. Slimy stuff.

Dear Chef of Hearts,

My husband has a gas problem...

    Seriously? Do I really need to know that?

Dear Chef of Hearts,

My boyfriend wants to know if you'd consider a threesome...

    I can tell this column is going to bring out the weirdoes.

Dear Chef of Hearts,

Do you know any good recipes for dog biscuits?

    Hello? Who am I, the Dog Whisperer?

```
Dear Chef of Hearts,


My boyfriend has never liked my best friend.
From the beginning, all they ever did was ar-
gue around me. And it really bothered me be-
cause I loved them both. But then I found out
my boyfriend...
```

There it is. The perfect letter. It's time for The Chef of Hearts to work her magic. I'm like a cooking sorcerer. Or is it sorceress? Is there a feminine form of the word? Regardless, I flick my wand, excuse me, my whisk, and dispense magical therapy and recipes.

The phone rings and I reach over to pick it up. "The Chef of Hearts... Just!"

• • •

Let's see. Mushrooms. I scan the index. *Ahhh, stuffed mushrooms.* I turn to page 516 in Julia Child's cookbook. Champignons Farcis. I roll the words around on my tongue. Lovely sounding French words. If only Justy could hear me now, she'd be so impressed with my accent. But alas, she's probably on one of her clothes shopping sprees in Paris, Milan, or London.

Justy's clothes shopping sprees are notorious. A few times a year, she and her girlfriends get together and go nuts buying Miu Miu, Louis Vuitton, and goodness knows who else. This year, she told me she just had to have some vintage outfit she'd been ogling that costs more than a month's worth of groceries and utilities for Cat and me. Imagine if Jean Paul didn't keep her on a budget. Kind of makes me feel like I can rationalize buying that Target green sparkly cardigan I've been eyeing.

I go back to skimming the index and am discouraged by my choices. Julia, I'm surprised at you. Where's the meat? Who wants mushrooms stuffed with just breadcrumbs?

I abandon her cookbook and open *Joy of Cooking. Mushrooms. Stuffed with clams or oysters.* No thank you. I don't like slimy stuff.

Mushrooms. Stuffed with seafood or snails. I don't think so. I don't like crawly stuff. Come on, Irma! Where are mushrooms stuffed with Italian sausage? I bought a whole package of Italian sausage links so I could stuff it into my 'shrooms. How hard can it be?

I look up sausage. Maybe I need some background information. Then I'll just concoct my own recipe. A little Julia, a little Irma, a lot of Maggie. That'll work. I'm a multi-faceted chef. A hybrid chef, if you will. And an educator.

"Cat," I call out, "listen to this." I turn my head to look at her in her crib and find she has rolled over. "Oh, Cat! You did it! You rolled over onto your tummy! My girl is a genius, yes she is." In response, she lifts her head and blows a spit bubble. Okay, maybe she's a work in progress, a genius in progress, so to speak. All genius have to start out as babies, right?

I begin to read out loud. "*Sausage is one of the oldest of processed foods; 3,000 years ago, grinding meat into sausage was an old Mediterranean custom....*"

Well, there you go. Sausages have been around for thousands of years. I bet those Mediterraneans knew how to stuff their mushrooms with sausages.

I study my sausages. Cute little fellas, all neatly lined up in a row. They seem to have some kind of covering over them. I bend down closer and examine them. A casing. Hmm, I guess the meat's in a protective casing. Makes sense. It's safety meat. Well, little fellows, time to be brave and come out to play. I poke a hole in the end of one the links with a toothpick and attempt to squeeze the meat out. It seems to be stuck in its casing.

"Come on sausage," I urge. "You can do it! Push!"

Back to Irma. Casings, casings... right under sausages, pages 797 and 812. Aren't you thorough, Irma. I'll start with page 812 and see how it goes.

Back to my sausage. "Push! Ah, there's my little meat. Come to Mama." It feels as though I'm about to give birth.

Irma: "*There are three major types of sausage: fresh or "country"; cooked, lightly cured and partially dried or dried....*" Hello-o-o, too much information.

Sausage: I watch as the meat pushes out of the casing. *Oh my.* That looks, well, nasty. Not at all like I expected. Kind of like vomit. The meat curls onto the countertop, and I'm left holding an empty casing. Excitement, awe, and nausea join forces and roll over me. I am the proud mama of a raw, case less sausage. One day it will grow up to be yummy mushroom filling.

Irma: *"The long natural casings made from…"* I read on and drop the casing like a hot potato. I don't care that I have given birth to an Italian sausage. I don't care that I'm an adult, a renowned chef and prize-winning columnist.

*There is no…*I grab the casing, careful to hold it between just my thumb and fingertip, and toss it into the trash can…*hot doggin' way.* I seize the meat and chuck that into the trash too, then spray the counter with disinfectant and wipe it down with a pile of perhaps forty paper towels. Then I remove my protective gloves and suds up the outside of them real good, turning them upside down to dry. *I am going to cook with intestines from sheep, hogs, and cattle. End of story.*

```
*Note to myself: Never de-case Italian sau-
sage.
```

I cross that out.

```
*Never buy raw Italian sausage. Buy ready-
cooked sausage. Get more paper towels. Pur-
chase bottle of Jack Daniels.
```

I gaze at my expanding wall collage of *Cooking and Women* covers and my disgusted feeling melts away. It's hard to stay grossed out about sausage when your trophy wall is displayed in front of you. I can't help being impressed. That might sound conceited, but there it is. I'm impressed with myself. Not even a year ago, I couldn't cook and didn't have a job. Now my column is called out on four magazine covers. I'm an actual chef. Okay, a fabricated chef, but why quibble? And I have a decent salary. Not bad for an ex-housewife. Not bad at all.

Chapter Fifteen

"If only one could tell true love from false love as one can tell mushrooms from toadstools."
—*Katherine Mansfield*

From: Maggie Malone
To: Peg Winthrop
Subject: *Pickin' Tomatoes* column

Peg,

Here's the column for January. Hope you had a nice Thanksgiving!

Maggie

Pickin' Tomatoes

Dear Chef of Hearts,

My boyfriend has never liked my best friend. From the beginning, all they ever did was argue around me. And it really bothered me because I loved them both. But then I found out my boyfriend had slept with my best friend

while I was out of town. I kicked my boyfriend
out and haven't spoken to my friend since. Now
my *ex*-boyfriend wants to come back and my *ex*-
girlfriend wants to apologize. They said it
was an accident. Should I forgive them?

Torn in Love
San Diego, California

I pause from my typing for a moment, overcome by emotion. *What is this woman thinking?* Some things you just can't forgive or forget. Some things will be forever etched upon your heart, and time just deepens the lines. I had way too many of those lines engraved upon my ticker these days.

The phone rang and I stopped cleaning to answer it. Dad was in the hospital, awaiting tests, and I was keeping myself occupied. It was my mission to clean his house thoroughly, from top to bottom.

"Oh, it's you Richard. What do you want?" I clipped as I opened the refrigerator door. I wasn't even going to try to be civil after the big blowup we'd had. I was still steamed over the "I need space" speech. Good God. What is that creature residing on the fridge shelf? It looked like it might be able to walk at any moment. I grabbed a spoon and prodded the moldy green and brown spotted blob with hairy tentacles.

"No, I don't have a minute. Dad was rushed to the hospital last night with chest pains. They told me not to worry so I think he's going to be okay...I don't know, they're running tests today...Fine, I'll tell him. Listen, I have a lot to do so...No, I haven't talked to Adam."

I stopped cleaning the refrigerator and stood up, stretching my back for a moment. Man, I was tired. Eight to nine hours of sleep was not enough these days. I was even resorting to little catnaps in the afternoons.

"You're sorry? Well, you should be sorry. You said some mean things, Richard. And it hurt my feelings that you wanted to have a bre...what do you mean? What's going on? You're where?"

My legs collapsed under me and I sat down hard on the linoleum floor.

"In the Bahamas? With who? Celeste?"

Dear Torn in Love,

How do I put this nicely? Wake up! You just don't sleep with someone and say, "Whoops, it was an accident. Sorry."

Anybody who loves you, really loves you, wouldn't do this to you. Not your girlfriend and especially not your boyfriend. My advice to you is move on and never look back. Friends and lovers should be like stuffed mushrooms. When push comes to shove, they need to be made of the right stuff or they are just slimy fungus.

The Right Stuff Mushrooms

Preheat oven to 400° F
Serves 8-10

Ingredients:

28 extra large, cleaned white mushrooms
1/2 cup Italian bread crumbs
1/2 cup already cooked breakfast sausage, chopped (follow instructions on package)
2 green onions, minced (white and green parts)
2 garlic cloves, minced
1/2 cup grated Parmesan cheese
8 ounces mozzarella shredded cheese
1 tablespoon olive oil
4 tablespoons minced parsley

1 teaspoon Italian seasoning
Salt and pepper to taste

Cut off stems of mushrooms, carving out cavity in mushroom top. Put tops in microwavable dish, cover loosely and heat on high for three to four minutes. Turn mushroom caps upside down to drain on paper towel and set aside Mince remaining mushroom parts and put in bowl. Add garlic. Microwave on high for three minutes, draining well when finished. Mix in remaining ingredients with minced mushroom pieces. Ladies—you can use Italian sausage. Just remove it from its casing and cook it. But if you want to save time, use already cooked breakfast sausage. Tasty and easy!

Combine well. Add filling to mushroom tops. Place on cookie sheet. Drizzle olive oil over mushrooms and sprinkle mozzarella cheese over each of them. Bake until cheese is melted, about five minutes.

Enjoy with "Right Stuff" friends and lovers!
—The Chef of Hearts

• • •

If I hear another Christmas song, I will vomit. Totally vomit. I've been hearing Christmas carols on the radio, in the grocery store, in the mall, in public restrooms, for crying out loud, for close to two months now. And there's still three weeks left until Christmas.

• • •

"Come on Kit Cat, you can do this. Yes, you can," I coo in my most encouraging voice. "This is Santa Claus. Nice, sweet, Santa Claus." I make one final attempt to pass Cat over to the white-bearded old man in the red velveteen suit and shiny black boots. He's perched on a huge, velvet throne in the middle of the mall. To be perfectly honest, I wouldn't want to sit in his lap either. He smells like moth balls and bourbon. Couldn't the mall have sprung for a classier Santa? I contemplate tossing in the towel when I look back and see the long line snaking behind me. All these moms are just like me, determined to get the holiday photo, even if it means putting their little ones in jeopardy of being jailbait. Nice. Well, if they're not afraid, neither am I.

Cat lets it rip one more time. Piercing wails and hysterical screams. All the while, the intercom blasts, *"Rudolph the red nose reindeer, had a very shiny nose. "*

Christmas. Bah humbug. It just leaves a bad taste in my mouth.

• • •

It's 5:45 in the morning and I've just finished feeding Cat. She stares at me with her big brown eyes, and I watch transfixed as they begin to droop. Closing. Closing. Closed. I rock gently, holding my daughter, and wonder, is there any better Christmas present than a child? Somehow, with all the commercial chaos and noise of the holiday, I forgot what Christmas is really about. The birth of an amazing baby boy. And now I have my own baby. I am a mother. How miraculous is that?

Throughout my childhood, my father made a point of telling me a story about my mother each night at bedtime so I could go to sleep with her in my heart. My most poignant memory is when he told me about Mom one last time.

I stared at my father and I knew.

The doctors said his triple bypass surgery was a success. His vital signs were good. His heart was beating strong. There were multitudes of machines and tubes hooked up to his body that monitored his condition. But I could tell. He had given up and was going home to my mom today.

I sat on the edge of the hospital bed. "Hello, Daddy," I whispered, taking his hand in mine and stroking it. His skin felt paper thin, soft as a whisper, like tissue paper covering a fragile gift.

Dad opened his eyes. "Hello, Mag-pie."

I tried to give him my best P.C.B., but I couldn't seem to find it anywhere. Do smiles reside only in happy people? Don't sad people have an arsenal of smiles? I tried to force ay P. B. C. onto my face, but a mouth twitch was all I could muster. "I have some good news to tell you," I said, changing tactics. If I couldn't cheer him up with a smile, then at least I could cheer him up with some positive news.

Dad stared at me, eyes as piercing as ever, and the seconds marched by. "You're pregnant, aren't you?"

I inhaled a slow breath and felt tears knocking at my door. How did he know? Of course, he knew. Dad always knew everything about me. Almost everything. I hadn't told him the latest news about Richard. I bobbed my head in affirmation and searched for my smile once more. She still remained elusive.

"I always knew you'd be a mother, Maggie," he breathed. "And Richard, is he happy?"

Richard's name dashed away any hopes for a smile. There it was, my secret. How could I tell Dad when he was so sick? But now that he knew about the baby, how could I not tell him?

"Um, Daddy, Richard and I, we're splitting up. We're getting a..." I faltered, unable to say the word divorce. It was one thing getting a divorce. It was another thing telling people about it. Especially people you love. A tear escaped and fled down my face.

"Ah, Mag-pie. You don't have to explain. I knew he wasn't the right one for you."

I wiped at my face with the corner of my sleeve. "I wish you'd let me know," I said, trying to add some levity to the situation.

"Some things you have to figure out for yourself," he replied, licking his chapped lips. "Picking the right soul mate is like picking a tomato. It's not the outside that counts. It's the inside. You'll find Mister Right one day, and you're going to be a wonderful mother. I just know it."

"How do you know? I could be a horrible mom." I replied, looking down. My hair fell around my face, shielding me like a curtain.

He lifted a shaky hand and tucked my hair behind my ear just as he had all my life. "Because your mother was amazing, and you're just like her."

I carefully climbed onto the hospital bed beside him, folding my long legs like an accordion. "Tell me about Momma again," I whispered, laying my head on his pillow

"Your momma had red hair just like yours..." Dad began, his voice fading to a murmur.

"She used to wear it long," I continued for him. "And she liked lavender. She said it was the color and smell of heaven."

For a time, we stayed like that, curled up in the hospital bed together. Joined by memories and hearts. Until I felt his body begin to relax and his eyes closed.

And he went home to Momma.

It was time I told Cat about her grandparents. "Your grandmother had red hair just like you," I whisper to Cat. "And your grandfather loved her very much."

I drift off to sleep, both my parents and my daughter in my heart. You can't have a better Christmas than that.

Chapter Sixteen

"Learn to let your intuition—gut instinct—tell you when the food, the rela-
tionship, the job isn't good for you…"
—Oprah Winfrey

I glare at the television, willing the peach, Atlanta's version of the Times Square Waterford crystal ball, to drop faster. Ryan Seacrest has been narrating the descent of that lit up fruit for the past hour. It's hard to be excited about the future when the symbol of the New Year is moving at a snail's pace.

Cat's whimpers come through the monitor, and I sit up, straighten out my sweat pants, and pull up my holey gray wool socks. Forget the peach ball. I am going to celebrate the New Year with my daughter. I walk upstairs and creep into her nursery. A slash of moonlight has seeped through the closed slats of the wooden Venetian blinds and it highlights Cat's sleeping body. She looks so tiny and alone. A moment of weakness overcomes me and I begin to doubt my choices. *Should I have told Richard he has a daughter? Surely Cat deserves to have two parents around.* Thinking about two parents makes me flash back to the night she was conceived, my birthday party.

"Maggie!" Adam, shouted, weaving and stumbling as he ambled toward me.

I giggled as I reached for his arm, trying to support him with my body but only half succeeding. Somehow my balance and coordination had gone missing. Maybe the celebratory champagne had something to do with it. But I didn't care. It was my birthday and Richard had thrown a huge party for me at Diamonds on the Plaza. It takes weeks to book a reservation at this nightclub, and my husband had managed to book a whole party. A glow of happiness still enveloped me.

"I've got to find Richard!" My "Birthday Girl" tiara slid down over my eyes and I peered through the holes of the sequin-studded letters to scan for him. "There he is!"

I pulled free from Adam, straightened my tiara—a princess always should look her best—and strutted over to Richard who was slow dancing with Celeste. Sometimes it irked me they were such good friends. I smiled at Celeste, and eased my body between them.

"You're mine," I whispered in my sexiest voice into Richard's ear.

"What? I can't hear you. I'm swine?" Richard shouted.

"You're mine," I yelled, exasperated by the loud music.

"You want some wine?" he bellowed.

I sighed and gave up on words. I grabbed his face, instead, and locked him in with some universal sign language, a long and passionate kiss. He got my meaning real quick and we topped off my birthday in the coat room of Diamonds on the Plaza.

What the fu…noodles am I thinking? Richard didn't deserve to know I got pregnant that night. He probably followed up our little coat room appetizer with a meal of Celeste.

*New Year's resolution: Find Mister Right for me and my daughter.

• • •

The heart is the tender central part of baby artichokes; it includes the inner core of leaves, the choke, and the bottom. I pick up the prickly green cone vegetable and scrutinize it. How do chefs get past the prickly leaves?

Choose the largest artichoke you can find. Hmm. Bigger is better. I've always thought that too. *Break the stem off close to the base of the artichoke.* I gaze at the illustration in Julia's cookbook, grasp the stem, and yank on it. Nothing happens. I yank harder and the artichoke shoots out of my hand, airborne. Straight into the kitchen window like a target hitting a bull's eye.

"Sugar!" I cuss. A small starburst crack explodes on the glass and tails radiate outward like a Roman Candle on the Fourth of July.

Well, it could have been worse. I could have broken two windows. I pluck the artichoke from the sink and this time, stepping far away from the window, grasp the stem, and jerk it hard to the left, than hard to the right. Nothing. It must be a flexichoke, masquerading as an artichoke. Okay, Julia, you obviously were much stronger than I am. Maybe I'm going to need some kind of culinary tool.

I eyeball my knives. Nope, something stronger. Perhaps, one of Dad's garden saws. It'll be perfectly sanitary. I'll just wash it with some Palmolive. Five minutes later, a foot long, no-nonsense saw is in the kitchen sink. Sharp and clean. I don my protective gear, which I had to dig out of the trash the other day because Justy tried to dispose of it, and carry the saw over to the plastic cutting board.

"Come here, flexichoke, come meet your master." Mindful of my yellow plastic-gloved, duck-taped fingers, I saw the choke with an aggressive back and forth motion, which severs the stem from the vegetable. The only problem is, it also cleaves the cutting board in two and lodges itself in the avocado colored Formica countertop.

Okay, not good. I push aside the stem, the artichoke, and the two pieces of cutting board and pull on the saw. Nothing. I yank it harder and the saw begins to chew deeper into the Formica. What would any logical woman do now? This is a no-brainer—toss a kitchen towel over it. Out of sight, out of mind.

Holding the artichoke bottom up, bend a lower leaf back on itself until it snaps. Then pull it off. Done, and very neat and tidy too. *Continue all around the artichoke.* Hey, this is fun. Like plucking the petals off a daisy. *Cut off remaining cone of leaves close above top of artichoke bottom.* Now it's easy to finish stripping off the leaves and trim it like Julia says. What's left of the artichoke? The bottom. Isn't that special.

Immediately rub the cut parts with lemon juice to prevent discoloration. Lemon juice? I forgot to buy lemon juice! I search through my refrigerator and spot a bottle of apple juice. Why not? Juice is juice. I plop the heart in a bowl and pour a good dose of apple juice all over it. I'm not much of a rubbing girl, I'm more of a pouring girl.

A blanc is a solution of salted water with lemon juice and flour. It is used for the preliminary cooking of any food which discolors easily, such as artichoke bottoms, salsify, calf's head. What's up with the nasty parts of animals in recipes? First sausage casings made from animal intestines and now calves' heads. And I don't even want to know what salsify is. I prefer to think that it is satisfying salsa.

Flour and lemon juice blanch the food and keep its whiteness. I fill up an old iron sauce pan with water and pour in a few swigs of apple juice. I bring it to a boil and remember that I should have put in some flour, so I toss a scoop of that into the boiling apple juice and watch as blobs of flour rise to the surface.

Add the artichokes. Bring liquid again to the boil, then simmer 30 to 40 minutes. Perfect. The Chef of Hearts will now take a thirty-minute cat nap while the flexichoke simmers. I set the timer and relax on my comfy couch.

• • •

Beeping awakens me and I wake up crying. I dreamt about the day my father died. How do people get over losing a loved one? Sometimes I feel like I'm stuck in a pot that's constantly boiling over. And I'm just trying to clean up from day to day.

Come on, Maggie, pull it together. You've got a meal to cook. I wipe my cheeks, stand up, and trudge into the kitchen to turn off the timer.

How's my little artichoke? I peer into the pan and see that it's happily simmering away in the flour/apple broth. I remove it from the liquid and stick it on one of the halves of the cutting board. The artichoke seems to be all gray and shriveled up, not so happy after all. Time for a bit more reading on the subject.

Scoop out the choke with a spoon, and trim off the remaining leaf ends. What the heck is a choke? I analyze the gray, pruny-looking artichoke bottom and decide the choke is the hairy looking thing tufting out of it. That's got to be it. I'd choke on that too. I get a spoon and dig away at it. The hairy stuff comes out but so does the rest of the artichoke bottom. I'm left with crumbled up blobs of gray matter. No worries. Cooking is all about being creative. I've just created an alternative artichoke heart, that's all. It's a broken heart. A gourmet broken heart. Let's see… *oven Preheated*…blah, blah…*get out some butter and some salt. Melt butter in casserole dish. Add some cut up onions and the artichoke crumbles. Cover and bake for twenty minutes.* Done.

I throw together the ingredients for the Béarnaise, stick it in a pan, and crank the stove on, then slather a couple of filets with oil, shake on some herbs, and toss them into the skillet. Presto. I am a culinary guru.

I glance at my watch. *Ice cream and cake, it's 4:03*! Matthew Fox is on Oprah and he's going to bare all. I can't miss that. I rush over to the couch and fifteen minutes later, smell something burning.

My Gourmet Broken Heart! My Béarnaise! My filets! My nose guides me into the kitchen and to the stove, where I come to a screeching halt. The cremated remains of my filets lie charred in my pan. The Béarnaise, too, is nothing but a brownish-blackish-greenish crust of ashes and—I open the oven door—my heart dies a twitchy death before my very eyes.

I have murdered my entire meal.

Oprah calls out from the television, "Sarah Jessica Parker has a new passion." *Wow. What's her new passion*? For a moment I consider the delicious possibilities. I bet it's shoes. She always has cool sh…. I shake off Oprah's lure and focus on the matter at hand.

The Chef of Hearts has become a meal assassin.

```
*Note to myself: Stay away from windows when
cooking. Do not use garden saw to cut vegeta-
bles. Call handyman to fix counter and replace
window. Never cook while watching Oprah.
```

Chapter Seventeen

"A woman is like an artichoke, you must work hard to get to her heart."
—Inspector Clouseau, The Pink Panther

From: Maggie Malone
To: Peg Winthrop
Subject: February Pickin' Tomatoes column

Peg,

Here's the February column.

Maggie

Pickin' Tomatoes

Dear Chef of Hearts,

My husband is no longer interested in me. We
don't even have sex anymore. It's like we're
cohabitating. How do I get the romance back in
our marriage?

Frustrated and Lonely
Tallahassee, Florida

Dear Frustrated and Lonely,

I hesitate in my typing. I can relate to this lady because I was so frustrated and lonely during the last part of my marriage. There was no romance. No love. No togetherness. But it wasn't always that way. I remember a time when Richard couldn't keep his hands off me. And romance? Well, romance was his middle name.

I walked through the front door and stopped dead in my tracks. A path of red rose petals wove from the door, down the hall, and into the bedroom. Rachmaninov's Rhapsody on a Theme of Paganini was serenading in the background. I sniffed the air. Is that something chocolate?

I followed the rose petals down the hall, through the bedroom, and into a candlelit bathroom. There, immersed in the tub with thousands of bubbles, was my husband, a bottle of champagne chilling in a bucket beside him. Two glasses, a couple of spoons, and a large covered china dish on a small table. And a large bowl of whipped cream.

"What ya got there, big boy?" I purred, as I drifted closer.

"Oh, just a little champagne," he said, "and some chocolate soufflé from Double Delight." He dipped his index finger into the white, fluffy whipped cream and popped it in his mouth. "Come on in, the water's great," he invited, giving me a Cheshire cat grin.

I laughed, shedding my clothes as fast as I could. "I thought you hated bubble baths."

"Not today, my sweets. Happy first anniversary, Margaret."

How do you slide from "go romance!" to "no romance?" No wonder I was frustrated and lonely.

Dear Frustrated and Lonely,

It is quite typical to have stagnant periods
in a relationship. Whoever said love is easy

lied! Romance is like a flower. Right now that flower is wilting and in need of watering and fertilizer.

Ladies, listen up! Cooking is not always about food and fancy recipes. This holiday season give yourself and your man a present of romance. Buy some lingerie, put on some mood music, have a little wine, and cook an easy meal. Your hearts will bloom tonight, I guarantee it.

And if all else fails, have a little chocolate. It's good for you and your heart. Happy Valentine's Day!

Filet and Hearts

Serves 2

Ingredients:

1 can of artichoke hearts in water
2 filet mignons
1/2 tablespoon butter
1/2 tablespoon olive oil
1/4 cup Madeira or dry white wine
1/4 cup beef stock
1 package prepared Béarnaise Sauce

Prepare Béarnaise according to package. Drain artichoke hearts. Add hearts to Béarnaise sauce. Set aside. Put butter and olive oil into skillet and heat on medium high. Add steaks, sautéing three to four minutes per side until desired temperature. Remove steaks and wrap in foil to keep warm. Add Madeira and beef stock to pan, stirring well to scrape up the bits of flavor. Simmer for a few minutes. Place steaks on plate, spoon wine sauce over them. Top with artichoke and Béarnaise Sauce.

Vive L'amour!
—The Chef of Hearts

• • •

Facebook

The Chef of Hearts – Tasty Therapy

416 Likes • 32 Talking about this • 159 were here

Getting people to like you is like trying to pour ketchup. Could it go any slower?

Ladies, don't settle for slimy fungus when you can have the right stuff. *Read Pickin' Tomatoes*, January issue of *Cooking and Women*.

Twitter

Chef of Hearts
@PickinTomatoes

Slime is a crime. *Pickin' Tomatoes*, Jan. issue, *Cooking and Women*. #Torn in love.

Well, ain't that the truth. Slime is a crime. In fact, marriage should come with de-slimer medicine. Take two whenever you feel the urge to be slimy. Probably would save a bunch of marriages.

A notification icon flashes. *Ooh, e-mail.*

```
From: Peg Winthrop
To: Maggie Malone
Subject: Salary meeting


Maggie,


I would like to meet with you tomorrow at 2:00
p.m. to discuss your upcoming salary. We're
located in the Worthington Office Park in Smyr-
na, 2 miles south of the Big Chicken. I assume
you know the Atlanta landmark, the Big Chick-
en.


Peg
```

Yes, Peg, I know the Big Chicken. How can you live in Atlanta and not know the Big Chicken landmark? It's like seven stories high. Must you always be so snarky in your e-mails? But who cares about stuffy old Peg? The Chef of Hearts is going to get a salary! Wahoo!

Chapter Eighteen

"How do you like them apples?"
—Matt Damon, "Good Will Hunting"

"Come," Peg barks from behind a closed door.

I enter the office, glancing around as I go. It's as if all color has been sucked from the room. White furniture, white statues, white walls. Good Lord, that's a lot of white. The only color relief comes from the framed artwork, a hodgepodge of diplomas and *Cooking and Women* covers. One of them features a smiling Martha Stewart holding out a wooden spoon-ful of some culinary concoction. "It's a good thing!" is scribbled diago-nally across the front of the photograph in black magic marker.

"Have a seat," Peg commands, perched atop the edge of her desk, her black stocking-encased leg swinging back and forth like a pendulum. I can't help but notice she has very muscular calves. If I wore four-inch stilettos, would my calves look like that? I sit in a chair with white curvy body and spindly white metal legs that looks like some sort of armless alien from a cheesy sci-fi movie. The slick, scoop-like surface of the seat makes it difficult to remain upright and I have to dig my feet into the floor to prevent myself from sliding down it like a super slide.

"So, Maggie, are you enjoying writing *Pickin' Tomatoes?*"

"Very much, Peg. I've…"

"You know, I find it intriguing that you've cooked dinner for Brad Pitt and Angelina Jolie," she interrupts, eyeing me as if I'm a tasty dessert. "What were they like?" She slithers off the edge of the desk, pulls up an-other alien chair next to mine, and sits in it without sliding one single bit. Perhaps Peg is from the mother ship and the chair recognizes her butt. She leans in towards me. "What'd they eat?" she asks, her voice becoming as velvety smooth as her mega-Botoxed forehead. "Did they have wine? Tip well?" A breath of minty, rancid air wafts towards me, and I can't help but wonder if she had fish for lunch followed with an Altoids chaser.

"Peg, do you have a minute?" a voice calls from behind us.

Peg and I turn as one and there is Peter, looking mighty sexy in a brown blazer, a white button-down oxford, khakis, and little wire-rimmed glasses.

"Maggie! I didn't know you were here yet." A slow smile spreads across Peter's face like warm butter.

I find myself grinning like a two-year-old. A forty-year-old two-year old, that is.

"Of course, I always have a minute for you, Peter," Peg interrupts as she rises from the chair, charm oozing from her like primordial alien slime. She slinks over to the door, grasps him by the arm, and looks up with moony eyes, like a lovesick teenager. Her head is tilted ever so slightly a come-hither glow on her face.

Hello? Is anyone in there? Gag me. I remind myself never to look like that.

"Maggie, why don't you wait outside."

"Actually, Maggie can stay. I primarily came here to talk to her about her column." Peter slips from Peg's grasp and takes a seat beside me in her vacated chair. His butt immediately begins to slide south, and after a few failed attempts of remaining in the middle, he settles on the edge, swinging around to face me. I slide to the edge of my seat too, relieving my quivering calves and thighs. Who knew sitting in a chair would be such a workout?

"Maggie, I want to congratulate you. Your column is terrific and the response has been amazing." I notice his breath smells clean and minty, like toothpaste. Not a hint of fish. Lovely.

"Why, thank you, Peter," I reply, trying to sound professional while fighting a giggle creeping up inside my throat. *I will not turn into a moony teenager. I will not...*

"In fact, sales have been up two percent since your column began. Two percent!" he emphasizes, his smile widening and his dimples engaging.

The giggles wrestle free from my resolve. "Hee, hee-hee." *Good Lord, The Chef of Hearts has turned into the Teenage Chef of Hearts.* I bite my lip, squashing the giggles.

"Now, I know Peg was going to talk to you about your salary today, but corporate wants me to be more involved in your career. So, I took the liberty of running up some numbers. You know salary, benefits, bonus potential—the usual. Take a look at these figures and see if they meet your approval."

Money! I have to restrain myself from grabbing the papers out of Peter's hands. I reach for them and peruse them at leisure, all the while sucking down the information like a chocolate milkshake and trying not to pass out from the brain freeze onslaught.

Success. It's so close, I can taste it. And I've got to say, it tastes wonderful. What do you think about them apples, Richard? You didn't want me to be successful from the get-go.

"I don't know, Richard." I studied my reflection and frowned. Did my bleached blond hair make me look washed out? Maybe I just wasn't used to looking sophisticated and elegant. But the makeup, good God, I could do without all that goop! I took a tissue and started to wipe it off my face.

"Darling, don't! It looks wonderful. Trust me. They know what they're doing at Material Girl Salon. All the girls in the office say it's the hottest place in town, and my paralegal, Amanda, said their products are made with essential oils and minerals. I think that's a good thing, right? No harsh chemicals on my sweet's tender face." He took away my tissue and balled it up, making a hoop shot in the bathroom trash can.

"I appreciate the complimentary makeover and gift certificate, Richard, I really do, but don't you think the makeup's too much? It looks cakey, and the blue eyeliner is making my eyes hurt."

"Nonsense." He cut me off, turned me around, and touched the tip of my nose with his fingertip. "A little makeup just enhances your natural beauty. It hides all those imperfections you women worry about so much. Besides, you're a Thompson now, not a Malone, and you need to look your best at all times. No wife of mine is going to play second fiddle to my partners' wives. So live it up a little. You don't have to work anymore. Enjoy, Margaret. You deserve it," he said, his fingertip tracing a soft zigzag from my nose to my lips to the crook of my neck.

"Well, Richard, I've been thinking about that. I know you'd like me to be a stay-at-home wife, but I would really like a job, maybe something in…"

"Margaret, that's silly. We have plenty of money. Just ask me when you want something. Why would you need a job?"

"Because I want one, Richard. Remember when I worked at your office? I was busy every minute, but it felt like I was making a difference. It gave me a feeling of satisfaction." I might have added self-worth, but that would have opened another can of worms. With Richard, it had to be baby steps.

"Of course, I remember that, Margaret. You were the hottest thing in the whole building."

Okay, itty bitty baby steps. *"Richard, in a few years, I'll get pregnant and then it'll be too late for a successful career. I'll be a mom and wife full time."*

I sat down on my vanity stool, opened the Material Girl Salon bag with its two hundred dollars in makeup: foundation, primer, blush, eye shadow, and two other compacts. I lined up the exquisitely packaged assortment in my vanity drawer, all tidy, fresh, and new—as they would remain through all eternity as far as I was concerned—and tried not to cry. It's not that I was unhappy. I just needed something more in my life than being Mrs. Richard Thompson.

Richard chuckled as he walked towards me. *"What a funny egg you are. You don't need to be successful. I'm successful enough for the both of us."* He ruffled my hair. *"Tell you what. If you really want, you can do some charity work. Find some cause you're interested in. But don't forget that I need you to manage the home front. And that will always be your primary job. Can you do that for me, Margaret?"*

I looked up and blinked back my tears, nodding my head.

"Now, don't forget my dry-cleaning tomorrow. And while you're out and about, why don't you pick up some new sexy underwear? You know the kind I like on you, those low-cut bikini ones. Oh, and it's my secretary's birthday— can you send her some flowers? Maybe some yellow roses. She likes those."

I stood up, turned around, and wrapped my arms around him tight. I was so lucky to have found Richard.

"This looks wonderful Peter," I exclaim. "When does it go into effect?"

"Immediately. Corporate wants you signed up and official. They think you have enormous potential." He claps me on the shoulder, grinning ear to ear. "The Chef of Hearts is going to be a star one day. I just know it."

• • •

"Hello?" I holler, striding into the kitchen and heaving my purse onto the desk. Good God, that thing is heavy. It must weigh twenty, thirty pounds, minimum. Why do women carry so much junk in their purses? Wallet, makeup, phone, that's all we need. Okay, maybe a little baby paraphernalia. Got to have a backup pacifier, diaper, and wipes. A couple or three Snickers Bars for those essential snacks, a Kindle for reading while waiting in the pediatrician's office, an iPad so as not to miss any critical communication, and a pair of comfy shoes in case you wear killer stilettos to lunch to flaunt your legs and then can't make it back to the car because your feet hurt so much.

Well there's my answer. Women carry so much because it's better to take too much and not need it than to need it and not have it. The good ol' American motto, *more is better.*

My colorful cover collage wall catches my eye. Wow, *Cooking and Women* really nailed that February cover. The whole page is bubble gum pink with large, floating valentine heart candies and each candy holds a topic in the magazine. *Dark Chocolate Recipes—They're More Than Sweet, They're Savory! Schnitzels and Schnapps…Valentine's Day German Style. Raising Teen Girls, It's Not For The Faint Of Heart.* And of course, my personal favorite, printed on a light green candy with red lettering, *Pickin' Tomatoes—Make Your Heart Bloom Tonight With The Chef Heart's Savory Solutions.* Quite catchy if I do say so myself.

I stroll into the family room. *Where is everybody?* I'm just about to panic. Did Mrs. Maroni, the babysitter, abscond with Cat and hitch a plane to Mexico? Laughter answers my question and I follow the laughter to Cat's room upstairs. There, on the floor, is Cat, squealing like a pig, and she's rolling from one corner of the room to the other. Mrs. Maroni is in the rocking chair, chuckling.

I stand in the doorway, stunned. "What's she doing?"

"*Ciao, cara,*" Mrs. Maroni comments, looking up. She breaks into fluent Italian and I simply nod, clueless. The woman is the capo di tutti capi of babysitting. Efficient, organized, and, most of all, Cat loves her. She's a Mary Poppins. No, better yet, she's a Mrs. Doubtfire, a mafia Mrs. Doubtfire. She looks like Robin Williams in drag, I don't understand anything she says in Italian and some guy wearing a suit and driving a black car always picks her up. But I don't care. As my daddy used to say, she's like money in the bank.

I crouch down in amazement and watch the spectacle of my daughter "motoring" across the room. Doesn't she get dizzy from all that rolling? I thought babies were supposed to crawl first.

"Cat?" I call, stretching out my arms to her. "Come to Momma." Cat looks at me, smiles a toothless smile, and tumbles over and over until she reaches my side. I laugh and stretch out my arms. "Come here, my little tumbleweed."

Motherhood. Got to love it.

Chapter Nineteen

"The poets have been mysteriously silent on the subject of cheese."
—*G. K. Chesterton*

Oh my God. The cheese. It's…it's…it's alive! How could I have created this monster? I only meant to experiment with a cheese sauce for my fish and crab recipe for March in honor of St. Patrick's Day.

I flee from a viscous blob of Gruyere rising from the little saucepan like a creature of doom emerging from molten slime rivers. It rises higher and higher until I cower in fear. My cheese is possessed!

I respond like any frightened woman and grab the broom, the savior broom that rescues women around the world from spiders and roaches and other threatening creatures. The broom that beats smoke detector senseless when we burn the toast, and which happens to be standing by because I used it earlier. In my haste for coffee, I split open the entire bag, dispersing thousands of coffee grounds throughout the air, onto the countertops, and in the crevices of the cupboards.

Yes, the Heroic Broom. I grab it and fight down the evil blob of dairy spawn. Take that! And that! And…uh-oh. I survey the oozy, gooey bristles. Maybe the broom isn't the best weapon against melted cheese after all.

Cat chortles at my antics like I'm Big Bird sweeping Sesame Street. Maybe I should have my own TV show. I could be a superhero. Supermom! Able to defeat monsterish, bubbling cheese with a broom.

What can I say in my defense? My brain cells were denied their morning elixir.

I sigh and begin cleaning up my mess. Do superheroes have to clean up their own messes? I think not.

*Note to myself: Buy new broom. Never dye cheese sauce green for St. Patrick's Day recipe. Buy coffee!!

• • •

From: Maggie Malone
To: Peg Winthrop
Subject: Pickin' Tomatoes column

Hi Peg,

Enclosed is the March column.

Maggie

Pickin' Tomatoes

Dear Chef of Hearts,

My boyfriend and I have dated for two years. I am widowed and he is divorced. We have always had a great relationship, but this year he moved in with me and things have changed between us. All we do is fight. Money, chores, friends—you name it. He says all I do is nag and stick my nose into his business. I say all he does is drink beer with his buddies and live like a slob. Any ideas how to sort things out?

Nagging Girlfriend of a Beer Buddy
Bloomfield, Kentucky

Dear Nagging Girlfriend of a Beer Buddy,

First of all, the word "nagging" should be banned from man's vocabulary. It is a vague, overused word that probably originated with the caveman. I wouldn't be surprised if it was the very first word he ever spoke. The caveman didn't like it when the cavewoman told him to stop playing bone hockey with his buddies, or to stop drinking berry wine, so his grunts articulated as he got angrier and angrier. It probably went something like this: "Errr awww grrrr naaaa nagging!" Hence, the nagging word was born in men's vocabulary.

I'm not saying that the fault all lies with your boyfriend. It doesn't. Women have a bad habit of confronting their man at the exact moment a problem arises. And that is usually the wrong timing. My advice to you is to sit down with your boyfriend when things are going fine between the two of you and talk it out calmly and logically. Make lists of finances, charts of chores, whatever it takes.

Look at it this way: Men are like fish and women are like crabs. They both live in the same ocean, but it is very easy for fish to get fishy and crabs to get crabby. If you compromise with your man, you can work it out.

Life is too short to live alone in the deep blue sea, don't you think?

Fish and Crab in Harmony

Preheat oven to 400° F.
Serves 4

Ingredients:

2 pounds Orange Roughy fillets
1/2 teaspoon lemon juice, plus 1 lemon
1/4 teaspoon Chesapeake Bay Seasoning
1 (8-ounce) lump crab meat (ready to eat)
1/2 cup Duke's mayonnaise
1 tablespoon fresh chopped dill
1/2 cup panko bread crumbs
1/2 cup shredded Swiss cheese
Salt and pepper

Spray casserole dish with cooking spray. Set
aside. Squeeze juice of one lemon over fish,
top and bottom. Season both sides of fish
lightly with salt and pepper. Combine crab
meat, mayonnaise, dill, Old Bay, and 1/2 teaspoon lemon juice in small bowl. Using knife,
spread crab mixture over top of fish. Roll up
fish (with crab inside) and set, seam down,
in casserole dish. The dish should fit snugly
around the fish. Bake for twenty minutes.

Enjoy and here's to compromise!
—The Chef of Hearts

Compromise. Now there's a fallacy. Who compromises? I make a face
at my bitter thoughts. People compromise, I know they do. And so did

Richard and I when we were first married. The problem is we both gave up on it.

"Why? Why do you drop your workout clothes all over the floor? It takes just a minute to toss them in the dirty clothes hamper." I bent over and picked up another sock. There was a trail of dirty clothes winding through the room like a dirty laundry road in the Land of Oz.

Richard walked over and wrapped his sweaty arms around me. "That's why I have you, my sweets. You can pick them up for me."

I jerked out of his embrace. "That is not why you have me! You always used to pick up your clothes. I'm not your maid and I'm sick and tired of…"

"What's up with you lately?" Richard pulled his white muscle shirt over his head, exposing his six pack of abs, and dropped another piece of clothing on the floor. "All you seem to do is nag, nag, nag."

"I am not nagging." Resentment bubbled up inside of me like a witch's brew. "I just think you could pick up after your—"

"Margaret!" his voice cut through my sentence like a knife. He began to pace back and forth like he was grilling one of his defendants. "Is it not true that I bring in the majority of money in this family unit?"

I opened my mouth to answer but he continued.

"And I work sixty-plus hours a week, while you stay at home?" He caught his reflection in the mirror and paused in front of it, flexing his arm muscles. Then he turned toward me, arms crossed, and raised his eyebrow. "Well?"

"Yes, you do, but…."

"No buts. Just answer the question."

"Yes."

"And all I ask in return is that you do a few household chores and look pretty when we go out. Is that unreasonable?"

Damn, when he put it that way, of course it didn't sound unreasonable. I didn't have to work those long hours. Just the other day, he was gone from five thirty in the morning to two the following morning. And who could fault someone who just wanted you to look your best? Resentment began to evaporate and guilt crept in. "No, Richard, of course not "I just thought…"

He tilted my chin up with his finger and kissed me on the lips. "Well, there's your problem. Don't think." He tousled my hair, stepped away from me, and stripped off the rest of his clothes, adding them to his dirty laundry road.

"Don't count on me for dinner tonight, my sweets," he called out, as he walked toward the bathroom. "I have an out-of-town overnighter."

"Another overnight business trip? I thought we could spend a little time together. Maybe, have a date night like we used to."

"Sorry darlin', this is the price I must pay to keep you in the lap of luxury. Oh, I meant to ask you, can you reorganize my closet? I was thinking one of those closet systems. Maybe Macy's has one in their home section."

I followed the dirty laundry road around the room, resentment resurfacing. Sure, why not? Just call me Toto.

And that would make Richard…?

I anchor March's cover to my wall. *Now there's compromise.* I wanted a job and *Cooking and Women* wanted a columnist. We both had to give a little and take a little. And look what we came up with, The Chef of Hearts.

Time to twit a bit. Okay, not twit, Tweet. But twit rhymes so much better.

Twitter

Chef of Hearts
@PickinTomatoes

Food for thought: Romance is like a flower-fertilize it or it doesn't bloom. *Pickin' Tomatoes*, Feb. issue, Cooking and Women. #Heart.

Facebook

The Chef of Hearts - Tasty Therapy

602 Likes • 20 Talking about this • 184 were here

Ladies, this Valentine's Day, cook up a little romance with beef and artichokes. Isn't your heart worth it? *Pickin' Tomatoes*, February issue of *Cooking and Women*.

Chapter Twenty

"I will not eat oysters. I want my food dead—not sick, not wounded—dead.
—Woody Allen

Dear Chef of Hearts,

My husband likes weird sex and...

Gross.

Dear Chef of Hearts,

Do you want to go out sometime? I am an attractive woman of forty-four.

Where are all the normal letters? Doesn't anyone need good old-fashioned advice these days?

Dear Chef of Hearts,

Have you ever felt lost in love?

Boy, there's a biggie. I bet everyone's felt that at one time or another. I pull open my desk drawer and remove the only remaining picture of Richard and me that has not been chopped up with scissors. I keep it there with the overdue bills not as a reminder of our love, perhaps, but of overdue happiness.

Well, that's a load of liver and onions. I keep it there so I can use a wipe-off marker to doodle on it. Richard is currently sporting warts, fangs, and a tail. I rub off the marker with the tip of my index finger and study the picture, searching for a clue, for some precursor of what was to go wrong with our marriage. In the photo, Elvis and a big-haired receptionist are in the background, Richard is playing the air guitar, and I am grinning a two-foot long smile. I was twenty-two, sunburned, hung over, and suffering from a bad case of diarrhea, but I was marrying the man of my dreams.

What could be wrong with that? At the time, I was, or at least thought I was, insanely happy. I would later regret that Richard talked me into our impromptu Vegas wedding, and that Dad and my friends didn't get to come to it. *And* that I was wearing jeans on the most special day of my life when I'd always wanted to wear a white, strapless Vera Wang wedding dress with a long train and have my father give me away.

I guess that sums up what went wrong in my marriage. Happiness. Put aside Richard's infidelity, how could Maggie Malone's happiness have gotten so lost in Richard Thompson's happiness?

A sneakyfeeling tiptoes into my heart, whispering the blame lies with both of us. Richard might have talked me into his idea of the perfect wedding, but I didn't care at the time. I was madly in love with him and would have agreed to any kind of marriage anywhere. From the very first moment, I was smitten with Richard Allen Thompson and that's all I cared about.

"Can I get directions?"

I looked up from my book, Hollywood Wives, *and squinted at the dark shape looming over me as male features came into focus. "Where to?" I asked, shading my eyes.*

The guy pushed aside the remnants of my lunch—a yogurt container, a half-full can of coke, and a candy wrapper—and sat down next to me on the park bench. *"To your heart,"* he declared, his eyebrows slightly raised and a hand over his heart.

I burst out laughing, shaking my head. "Sorry, not interested," I replied, lying through my teeth. What girl wouldn't be hooked with that line? The man looked like Richard Gere when he was in An Officer and a Gentleman. But I had a dating guidebook that said it was important to play the game when a man was flirting with you. If you acted too interested, there was no challenge and the guy would give up.

He flashed an incredibly white smile, shrugged his shoulders as if to apologize, and leaned back on the bench, hands linked behind his head. I scooted a little away on the bench and went back to reading my book. Or tried to. All I could think about was Richard Gere sitting next to me. Say something, I willed. Please God, make him say some...

"Don't you know me from somewhere?"

Wow, God must listen to dating prayers. I casually put down my book and gave a theatrical sigh. "Listen, no offense, but I don't know you. I just want to do a little reading on my lunch hour." I picked up my book and resumed reading. Okay, not reading, staring blankly at the page.

He chuckled, reached over, and turned my book around.

Crap, I hadn't noticed my book was upside down. No matter, just stick to the game, Maggie Malone. Stick to the game.

"Well, you should know me," he chided.

I sighed another sigh, this one worthy of a heroine in one of Jackie Collins' books, with just enough oomph in it to portray how exasperated I was. "And why, exactly, should I know you?"

The guy beamed his ever-brights. *"Because, I'm Richard Thompson. From the tenth floor of Whitman, Thompson, and Allen."* I stared at him, my mind a blank. *"I believe you answer phones for me."*

I draw a fresh doodle on our wedding picture. Richard is now decked out in high heels, with heavily made-up eyes and long eyelashes. He makes a good-looking woman too. I stuff the picture back into the drawer and return to the task at hand—finding a recipe for my "Lost in Love" column. Maybe seafood again. I haven't done lobster yet. What woman wouldn't go for a tasty lobster recipe?

• • •

MIKE'S EDIBLE SEA TREASURES.
THE BEST SEAFOOD STORE IN TOWN.
FISH, SHRIMP, LOBSTERS, EELS.
WE HAVE IT ALL.

Hmm. Kind of like a pet store. Except people come here to pick out dinner, not pets. Now there's a sick thought. Cat and I stroll through the front door and a large man with a green T-shirt that says "Got Fish?" walks right up to us.

"Need help, ma'am?" he asks, crossing his arms over his chest like he is a guardian of *Mike's Edible Sea Treasures* instead of an employee. The short sleeves of his tee stretch taut over his bulging muscles and the front nearly explodes with his rotund belly. Methinks he has been sampling instead of guarding the sea treasures.

"Um, yes. I'd like a lobster please," I reply, jiggling Cat on my hip.

"Got you covered," he grunts, walking ahead of us toward a side tank with lobsters. "What kind you want?"

"Oh, something tasty."

He plunges his hand in the water and plucks out a mottled dark blue-green lobster. It wiggles its legs and antennae like it's doing air aerobics.

"Isn't he a little, uh, spunky?"

The man grins yellowed teeth at me. "Yes, Ma'am. Spunky is goo-oo-ood eating."

I begin to feel a little bit squeamish.

"You wanna just carry this spunky whippersnapper home in that there diaper bag?" He brandishes his lobster in the air and advances on Cat and me.

"Excuse me?" I recoil, stumbling into the canned tuna display behind me, knocking down twenty or so of them.

The *Got Fish* man chuckles and backs off. "Sorry, ma'am, couldn't resist. I'll just pack this here lobster on some ice and you'll be good to go." He swaggers toward the back of the store, bellowing, "Clean up on aisle two!

Good God. What a nut. What in the world am I doing in this freak store? It's dangerous. But The Chef of Hearts is nothing if not courageous.

• • •

While Cat is napping, I put the box with Sparky—I nicknamed the lobster on the way home…it seemed like a good idea at the time—on the kitchen counter, unfold the ironing board, and plug in the iron.

Cooking is the perfect time for multitasking. Why waste my precious time focusing on cooking when I could be ironing too? Plus, I left the wash in the dryer for a week and all of our clothes look like they came out of a bag lady's grocery cart.

I open up *The Joy of Cooking* and read a bit aloud as I iron. "*To store live lobsters until ready to use, place them in the refrigerator, but not directly on ice.*"

Son of a sea cook! Sparky's on ice. I'm going to kill him before I'm ready to kill him! I immediately throw down the iron and snatch Sparky off the ice in the box.

"Shhh, it's alright Sparky. It's okay boy." Yes, I realize it's odd that I'm comforting a crustacean while I was just reading about killing lobsters, but I can't help myself. This is what mothers do, they comfort.

I hold Sparky up and his gentle eyes seem to communicate a quiet understanding. *"It's okay, Maggie, I understand you need to kill me. I forgive you."* His once spunky claws, now bound together by a rubber band, flop dejectedly downwards, and I feel a sob coming on.

How can I do this? It's one thing dealing with a dead chicken. I didn't have to kill it. It's a totally different thing having to kill a living creature. I stare into Sparky's orbs of sea intelligence and tears form in my eyes.

A burning smell begins to engulf my senses. *My iron!* I dump Sparky back into his box and seize the culprit. A black-iron-imprint covers the back of one of Cat's frou-frou little girl dresses. Not good. Not good at all. Maybe I can rig up a giant pink ribbon bow and sew it to what's left of the back, disguising the burn and my lack of housekeeping skills. Probably not.

It's at this late point, I am proud to announce, a glimmer of sanity returns. The whole burning process is like a splash of seawater in my face. *This lobster is a sea bottom dweller, for Pete's sake!* I grab Sparky, open my refrigerator, and plop him firmly on the middle shelf. Irma says to store him in the refrigerator and that's what I'm doing, by golly. I will wait until he is fully chilled, and then I will do the deed. *Hasta la vista, Sparky.*

Twenty minutes later, after studying Irma and Julia, logging onto Food Network and watching their seafood videos, I feel sufficiently steeled to cook myself a lobster. I am proud. I am educated. I am The Chef of Hearts, after all. And I have finished my ironing.

I put down the iron, careful to stand it properly on the ironing board and walk over to the refrigerator and open the door. All I see are claws, coming at me from every direction. And blood sucking pinchers. And evil, beady eyes.

My God, the horror! Sparky has turned into the Sparkinator. I defend myself bravely, karate chopping at the mutant crustacean, dodging and kicking away. But I never had a chance. I made a fatal mistake and underestimated Sparky.

I had failed to notice earlier that while Sparky was staring at me with those deceptively innocent eyes, his claws must have been working the rubber band. Working to get free. Plotting to overtake me. The Chef of Hearts has been defeated by a two-pound lobster. And to top it off, I knocked the iron onto the stack of freshly pressed clothes and it had burned right through them. All of them.

That makes me so angry, I run to Dad's basement and grab my old butterfly net. I scoop up that psychotic shellfish and dump him back into his Styrofoam box. Fifteen minutes later, Cat and I return the evil lobster to *Mike's Edible Sea Delights*. The "Got Fish" man refunds us the money, no questions asked. Perhaps he is feeling guilty for selling us what obviously was an over-eager lobster. Or maybe he just wants to get the psycho woman away from him.

One thing's for sure, I'm back to square one with the seafood recipe and lobster is not on the menu. Maybe shrimp? They're already dead.

```
*Note to myself: Never cook live lobster. Nev-
er iron while battling crustaceans. Go clothes
shopping.
```

Chapter Twenty-One

"Home Cooking: where many a man thinks his wife is."
—Author Unknown

Twitter

Chef of Hearts
@PickinTomatoes

Don't get fishy, don't get crabby. *Pickin' Tomatoes*, March issue, *Cooking and Women*. #Compromise.

Facebook

The Chef of Hearts – Tasty Therapy

714 Likes • 31 Talking about this • 164 were here

Compromise with this dish, "Fish and Crab in Harmony". *Pickin' Tomatoes*, March issue, *Cooking and Women*.

From: Maggie Malone
To: Peg Winthrop
Subject: April Column

Hi Peg,

Here's April's column.

Maggie.

Pickin' Tomatoes

Dear Chef of Hearts,

Have you ever felt lost in love? I have been
living with a guy for a year and I feel like I
am losing my sense of self. When I met Sammie,
I knew who I was, what I wanted. Then everything changed. Now I live in Sammie's house,
go to parties with his friends, and do things
he likes. I even dress to please him. Is it
wrong to feel bitter and lost when you are in
love?

Lost in Love
Seattle, Washington

Dear Lost in Love,

It's very easy to lose your sense of self in
the game of love.

A ring of truth. Finally, I'm typing something I believe. I totally got lost in my relationship with Richard, and because of that I felt bitter. There's something wrong with that. Not that every minute of being in love is all wonderful. It's not. It's hard work sometimes. But you've got to keep your head. You've got to have some kind of internal compass to guide you home when you find yourself wandering. The minute you become lost in a relationship, with no identity of your own, your defenses are down, and then you are exposed to danger. That's the one thing that quack of a shrink said that I concurred with. But it was the only thing.

Why in the world did I agree to Richard's choice of marriage therapists? No matter that the guy was accredited. Accredited by the Institute of Male Chauvinism maybe. Bottom line, he was a nut.

"Mawwiage," Dr. Snelling droned in his Elmer Fudd lisp, "is a sacred union of minds and bodies." He stirred a package of artificial sweetener into his Styrofoam cup of coffee with a wooden stick. "When the minds are not in synch, the bodies can be threatened by outside dangers."

I rolled my eyes at the therapist's accent. Why was I here? I didn't want to be here. I didn't need to be here. I should have left when I discovered Richard was having an affair. In fact, I was all packed and ready to go. But then I found out I was pregnant and then Dad died, and things weren't so cut and dry. I stayed and agreed to counseling, hoping to fix our marriage. But I wasn't telling Richard about the baby. Not until I was sure there was a marriage to fix.

"To discover how our minds have gotten out of synch," Dr. Snelling continued to stir his coffee, "we must delve into our pasts. Wichard, let's begin with you. Tell me about your childhood. What was your upbringing like? Did your mother work? Stay at home? Did you ever feel abandoned as a child?"

There was silence.

Up until now, Richard had been secretly texting on his Blackberry, hand held low, beneath Dr. Snelling's range of vision, but well within my range of vision. It was good to know my husband was serious about fixing our marriage.

"Wichard?"

I kicked him and he looked up, slightly startled.

"My childhood?" he mumbled.

I couldn't help but feel vindictive. Busted, you little shit. You have no idea what he was talking about, do you? Go get him doctor.

"Actually, now that you mention it, doctor, my mother didn't work. She stayed at home and..."

Oh, of course. I should have known he was paying attention. He did this in trial all the time. It was his trademark trial attorney strategy. Act clueless and dive in for the kill.

"...so I guess in response to your question, doctor, no, I never felt abandoned as a child." Richard summarized. He slid his Blackberry into his coat pocket.

Dr. Snelling nodded his head. "Interesting," he commented as he tore open another package of artificial sweetener, poured it in, and continued to stir. *Hello? Are you ever going to drink that coffee? Or do you just get a high off the artificial sweetener and the stirring? I began to have doubts about this doctor. Maybe he had a few issues himself.*

He glanced down at his clipboard. "Ah, yes. Just as I thought. I see Margawet works part time."

I nodded my head in affirmation and opened my mouth to delve into my past. It was my turn now. "Yes, doctor, I..."

"Wichard, perhaps you feel abandoned by Margawet?"

"To be honest, I do."

My mouth dropped to the floor. I was flabbergasted. Richard felt abandoned by me? Was it because I had a job? He didn't even know I had a job. He thought I did charity work from time to time and that was it. This was exactly the reason I didn't tell him about my job in the first place. Give me a break. Millions of women have jobs and happy marriages.

Richard settled back into the leather armchair, stretched out his legs, and crossed them at the ankles. "Frankly," he sighed, "I'm disappointed. When we got married, the agreement was Margaret would stay at home. She would manage the house. Pay the bills. Do the chores. Be there one hundred percent for me. I, in return, would bring in the income. Here we are, seventeen years later, and she is not fulfilling those duties. And that charity fundraiser. It's become all consuming. We've had to hire a cleaning service. And she doesn't even cook, unless you call frozen meals, takeout meals, and canned meals, cooking. What kind of woman does that? In all these years of marriage, she's never cooked. Oh, she may have given it a try once or twice with rather, uh, disappointing results. At first, it didn't seem that big a deal. We'd get takeout *or go somewhere for dinner. But, after a while, it got old. I even offered to send her to cooking school, which she adamantly refused to do, doc. Maybe I need more. Maybe, I need a home cooked meal, once in a while. And..."*

What did all of this have to do with Richard shacking up with Celeste? I didn't cook so he screwed our next door neighbor? "Richard! That is not what this is about. This is about you and Celes..."

Dr. Snelling held up a hand. "Now, Margawet, wait your turn. Wichard, please continue expressing your feelings. And don't be afraid of honesty or waw emotion."

"And my stress-o-meter is maxed out these days with my workload. Clients. Billable hours. Trials."

His stress-o-meter? What about my stress-o-meter? Try finding out your husband is having an affair and you're pregnant! Try having your dad die!

Richard rambled on, Dr. Snelling nodding his head while taking notes.

"Richard!" I exploded.

Richard ignored me, branching off into a man's needs.

"Doctor!" The doctor ignored me, bobbing his noggin like a bobble head in the back window of a speeding vehicle.

Fine. You like raw emotion, Dr. Sniveling, Sniping, or whatever your name is! I'll give you raw emotion. And stress!

I leaned forward in my chair, turning slightly, wound my arm back, and decked Richard with an open handed slap across the face.

"You are not pinning the blame of your screwing around on me, Richard Allen Thompson. And you want some stress? Some real stress? Try being pregnant. There's stress, you conniving little rat!" I leapt from my chair, walked around Dr. Snelling's desk, and dumped the contents of his coffee in his lap. "And my name is Maggie! Stir that, you quack!"

There's something to be said about raw emotion.

Strike that. Waw emotion.

Dear Lost In Love,

It's easy to lose your sense of self in the game of love. But look at it this way: A re-lationship is like a email—a little of you, a little of him, combine and cook. If you don't have all the ingredients, you're not going to

like what you cook. So my advice to you is to
throw it out and start all over again. There
are plenty of emails out there to try

True to You Shrimp Kabobs

Serves 4

Ingredients:

1/3 cup honey
1 teaspoon grated fresh ginger
4 teaspoons fresh lime juice
1/8 teaspoon Old Bay seasoning plus extra for
shrimp
1/2 teaspoon hot sauce
4 bamboo skewers
8 slices bacon
16 medium peeled and deveined shrimp
2/3 cup teriyaki sauce

Combine honey, ginger, lime juice, 1/8 teaspoon Old Bay, and hot sauce. Divide into two
separate bowls and let sit at room temperature
for thirty minutes. Soak bamboo skewers in
water to prevent burning while grilling. Microwave bacon four minutes and cut each slice
into half. Season shrimp liberally with Old
Bay and wrap bacon around shrimp. Brush shrimp
and bacon skewers with teriyaki mixture from
one bowl, discarding any remaining sauce from
bowl. Grill shrimp three to four minutes or
until no longer pink. Serve with extra sauce
for dipping.

Emails, like love, require all the right ingredients. So pay attention, ladies, pay attention and happy cooking.
—The Chef of Hearts

Chapter Twenty-Two

"You should be on a Campbell's Soup commercial because you are mmm mmmm good."
—Author Unknown

From: Peg Winthrop
To: Maggie Malone
Subject: Lunch meeting

Maggie,

Peter and I need to see you. Can you make lunch at the Merci restaurant on Monday, 12:30?

Peg

    I knew it would happen. They hate the column. They hate me. They hate the column and me. I want to go to this lunch meeting like I want to have root canal, which interestingly enough, is scheduled for Monday morning. I am so blessed.

From: Maggie Malone
To: Peg Winthrop
Subject: Lunch meeting

Peg,

I'd love to have lunch with you and Peter on
Monday. I have a dental appointment scheduled
for that morning but it should be fine.

Maggie

• • •

"Maggie, how are you? Have a seat, have a seat." Peter stands, grasps my hand, and leads me to a chair next to his. His jacket is off, his tie loosened and his blond hair askew like he'd just run his fingers through it. He smiles and his dimples engage, like happiness beacons beaming goodwill across the world.

Yes, I know that sounds sappy. But it's true. Happiness beacons. And I have just been beaconed. If only I could enjoy it. All I can think about is the throbbing pain blossoming on the left side of my jaw. Let me just say, a root canal is not fun.

I try to smile but find it difficult as the numbness, although wearing off, is still quite prevalent in places. I manage a lopsided joker smile and discover drool is dripping down the corner of my mouth. *Nice, Maggie.* Wiping it away with the tip of my index finger, I glance around Peter's table for two. Where is Peg? Could she be beneath the table perhaps, wielding a spear? Ready to stab me in the foot? How silly. I drop my napkin and as I reach down to pick it up, take a gander beneath the tablecloth.

"Peg's not coming today," Peter comments as I straighten, my errant napkin in hand.

"She had to complete a rush assignment and won't be able to make lunch. But she sends her regards. Glass of tea? Wine?" He lifts his hand in the air to flag a waiter.

"Sweet tea," I try to mumble but it comes out as "wheat thee." I dab at the drool with my napkin.

Peter scrutinizes my mouth. "Dental work?"

I nod my head in affirmation.

"Just had some myself a couple of weeks ago," he commiserates. "It was horrible. Dentists are definitely up there with proctologists. Not my favorite people." He turns toward the waiter, "Two sweet teas, please," and then helps himself to the bread basket. He butters a slice of fresh bread, lays it on my plate, cuts off the crusts, and slices it into squares. Nudging it towards me like an offering.

I'm stunned. What kind of man does that? Cuts up your bread because you've had dental work and your jaw hurts? No man I know. I broke a tooth once and it was a whole day before the dentist could see me. My tooth hurt so much I couldn't eat, couldn't drink. Richard just patted me on the head. "Bad luck, Margaret." He brought home pizza and wings that night for dinner and I had to cut up my own slice of pizza into bite size pieces to suck on. Needless to say, the wings were a no go.

Peter butters a slice for himself and wolfs down the whole slice. "Maggie," he continues. "Corporate is thrilled with your work. The column is a huge success and letters are flooding your website. Because of you, sales are at an all-time high and tongues are wagging. Everyone wants to know—"

I can't resist the obvious question. "Know whath?" I burble, in between sucking on my bread.

"Who is The Chef of Hearts?" Peter declares.

"Argh…" I choke and he thumps me on the back.

"So I think to myself, let's give America what they want."

I gulp down some sweet tea and look at him, my heart going a mile a minute.

"An intimate profile of The Chef of Hearts' life. Her triumphs. Her tribulations. Her secrets. Photos of the master chef at home creating culinary works of art in her very own kitchen. Think of the publicity it will bring to *Cooking and Women* magazine!"

I guzzle some more sweet tea. *Yea, think of the publicity it will bring to me.* Is America ready for the real Chef of Hearts? Better yet, am I ready for America? I'll tell you what I'm ready for, a double Jack on the rocks. There's nothing worse than wanting something and not being able to get it. The story of my life.

• • •

Ah-h-h, good food. I recline in my chair and feel completely sated, like I've had amazing sex. What a meal. Who would have guessed that "Buffalo Rossini with Truffle and Foie Gras Sauce" would taste so good? Not really sure what the Foie Gras was, but it was one tasty little bugger. Maybe it was the truffles. I've always loved truffles.

"So Maggie, did you like the buffalo entree?" Peter scoots back his chair and reclines, fingers lacing together behind his head.

I nod my head as I dab my mouth with my napkin. The Novocain has worn off and the drool has dried up—but you never know, some rogue drool could still escape. "It was amazing, Peter. Thank you for recommending it."

"I thought you'd like it. It's my favorite entrée here. And I just can't get enough of that Foie Gras."

"Me too. Love it." I kiss my fingers. "Love everything about it."

"Do you make Foie Gras, Maggie?"

Are you kidding me? I don't even know what's in the stuff. "Of course. Who doesn't?"

I take a big sip of sweet tea, enjoying the slight sugar rush and wishing the Georgia legislature had passed that tea law, the one making it a misdemeanor for a restaurant not to offer both regular and sweet tea. It should be a crime not to offer good ol' sweet tea.

"Where do you get your duck livers? Do you import them?"

At that, my sweet tea sprays all over my pink silk blouse and charcoal gray blazer. Good lord, that's what Foie Gras is? Duck livers? Daffy Duck livers?

Peter looks at me in alarm."Are you okay?"

"Yeah, fine. My tea went down the wrong pipe." I pat my throat with my napkin, and then my shirt and my jacket. The choke spray radius was huge. *Oh my God, is that a droplet on Peter's face? I will totally die if I nailed him with sweet tea.*

Peter grins like a schoolboy and leans forward as if to tell me a juicy secret. "Guess what? Upper management wants me to permanently transfer to the Atlanta branch and personally handle your column. Peg will still be indirectly involved, and you'll copy her on your column e-mails, but you would send them to me for comments and editing. I'll also be in charge of a publicity blitz to promote you." Peter leans back in his chair and smiles. "So what do you think? I think we'd make a great team."

I pause my napkin mid-dab and stare at him. Does he mean professionally? Of course, he does. "I think so too. Maybe we could, uh, even work on a recipe together."

"I'm not so sure about that one. I'm a horrible cook. But hey, I wouldn't mind watching you cook. Maybe I'd pick up a few pointers."

My heart does an odd little skip and a jump as I process his words. He hates cooking. He wouldn't mind watching me cook. I try not to smile but all I can think is I wouldn't mind watching you cook either. *Maybe we could cook up a little something in the bedroom together.* I kick myself under the table. *Focus, Maggie!* He's your boss. Not some guy on Match.com. He is not flirting with you. Man, I need to get out more.

Peter smacks his head. "I almost forgot to tell you. Somehow, I always get off on these tangents when I talk to you. Must be your southern charm." He waggles his eyebrows at me and I burst out laughing.

Okay, I might be middle aged and definitely out of practice, but I'm not dead. This man *is* flirting with me. Flirting hasn't happened to me since, well, since Richard. Even then it wasn't really flirting. It was more like aggressive pursuing. He knew what he wanted and he got it.

"How you doing, Margaret?" someone said. I was so immersed in writing my to-do list for the day that I startled and my pen scribbled across the message pad. I looked up, and there was Richard, lounging in the doorway to my cubicle.

"Um, fine, Mr. Thompson. And, uh, you?" What is he doing here? Since the day he sat by me on the park bench, I'd been running into him everywhere at the office: the copy machine, the lobby, the conference room.

"You know, you can call me Richard," he said. "I won't bite."

"Tee-hee." Oh, God, where did that giggle come from? I felt myself blushing. "Alright. Richard. And you can call me Maggie. All my friends do."

"Ah," he responded. He leaned inside my door until he was hovering above me and my heart began to race. "But I like the name Margaret. It's elegant. And maybe I don't want to be your friend."

"You, you don't want to be my friend?" I stuttered.

"Nope." He presented me with a red rose and I about died right there. "I want more than friendship. I want dinner. How about Chez Vous, seven o'clock tonight?"

There's something exciting about being pursued, and I fell for Richard hook, line, and sinker. Later on I would find out he was also domineering. And sexist. I could go on and on but I won't because I am a mature woman. And pig-headed. And left the toilet seat up. Nope. I'm done. Really. See? Closure. The lid is on that pot, and it's staying there.

The waiter appears with a dessert cart and Peter looks at me, tempting me.

"Oh, no, I couldn't. I'm stuf…is that strawberry cheesecake? Maybe just a small slice." How much exercise do you have to do to burn off ten thousand calories? Does playing with your infant daughter count?

"I've tentatively booked your first PR appearance. I thought it'd be great if you had a booth at Harry's Farmers Market in Marietta. You could prepare a little food and dish out some advice to customers. What do you say? Maybe Thursday or Friday of this week? I could even join you in the booth and be your sous chef."

Now there's an idea: Peter as my sous chef. What exactly does a sous chef do? Do they give back rubs?

"Sounds perfect Peter. Just perfect."

Chapter Twenty-Three

"How luscious lies the pea within the pod."
—*Emily Dickinson*

"Can I get you something?" the girl at the register asks.

I stop swaying and realize we're next in line. Wow, that was quick. Cat barely had time to fall asleep in her Baby Bjorn.

"Uh, yes, I'll have a…" The gold stud in the checkout girl's nose distracts me and I rub my nose with my finger. *Does that hurt?* "…a skinny grande cinnamon dolce latte, please." I try not to stare but I can't help myself. It kind of looks like a pimple. Now, if it were me, I'd put a diamond in my nose.

"That'll be $3.26," Stud Girl declares and I force myself to focus on the matter at hand. Money…I'm rooting in my purse for my wallet when my cell phone rings and Cinderella's voice sings out, *"A dream is a wish your heart makes."*

I look up and catch Stud Girl smirking at my ringtone.

"When you're fast asleep."

"My daughter likes Cinderella," I explain. Stud Girl stares at me like I've grown horns. Well, you can kiss *your* tip goodbye. I grab the money, toss it on the counter, and answer my phone. "Hello?"

Justy giggles on the other line. "Cherie? We're going to have a bébé. "

"We're pregnant?" I bellow and realize all the coffeehouse patrons have grown quiet. "Sorry," I call out and walk over to a table in the back of the room.

"Okay, tell me everything."

"Well, Jean Paul and me, we like to have sex. Ze morning, ze afternoon…"

"Just! I know how it happened. Give me the story. I thought you weren't trying anymore."

"*Oui, oui*, but now we are pregnant and I will be *Maman!*" She begins speaking in French, each word rolling off her tongue faster and faster, until her sentences blur together, and I can no longer catch any words. I can understand normal French but this is like a verbal onslaught.

"Just, Just, slow down. Take a deep breath. Hee hee ha, hee hee ha."

Nothing could make me happier than Justy having a baby. It's all she's ever wanted. It's all *we* ever wanted. Ever since we were kids. We always promised we'd be there for each other at delivery. And sure enough, during my last week of pregnancy, Justy flew in from Paris. I could never have gotten through Cat's delivery without her. Especially without a husband in the picture.

"Hee hee ha. Hee hee ha," I pant

"Bon, Maggie." Justy's face appeared over me, looking decidedly dewy fresh, unlike mine, which was dripping with sweat. She was wearing a new outfit she bought just for the delivery occasion. Black silk pants and a pink, silk shirt. "Imagine you are floating in transvestite water. So blue and calm…"

I gritted my teeth against the building contraction. "It's not transvestite water!" I grunt. "It's tranquil water" The contraction continued to grow. Get your freakin' English words straight, Florence Nightingale!" I doubled over in anguish. The baby was splitting me in two. I was a log being assaulted by an ax. "I want some pain medication," I moan.

Justy clucked her tongue like an overanxious hen. "Maggie, we talked about zees. You said you want the bebe au naturale. Now, repetez after me. Hee hee ha. Hee hee ha," she demonstrated, careful not to overexert herself.

Heaven forbid she wrinkle that pretty blouse or mess up her makeup. I'd seen her reapply her lipstick and powder twice in the past two hours alone when she thought I wasn't looking. I loved Justy like a sister, but did she have to look like Snow White when I looked like Grumpy?

Another contraction threatened to rip me apart and I tossed in the towel. That was it. I was so over this natural child birth thing. I leaned forward, "Get me…hee hee ha, hee hee ha…drugs…now!" I screamed.

Justy's eyes opened wide and she ran out of the room. Minutes later, I heard raised voices in the hallway. They escalated in volume and one of the voices broke off into a tirade in French after which Justy appeared with a nurse in tow.

I had to giggle, even through the onslaught of pain. Justy's hair was mussed up, her silk blouse untucked, and large sweat stains showed beneath her armpits. But that's not what tickled me. She had her fist practically around the collar of the nurse's uniform and was dragging her into the room. Which was quite a feat, considering the woman had about five inches and sixty pounds on Justy. If I hadn't been in so much pain, I would have split my sides laughing. No one messes with Justine Beignet.

Minutes later I found myself floating in tranquil water, so blue and calm, sipping a margarita.

"Hey, Cinderella, your skinny grande cinnamon dolce latte is ready," Stud Girl announces to the world.

Did she just call me Cinderella?

"Justy, got to go. We'll talk later. I'm so excited for you and Jean Paul!" I disconnect and walk up to the counter, narrowing my eyes into mailslot slits and delivering contempt to the snarky coffee girl. Two could play this game. I take my coffee and just as I am about to leave, rub my nose. "You've gotten a little something right there," I say.

Stud Girl raises her hand to her nose, feeling around. Nothing like a skinny grande cinnamon dolce latte with a side of poetic justice.

I leave the coffee shop, humming the theme from *Cinderella*. The sun is shining, the birds are singing. Maybe I *am* Cinderella. All my dreams are coming true. I'm getting the successful career I always wanted, I'm a mother, and now Justy's going to be a mother too. Life is good.

• • •

From: Peter Rudolph
To: Maggie Malone
CC: Peg Winthrop
Subject: Harry's Farmers Market

Hi Maggie,

I've got the PR appearance set up at Harry's
Farmers Market for this Thursday at noon. I
thought maybe you could wear your chef uniform. Don't forget to bring whatever you're
cooking plus any utensils, knives, etc. you
need. I'll get there early and set up the
booth for you. I was thinking I'd bring a
loudspeaker and microphone also. Looking forward to it and count me in for chopping! I may
not like cooking, but I love to chop.

Peter

    I chuckle. He likes to chop?

From: Maggie Malone
To: Peter Rudolph
CC: Peg Winthrop
Subject: *Pickin' Tomatoes column*

So, you're a closet chopper, are you? Good to
know. Heads up—keep an eye out for the Pillsbury Doughboy. That'll be me in my chef outfit.
See you Thursday.

Maggie

Chapter Twenty-Four

"Why, if I had a brain I could wile away the hours, conferrin' with the
flowers consultin' with the rain.
And my head I'd be scratchin'
While my thoughts were busy hatchin'
If I only had a brain."
—The ScareCrow, The Wizard of Oz

"Ladies, come on down and meet the one, the only, The Chef of Hearts!" Peter announces as if he were a commentator at a WWF match. I cringe. If I weren't sequestered in this booth, I'd run far, far away.

This whole afternoon has been crazy. I got to *Harry's* a few minutes before noon and Peter had already gone nuts with the hot glue. I mean really nuts. He had hot glued "Cooking and Women" covers to the side of the stand, red heart streamers to the top, and a large sign on the front with "Introducing The Chef of Hearts – America's Cooking Therapist!" Between all of this paraphernalia and my Pillsbury Dough Boy outfit, I now feel like a circus freak. And Peter, wearing a black T-shirt imprinted with, "The Right Stuff Mushrooms," doesn't help. Maybe I've died and gone to cooking purgatory.

I stare at some other booths promoting their wares in the distance, wishing I was anywhere but in the *Cooking and Women* booth. There's a "Fiesta Fruit and Dip" booth with exotic fruits and luscious dips like dragon fruit and acai yogurt dipping sauce. An elegant woman dressed in a black suit and a green silk blouse hands out tasty tidbits on toothpicks. Another booth, dubbed "Signature Sandwiches," has a man garbed in jeans doling out turkey and brie bites. Both booths look calm and normal. Why do I get stuck with the three ring circus?

"Chef! Ooh, ooh! I have a question!" a woman calls out, jumping up and down, waving her arms in the air like the smartest kid in the class.

I pause in the process of crumbling up tortilla chips and give her a warm smile. Let me tell you, a really warm smile. I'm so overheated right now, I could fry a burger on myself. *Man, this chef outfit's hot.* "Sure, go ahead," I call out, all the while wishing I could pepper Pollyanna over there with crumbled tortilla chips. How many questions am I going to have to answer this morning?

If one more rabid fan asks me another airhead question, well, tomorrow's *Atlanta Journal* headline just might be: *Chef of Hearts Incarcerated After Slicing And Dicing Woman*

"What are your tips on flirting and sautéing?" the woman continues, looking coyly at Peter. The assembled cougars titter like a group of apprentice blue hairs.

Peter pauses in his onion chopping frenzy, perhaps sensing the laughter involves him, and looks up like a deer caught in headlights.

"Well," I say, racking my brain for something witty and intelligent, wanting to deliver Peter from freak woman, "My…"

"Louder! We can't hear you!" roars a lady who looks like she's been sampling the freebies a little too much.

"My tip," I proclaim into the microphone, feeling like a DJ, "would have to be stirring. Flirting and Sautéing both need stirring. You've got to work at them. Because what do we ultimately want, ladies?" I stare at various women in the crowd to make eye contact and notice a woman in sunglasses, wearing a black fedora tilted to the side and a gray overcoat, collar turned up. Give me a break. Who dresses like that? Like Humphrey Bogart wearing stilettos? I crane my head closer. *Is that…*

A lady calls out, "What we want is to eat!" and everyone laughs.

I snap back into focus. *What was I saying? Oh yes.* "What we want" I bellow, "is perfection. The perfect dish. The perfect 'Mister Right.' So work on the stirring, ladies, and I guarantee you'll cook up something tasty for your dinner and your love life!"

A pandemonium of clapping erupts and I turn to Peter, muttering under my breath, "You owe me a meal for doing this, Mister Chopper. A big meal."

He laughs and mumbles back, "You're on." He turns to the ladies and announces, "You heard it here, ladies. The Chef of Heart's own words of wisdom. And I can tell you, as the token male here, we love some stir-ring!"

Amidst much cat calling and whistling, Peter holds up his hand for silence. He ladles up a cup of chili, and sprinkles some chips, cheese, and onions on it. "Now come get a cup of the Chef's Wise Chili and remember to check out her column, *Pickin' Tomatoes*, in this month's issue of *Cooking and Women!*" He holds up the March issue, moving it from right to left until he's satisfied that the smiling crowd has been tempted by the colorful cover. "Bon appétit!"

Wow. This man is good. He chops, he promotes, he flirts, he's good looking. He's kind of like the poster guy for Mister Right. Not that I'm looking for Mister Right. I'm not. No sir-ee Bob. I don't need perfection. I just need reliability. Perfection is like seeing the world through rose colored glasses. You just can't count on the world lookin' so pretty when you take 'em off. I'd rather have reliability any day. What you see is what you get.

• • •

I open the garage door and let myself into the kitchen, glancing around as I enter. No one's here but the dishes are done and the floor looks shiny like it's been mopped. Mrs. Maroni's been working her magic again. I creep up the stairs and peek into Cat's nursery. She's snoozing away in her crib, and Mrs. Doubtfire, excuse me Mrs. Maroni, is snoozing away in the rocking chair, as is her daily ritual. When three o'clock hits, she out like a light. Religiously.

I pat her shoulder and Mrs. Maroni opens her eyes. "Time to go," I whisper, reaching into my wallet for some money. I panic when I can't find any. How could I have forgotten to stop at the ATM? I'm rooting around in the dregs of my purse for loose change, when Mrs. Maroni lays her hand on my arm.

"Non ti preoccupare," she says, rising from the rocking chair.

Um, okay. I nod my head and smile in universal language and she pats my cheek. *"Mama buona."*

I'm still smiling as she leaves. I have no idea what she just said but hey, it couldn't have been bad. She patted me. Maybe it was bill me in Italian.

The phone rings, and I sprint out of the room to answer it. Why hasn't someone invented a house system where you can just clap, the phone is answered, and your voice immediately is on intercom? Kind of like "The

Clapper." I still remember that silly eighties TV jingle. *Clap on clap off, the clapper*! My name is Maggie Malone, renowned chef and inventor of....

"Hello?"

Crying answers me, and then the mangled words, "Mag-gie?"

"Justy? What's wrong?" All sorts of things barrel through my mind: Her husband left her, she miscarried, she's been in an accident....

"It's Jean Paul. He brought home pizza," she blurts out through her sobs.

"And, that upsets you? Why?"

"Because he got pepperoni and anchovy. He knows je déteste anchovies. Zat means..." The wailing begins anew, interspersed with several choice French cuss words.

"Means, means what?"

"He's having a liasion," she explodes.

I begin giggling, I can't help it."Just, come on. That's ridiculous. He's not having an affair. It's your hormones on steroids. You're pregnant. This is what pregnant women do. They blow things out of proportion. Now, repeat after me: Jean Paul is Mr. Right, Jean Paul is Mr. Right."

I collapse on the couch, preparing myself for a long, exhausting phone conversation. Who knew counseling would be such hard work?

• • •

Julia, Julia, inspire me. Show me your wisdom. I fan the pages of *Mastering the Art of French Cooking* and let it flop open to a page. Let's see, my next cooking experiment will be...I close my eyes and skim my finger down the page. My eyes flutter open and I read, "*Sweetbreads and Brains.*"

Brains? G*ood God, that's nasty.* Who would cook a brain? "*Sweetbreads and brains have much the same texture and flavor, but brains are more delicate.*"

I would say so. Yes, it's been my experience my brain is very delicate. Plus extremely sensitive and hugely intelligent.

I continue reading out loud. "*Both must be soaked for several hours in cold water before they are cooked, to soften the filament which covers them so that it may be removed, to dissolve their bloody patches and to whiten them.*"

I feel nauseous, I feel squeamish, I feel...amazed. Who knew brains could be cooked so many different ways? Braised brains, cold brains, gratin of brains, sautéed brains. Julia is certainly educational as well as creative.

Focus, Maggie! I am not cooking up animal brains. I'm cooking up an original Chef of Hearts recipe. I glance at the clock and note it's nine o'clock. Maybe my brain has excused itself for bed. Ridiculous. People stay up past nine all the time.

Okay. I'm writing for the May column, so it's gonna be warm, maybe lower eighties outside. And Memorial Day is coming up, so something grilled to celebrate it. Something spicy. I snap my fingers. That's it. The recipe I pilfered from that grocery story magazine this morning—Spicy Thai Grilled Beef Salad. I'll just Maggie-tize it a bit, and it'll be perfect for my "Love Hurts" column.

Love hurts. There's an oxymoron if I do say so—something that feels so good hurting so bad. Who hasn't experienced that? I plunk my tired head face down on the cookbook for a moment and get caught up in the memory of the last time I saw Richard. Now that's an example of love hurting. If only I could go to an exorcist and have all those memories purged from my life, maybe then I could find closure. Maybe then it wouldn't hurt anymore.

"I'm leaving, Richard," I declared as I sat on my bulging suitcase to zip it.

"What is it now, Margaret?" Richard sighed, running his hands through his hair. "I thought we worked that out last week with Dr. Snelling. The affairs are over, and you agreed to give me a reprieve. You in turn said you'd cut back on so much charity work and give cooking another try."

I stood up, shoving him aside. I should never have gone to see that crackpot a second time. It's just that Richard was so different after the first visit. Once he found out I was pregnant, things changed. He seemed so caring and interested in me and our baby, or at least I thought he did.

"A reprieve? This isn't court, Richard. I agreed to give you a second chance. And guess what, you've had it. Didn't you hear last night's phone call?"

"What phone call?"

"You didn't hear the phone call."

"No. I don't know what you're talking about."

I stared at Richard's blank face, devoid of any emotion, and didn't believe one iota of it. "Well, isn't that convenient, the ignorance plea from the best defense lawyer in town. Let me fill you in, counselor. Celeste called at two in the morning."

"Celeste? What on earth are you talking about?"

"How could you not hear her? I put her on speaker phone. The neighbors probably heard her! She called me a bitch and said she'd make my life miserable if I didn't leave you"

Richard shook his head in denial and snorted. "Honestly, Margaret, you must have dreamt the whole thing. That affair's done, over. You're blowing this out of proportion."

"Give me a break, Richard. I am so over your lies and your affairs. In fact, you know what? I am over you." I picked up my suitcase and attempted to barrel right through him. It was so heavy all I could do was drag it over his toes. He didn't even flinch.

"Where do you think you're going, Margaret? I am your whole life," he scoffed. "Your house. Your friends. Everything revolves around me and my money, my career, my social standing. You're nothing without me. You don't even have a paying job. How are you going to support yourself?"

"I don't know," I snapped, "but I'll figure it out. I'll start a new life, one without you!"

"Have you considered the ramifications of this action, Margaret? How it might affect my life? What will my partners think?"

"Your partners? Like I really care, Richard. They're all on their second and third wives anyway." I lugged the suitcase to the edge of the stairs. There was nothing he could say to stop me.

"And the baby?"

I stopped cold. Nice one counselor. But I was prepared.

"What baby? I don't have a baby anymore. I miscarried." I turned to him, tears blurring my eyes. "Love hurts, doesn't it Richard?"

I raise my head and realize I have cried all over the sweetbread and brains page. I feel like the Tinman from *The Wizard of Oz,* wanting a heart, a new heart. Maybe I should feel like the Scarecrow. My brain seems to be missing these days.

Chapter Twenty-Five

"You may want to rub your hands in the dirt for a while after handling the hotter peppers and sauces, then washing them (then playing in the dirt again, then washing them again)."
—Gnorb.net

Minced garlic. Got it. I dump in a jar of the stuff. *Lime juice.* Mm-mm, so citrusy and fresh. Kind of wish I were making margaritas instead of Spicy Thai Grilled Beef Salad. *Soy sauce, brown sugar.* I feel so professional, The Chef of Hearts, at the top of her game. I've even graduated from using safety gear. Professionals don't need safety gear. Besides, I finally had to retire my gloves when they became more duct tape than rubber.

Olive oil. Virgin or extra virgin? I have both of them, just in case. Let's see, I think The Chef of Hearts is feeling virtuous today. I shake in some oil from the extra virgin bottle.

Hot peppers. The Spicy Thai Grilled Beef Salad recipe calls for seeded jalapeño peppers but the ones at the grocery store looked all shriveled. This orange one has to be fresher, and it's so pretty. Pretty's better. Besides, I'm sure a habanera pepper is equivalent to a jalapeño pepper. A pepper is a pepper. I smile and begin singing slightly out of key, *"I'm a Pepper, he's a Pepper, she's a Pepper, we're a Pepper. Wouldn't you like to be a Pepper, too?"* Gotta love those old TV jingles.

I pull out my big chef knife and lay out the sacrificial pepper. *"Come here, you sweet little hot pepper. Come to Momma."* Two minutes later, I have masterfully minced up my habanera pepper and pushed the minced pieces and seeds into a nice orderly pile.

"Achoo! Achoo!" I sneeze into my elbow, just like they demonstrated on the evening news. I am so over spring allergies. They are a royal pain in the rump roast. Atlanta's got to have the worst pollen count in the whole world. Yesterday, it was somewhere around eight thousand particles per cubic meter of air. Not really sure how big a space a cubic meter of air is, but it can't be big. That means all those gazillion green and yellow particles are cramped in their little meters of home and basically house shopping. And my body is as good a home as anywhere. I feel a slight tingle on my upper lip and chin, so I give them a quick swipe. Then my nose starts tingling so I rub that too.

Cat's in her portable-crib, jabbering away. "Ba, ba, baba."

I walk over to her and swing her up into my arms. "What a good baby you are, yes you are. And so cute too." Cat's still wearing her short sleeve purple footy jammies with yellow daisies scattered all over them. Wouldn't it be nice to stay in your jammies all day? Watch a little Sesame Street, have some juice and crackers? A slice of Heaven, that's what it'd be. I massage my nose with my hand—*man my nose is tingly and itchy today.*

"Ba ba!" Cat declares, pumping her baby fist in the air like she's shaking a maraca.

"Ba ba," I reply, nodding my head in agreement. I pat her chubby cheeks, and then "beep" her nose with my finger tip. She giggles and I beep it again.

The tingling is intensifying on my nose, mouth, and chin. It revs up and becomes a major burning. "Holy Twinkie!" I swear.

What is wrong with my face? It feels like it's on fire. My eyes begin to water so I rub them with one hand while jiggling Cat on my hip with the other hand. She begins to cry and I jiggle her faster. "It's okay Cat, it's okay. Mommy's allergies are just acting up." I turn my head to look at Cat and there is an angry streak of red on her cheek and nose where I touched them.

She begins to wail, her anguished cries in tandem with the throbbing pain on my face, and I begin to cry too. What have I done?

• • •

I collapse on the couch, my hands and face still burning. Cat and I have spent the past hour and a half at Urgent Care. Dr. Patel finally had to give her a shot of Benadryl to reduce the redness and swelling from the habanera pepper. Thankfully, the injection knocked her right out but they didn't offer anything to me for my discomfort. Hey, haven't you people heard of the Hippocratic Oath? I guess the doc thought I was old enough to self-medicate, but he was just being downright mean and Machiavellian, if you ask me.

Who knew habanera peppers were so dangerous? I glance at Cat in her carrier. She's still dead to the world, and I struggle to my feet. I'm angry about this whole pepper fiasco and I need answers. I need to know what's in that stupid orange pepper. Thank God for the internet.

"Researchers state that the habanera is one thousand times hotter than the jalapeno pepper. Use just a little and keep hands covered at all times. You must take precaution with hot peppers and wear gloves or plastic sandwich bags on your hands. Never, ever rub your eyes or face or nose. Oil of peppers can be transferred from person to person. Peppers can cause second-degree burns that last for several hours."

Good God, I've practically incinerated my child. What kind of a mother am I?

```
*Note to myself: Always wear protective gear
when cooking! Is there baby-sized protective
gear? Never substitute habanera peppers for
jalapenos.
```

I cross that out.

```
*Never cook with hot peppers. Buy hot pepper
sauce instead. Take a nap.
```

• • •

"Maggie?"

"What?" I mumble into the phone. Who's calling at 1:20 on a Friday afternoon? Don't people know this is nap time for *MAWs,* aka *Mothers Around the World*? Get with the system, people.

"Hello? Yes!" I blink my eyes four or five times to focus. I realize I have the phone up to my ear upside down and fumble around to turn it right side up. "This is Maggie." My voice reflects irritation at having my nap disturbed and Cat awakens beside me. Her face crumples up like a piece of paper.

Great, now you've wakened the sleeping baby. I drag myself out of bed and pick her up.

"Oh, there you are. How are you, Maggie?"

Cat commences her infantile version of the "I'm tired and let me sleep" aria. Full of heartache and pain. Let me just say, it's not pretty.

I pick her up, juggling her on one shoulder and the phone on the other. *"Three blind mice, three blind mice.* I'm good and you?" I have no earthly clue who this is.

"I'm wonderful, actually. But that's not why I'm calling. The magazine wants to feature a piece on you and…"

Cat's voice begins to crescendo and I juggle her up and down, trying to appease her. Awareness dawns like the sun rising on a cloudy morning—you know it's there but it takes its' sweet time showing its' face. *Oh, it's Peter.* Without even thinking, I blurt out, "I had a lot of fun cooking with you at Harry's the other day."

He laughs and I envision those dimples. "I did too. That pack of women was a little scary, though. All those questions. And it looked like I was the only man there. Kind of felt that they were eyeing me like I was the main course."

"Naw, ya think?" I get off the bed and begin to jog around the room. Sometimes jogging distracts Cat from crying. Or not. I slow down when Cat's aria reaches an obvious operatic cadenza, cascading sobs punctuated with trilling shrieks and screams. Very impressive, actually. "They were just being friendly."

"Er-right. Do you have the TV on?"

"No, why? Oh, you must hear the baby."

"The baby?"

"My, uh, my mother's sister's daughter's baby. I'm helping her out today." Mother's sister's daughter's baby? *What planet am I from?*

Cat ceases screaming and begins to hiccup. Without warning, she turns bright red and becomes deathly silent.

My God, she's choking on a hiccup. I pat her furiously on the back and resume singing "Three Blind Mice." *"She cut off their tails with a…"* What the sweet nibblets did she cut off their tails with? *"She cut off their tails with a…"*

"*...carving knife. Did you ever see such a sight in your life as three blind mice,*" Peter chimes in.

"Hey, you know 'Three Blind Mice?'" This man is full of surprises. Cat's hiccups begin again and she smiles, a big, one-toothed jack-o-lantern smile. I can't help but grin back at her.

"Of course I know that song. My daughters love it. Personally, I think it's a little sick."

"You're married? You have children?"

"Divorced, actually, and yes, I have children. Twins. They're four now. Listen, I don't mean to take up your Friday afternoon but I wanted to see if we could do a phone interview."

"A phone interview?"

"Yeah. As I was saying earlier, the magazine is doing a piece on you. So I thought I'd do the interview part over the phone. After that, Corporate wants to fly you to New York for the shoot. We have a studio there. I thought I'd go with you and oversee things a bit."

I don't say anything as I attempt to absorb this latest information. Finally, it sinks into my brain. "Really? They want to fly me to New York?"

"Yup. Really."

A warm happy feeling spreads over me and I grin. "Peter! That is so cool! I'd love to. When do you..." Cat tenses up and I sense round two of Cat versus Mommy is about to begin. "Listen, I need to go. Can you call me later, and then we'll do that interview?"

"Sure. No problem. What about six-ish? Will that work or is it dinner time?"

"Yes, six is perfect. And Peter?"

"Yup?"

"Thank you."

"For what?"

"For giving me a chance with this column and believing in me."

There's silence. "You're welcome. Talk to you later."

After he hangs up, I stand there for a moment, ignoring Cat's burgeoning cries. It's been so long since someone believed in me. Did Richard ever really believe in me? I remember when I was having difficulty getting pregnant and Dr. Westinghouse, my gynecologist, had suggested a meeting with Richard and me. It hadn't gone well.

Richard strode ahead of me and barreled through the exit door, without even holding it open for me.

"Richard. Wait!" I called. "Richard!"

He got into his silver Lexus and slammed the door. I climbed in the passenger side and we sat in silence.

"So, I think Dr. Westinghouse has a good point," I began. "If I get hormone shots, it will increase the chances of..."

"Margaret, stop. Just stop. Didn't you hear what he said? You can't get pregnant."

"Yes, Richard, I heard him. Did you? He said I probably couldn't get pregnant the traditional way. But with the shots or maybe in vitro, I could."

"Listen Margaret, it's not going to happen. And frankly, it's a bit degrading. Accept the fact you can't get pregnant and let it go."

I turned towards him. "You know, if you had more faith in me, in us, maybe it would happen."

Richard exhaled, put on his seatbelt, and started the car. "It's not that I don't have faith in us. Maybe I've just changed my mind about having children, that's all. You know, work is requiring a lot more travel with this new client in New York. I think we have enough on our plates right now, without the stress of your trying to get pregnant. Just let it go, okay?"

It was not okay. How could it be okay? I couldn't have a baby, ever.

• • •

Twitter

Chef of Hearts
@PickinTomatoes

```
Lost in Love? Need a culinary GPS? Pickin' To-
matoes, April issue, Cooking and Women. #True
to you.
```

Facebook

The Chef of Hearts - Tasty Therapy

Wrong recipe for your relationship? Cook up some True to You Shrimp Kabobs. Coming home never tasted so good. *Pickin' Tomatoes*, April issue of *Cooking and Women*.

From: Maggie Malone
To: Peter Rudolph
CC: Peg Winthrop
Subject: *Pickin' Tomatoes* column

Hi Peter,

Here's the May column. Looking forward to the phone interview tonight.

Maggie

Pickin' Tomatoes

Dear Chef of Hearts,

Sometimes my boyfriend and I have big fights and we stay mad for days. How do we move on when things have been said and feelings hurt? Should I say I'm sorry, even if I'm not the one who messed up?

Love Hurts
Boise, Idaho

Dear Love Hurts,

Whoever said love is easy lied. Not only is
love not easy, fighting is not easy. Men tend
to have acid tongues when they fight and women
tend to get emotional. Words are spoken that
really hurt, and they keep on hurting, long
after the words are spoken. Do yourselves a
favor and wear protective gear for your hearts
when you fight. Stick to the facts of the fight
and try to be gentle with your words, because
you can't take them back. Fighting turns out
to be a lot like the burn from a habanera pepper. Long after the pepper is gone, the burn
can last and last and last. And love is too
precious to be burned by words.

As far as the "I'm sorry goes," it never hurts
to say it. But it definitely hurts not to say
it.
—The Chef of Hearts

Love Hurts Thai Beef Salad

Serves 4-5

Ingredients:

3 tablespoons minced garlic
2 teaspoons red pepper flakes
1/3 cup fresh lime juice
1 tablespoon water
1/3 cup soy sauce
1/4 cup teriyaki sauce

1/4 cup olive oil-extra virgin
2 tablespoons brown sugar
2 tablespoons ginger puree
1 cup bean sprouts
4 cups salad mix
1/2 cup shredded carrots
1/2 cup basil leaves, torn
1/2 cup mint, torn
1/2 cup cilantro leaves
1 flat iron steak (flank steak)
Olive oil
Grill Mates

Combine garlic, pepper flakes, lime juice, water, soy sauce, teriyaki sauce, olive oil, brown sugar, and ginger in bowl. Mix well. Let sit for at least an hour. Combine sprouts, salad mix, carrots, basil, mint and cilantro and spread on platter. Drizzle olive oil and liberally apply Grill Mates to meat and let sit 30 minutes on counter. Grill meat five minutes on one side and four minutes on the other or until desired doneness. Lightly cover with foil and let sit for 10 minutes. Cut against the grain into strips. Arrange meat over salad mixture and pour dressing over top. Serve immediately.

Chapter Twenty-Six

"If life gives you limes, make margaritas."
—*Jimmy Buffett*

From: Peg Winthrop
To: Maggie Malone
Subject: Pickin' Tomatoes column

Maggie,

Could you come to the office at noon on Monday?
I have some things I'd like to go over with
you.

Peg

Huh? Okay, that's interesting.

From: Maggie Malone
To: Peg Winthrop
Subject: Pickin' Tomatoes column

Peg,

No problem. I'll see you then.

Maggie

The phone trills and I know it's Peter. Should I pick it up or let it ring a few times? It's important to appear nonchalant when answering someone's phone call. It's not like I've been sitting by the phone for an hour and two minutes and, let's see, forty-three seconds waiting for it to ring. I lunge for the phone and answer it before it rings a second time. *I am so pathetic. I have no life…*

"Hello?"

"Hi Maggie, it's Peter."

"Hey, Peter. "

"So you ready?"

"Ready for what?" *As if I don't know.* I'm good at nonchalance, aren't I? See? I do have a life.

"The interview. Okay, here's how it'll go down. I'll ask questions and you answer: it's as simple as that. Just try to be as honest as you can. If I need to edit, I will. The main thing is we want to give readers insight to the real Chef of Hearts."

"Sure. Bring it on. I'm game."

"Alright. Chef, you're definitely the columnist du jour. Single-handedly dissecting love problems with a paring knife and dishing out tasty solutions in appetizer and entrée therapy. But the public needs more. They want juicy details…secrets. Secrets from the real Maggie Malone."

Good God. "Peter, you know I can't tell you my secrets. Then they wouldn't be secrets anymore. A woman has to have *some* secrets. Let me rephrase that understatement. Women have to have a lot of secrets, especially from men. If we told men everything, they'd be disgusted. Do they really want to know what's going on with us mentally and physically? I don't think so. They couldn't handle our moods, let alone our more, let's just say, unappealing bodily functions."

Peter bursts out laughing. "Okay, you've got a point there. How 'bout we start with the basics. Your full name."

"Margaret Elizabeth Malone. But if you call me Margaret, I will never speak to you again."

"Fair enough. When were you born?"

"February 2, if you must know. But there's no way you're getting the year. Secrets, remember secrets…"

"You are one tough Aquarian. Remind me never to mess with you. Back to business. Hometown?"

"Atlanta, Georgia."

"Ah, a southern peach. Education?"

"I received a B.A. in business administration from Georgia State."

"Come on, Maggie, give us some details. America wants to know! What happened after Georgia State? How did you train to become the amazing Chef of Hearts?"

I sigh, all the while spinning a tale in my head. Come on Maggie, get on the BS bus! You are the maestro of misinformation. "Well, after I graduated from Georgia State, I went to France to live with my best friend's family for a while. I took a job as a prep chef at a popular local restaurant, Lavande. I guess I was in the right place at the right time. Although I couldn't cook a thing at the time, they needed help and I needed money. After quite a bit of hands-on training, and many cut fingers, I got promoted to sous chef and realized I had a flair for cooking. My surrogate French family encouraged me to apply to the French Culinary Institute and I was accepted. But a few months later, Lavande offered me the position of senior chef, so I quit the Culinary Institute to work full time." Yeah, that's it. Sounds good.

"So that's when the real chef emerged. Next question: Everyone knows you're single. Any men on the horizon?"

"You are a pathetic, little man to ask that. And if you quote me, I will hunt you down. But off the record, no."

"Hey, I'm not pathetic. A man has to jump at his opportunities, doesn't he? Besides, sharing secrets is fun. So, how 'bout your favorite cookbook?"

"I'd have to say it's a tie between Irma Rombauer's *Joy of Cooking* and Julia Child's *Mastering the Art of French Cooking*. I'm sort of a hybrid cook, influenced by many styles and many cooks." *Yeah, really influenced. I'm a blank book.*

"Favorite cooking show?"

"I love all the shows on Food Network, but I guess Paula Deen's is my favorite. She's funny, down to earth, and isn't afraid to be herself. And she doesn't mind getting her hands dirty. I suppose I cook the same way. I love digging my hands into raw meat and really massaging spices into it." *I'd rather poke a fork in my eye.*

"Wow, that's bold. Personally, I hate to touch raw meat. Secret passion?"

"Hmm…if I had to pick, I suppose it would be chocolate. I love chocolate. One of these days, I'm going to create an incredibly decadent chocolate dessert and I'll serve it to 'Mister Right'. But, got to find him first."

"Favorite magazine?"

"*Glamour!* Ha-ha, just kidding. *Cooking and Women* of course."

"Smart answer. Now, final question. If you could give someone advice about life, what would it be?"

"That's an easy one. Life is like a soufflé, soaring with success and falling with failure. When it soars, it's fluffy and beautiful, when it falls, it's flat and depressing. That's the natural order of life. What goes up must come down. But a good soufflé doesn't necessarily have to be fluffy and pretty to be tasty. And sometimes the best things in life are disguised. Bon appétit!"

"This is going to be great, Maggie, just great. Your readers will love this. I'll do a bit of editing and it'll probably be featured in the June issue. Let's see…what else do I need to fill you in about? Oh, right. I'm going to e-mail you the details of the upcoming New York photo shoot, and I'm also thinking I'll book you on one of the popular radio talk shows for some additional PR. You up for that?"

"Sounds wonderful, Peter. Just wonderful. I meant to ask you, do you know what Peg wants to talk to me about? She wants me to come into the office on Monday."

"Hmm…I have no idea. She didn't tell me about it. Maybe it's some paperwork. She prefers to be in charge of the office-related details. I'm sure that's what it is. Corporate and I are both thrilled with your performance so I know it's nothing bad. Listen, I'll go ahead and book you for that radio gig. And again, thanks for the great interview. Talk to you soon."

I hang up feeling alternatively psyched about the interview and perturbed about the upcoming meeting with Peg. Peter doesn't know anything about it? What are the chances of that? The guy's supposed to be in charge of my column. I have a gut feeling this isn't just a meeting about paperwork—there's got to be some hidden agenda on Stiletto Heel's mind.

I've learned to trust these sneaky feelings. The one time I didn't, I got out-scrabbled by Richard and Celeste—in more ways than one.

"Richard! You're bad!" Celeste gave Richard a little slap on the arm with her fingertips then ran them down his bicep.

A creeping feeling began in the pit of my stomach, working its way up. It was Mexican night and Celeste and Adam were here for a rematch of last week's Scrabble game. Richard and Celeste were supposed to be making margaritas for everyone while Adam put Mexican takeout on plates and I set up the scrabble board. Is this how you made margaritas, by flirting?

My creeping feeling morphed into a gut feeling: the kind that kicks you and says wake up, you're speeding—a police cruiser is behind the hedges. The kind that yells slow down when you're running down the stairs—there's a pair of shoes on the steps. The kind that plunks you in the head and says, "Hey, idiot, something fishy's going on there with your husband and neighbor."

Okay, I was just being paranoid. Celeste and Adam were a couple of our closest friends. We got together all the time for dinners, parties, outings, and Celeste was like a sister to me. Just the day before, she had come over and helped me organize Richard's closet. She was the queen of organization and makeup. Her makeup was always flawless. I don't think she had an oily day in her life and middle-age pimples? Forget it. Pimples didn't appear on lovely people like Celeste, just lovely wannabes like me. There was absolutely no reason not to trust Celeste. Besides, Richard had always been faithful.

My gut feeling had to be wrong. There was a first time for everything. Maybe gut feeling sour as we get older.

"Hey, guys!" I called. "Come sit down and help pick letters." I pointed to Adam. "You and Celeste are going down, my friend. The Thompsons are going to smoke you."

Adam laughed. "Promises. promises."

Richard ambled over to the table and sat across from me. I looked up in surprise. "Richard, what are you doing over there? We're partners. You've got to sit by me so we can pick our letters." Earlier that day, Richard and I had a blow-out about my wanting to work, but come on, we were still husband and wife. A team. Besides, we did make up afterwards—sort of. We both changed the subject and moved on. What was with this change in Scrabble teams?

"Let's mix it up a bit, shall we? The Thompsons are all about fair play. Adam, how about you going over and being Maggie's partner, and I'll take Celeste."

Celeste walked over, carrying a tray of margaritas. "Oh, yes. Let's live a little dangerously."

Adam shrugged his shoulders, and sat next to me. He put his arm around me and hugged me to him. "Don't worry, Maggie, I want you even if Richard doesn't."

I picked up my margarita glass, licked the salt off the rim, and took a big gulp. Margaritas always make everything taste better.

Even sour gut feelings.

Chapter Twenty-Seven

"Well, butter my behind and call me a biscuit."
—Southern saying

Peg's door is wide open so I cautiously poke my head in. "Hello? Peg?"

There is no sign of her, just her black leather jacket slung over the back of her chair and a half-eaten sandwich lying on her desk. She must have stepped out for a moment.

I debate waiting outside or going in and going in wins hands down. My appointment is for noon and I'm on time. Peg wouldn't have left her office open if she didn't want me to come in. I wander in and occupy myself by studying the framed diplomas and awards. Why do people always feel the need to advertise themselves? Must they plaster every achievement and noteworthy moment on their walls? They're like Facebook pages. Come see every moment of my life and walk down "Kudos Lane" with me. I restrain myself from sticking my finger in my throat and gagging as I walk down Peg's "feel good about herself" lane. BA degree in Magazine Journalism and Feature Writing from University of Florida. Second place in the national photojournalism award at...

"So, how's The Chef of Hearts today?" Peg oozes, slithering in from behind me.

Holy guacamole! I jump about ten feet into the air. "Um, just fine and you?" I crane my head around to look at her. It's never good to have a snake at your back.

"Wonderful, just wonderful," Peg comments as she shuts the door.

My hackles rise. When has Peg ever said "wonderful?"

"You know, your column's really a hit." She perches on her usual place, her broomstick, excuse me, desk. Back and forth her leg swings, back and forth, hypnotizing in its movement. It must be hard to ride a broom in those red stilettos.

"Thank you. I think it's going well. So, what can I do for you Peg?" I struggle to take control of the situation. I am, after all a professional, not some intimidated teenager.

"Well I just wanted to have a girl-to-girl chat. You know, see how you're holding up. You're quite the busy beaver these days," she says. She cocks her head and gives me a speculative look as if I'm a mouse she's thinking about gobbling up whole.

"Yes, well that's all Peter's doing. He's really working at promoting me."

"Ah, yes. Peter. I'm sorry I missed lunch with the two of you a couple of weeks ago. But it sounds like it was productive. I have to say, you guys make quite the team." She takes a pencil and repeatedly drums it against her thigh.

"Team?" My mind is a blank page. What is she talking about? I plaster on my P. B. C., my protective brain coating. If I ever needed protecting, it's now.

"Come on, don't play that game. You know, Harry's Farmers Market?"

My P. B. C. remains in place, secured with super glue. "Of course, the cooking demonstration. I didn't know you were there." *Yeah right. I thought those were your stilettos, you sneaky little…*"It was fun." I give her my best Mona Lisa smile. "A good turnout too."

"Did you know I've known Peter since college?" Peg interrupts, changing the subject. "We both went to the University of Florida. We actually even dated a bit our senior year. I hadn't seen him for years, and then out of the blue, he appeared last year as the senior editor for *Cooking and Women* in New York. Imagine that. Of course we immediately took up where we left off during our senior year. You know how office romances are. Hush, hush." She held her finger to her lips.

"Oh, sure. Totally understand." So that's what this is about. Peg's marking her territory. Well, butter my behind and call me a biscuit. Won't be touching that now. Not that I was going to…"So, if this is all, do you mind if I—"

The sound of the phone ringing interrupts me and Peg clamps her claw-like hand on my shoulder. "Just a moment, Maggie," she commands, giving my shoulder a little pat, and answers the phone. "Peg Winthrop." After a few moments, Peg cradles the phone against her shoulder. "Maggie, what year did you graduate from The Culinary Institute? I don't think you mentioned it in the article."

My breath is sucked out of my chest as if a vacuum cleaner has just done major cleaning on my soul. I begin to cough and sense the vacuum cleaner is clogged with sucked-up stories and half-truths. I swallow and clear my throat. "Uh, uh, I didn't mention it. I didn't mention it because I…I never graduated, that's why. Lavande offered me a fulltime chef position and I quit. I thought it was a wonderful opportunity I couldn't pass up."

"Oh, that's right, I remember now," she says, her voice dripping innocence.

Yeah, like I'm sure you forgot that important fact. Don't you even think about trying to trip me up, stiletto chick!

"You can go now," she commands, walking her fingers in the air.

"Well, I'm really glad we had this chat." I back away, nice and slow, right into the closed door. "Whoops. Door. My bad." I open it and stride through, intent on keeping my head high.

I'd like to say I at this point I glided from the building with the grace of a thoroughbred, but I didn't. As soon as I cleared the front doors, I ran like the devil was chasing me. And maybe he was. Wearing a mini skirt, stiletto heels, and looking like he had gone a bit heavy on the Botox.

• • •

"Hey there, Kit Cat, were you a good girl for Mrs. Maroni today?" I lift Cat into my arms and inhale her clean, baby powder scent. Mrs. Maroni is a godsend. She bathed Cat, washed the dishes, and put dinner in the Crockpot for me. I love Mrs. Maroni. Just love her. Someone should bottle her goodness and sell it. Eau de Maroni. It'd sell like hot cakes.

Cat smiles at me, displaying her one tooth like a badge of courage. "Ba ba."

"Ma maaa," I encourage. When is she going to be out of the babble stage? She's ten months old! I point to my chest, and pronounce, "Ma ma," then immediately regret it. Why should I rush her to speak English when she's obviously fluent in Baby-ese?

I nod my head and converse in her language. "Ba ba."

It's important for a mom to be fluent in all the different languages of children. But heaven help me when Cat reaches her teens, because Teenage-ese is not a language I'm fluent in.

I remember one time when I was thirteen. Dad was getting on me about dancing when I should have been studying. He obviously didn't know how to speak Teenage-ese either.

"Maggie! You can't dance and study! And turn that stereo down!"

I kept dancing. "Like a Virgin" was not a song to be ignored. "Just a sec, Dad." I called out as I twirled around and shimmied my hips. I was wearing a short black skirt over purple leggings and a black bra with a see-through lacey white shirt just like Madonna's, and I was determined to move just like her. This was as important as studying, in my opinion. More so. Studying could be learned. Dancing had to be cultivated over time and with lots of practice.

He walked over and turned off my stereo. "No, not just a sec, right now. And good God, what are you wearing? Cover yourself up! I can see your bra!"

"Pa-lease, Dad! Everybody's wearing this blouse. It's like awesome." I twisted my big gold hoops so they hung straight and patted my hair to make sure my black bow was still there. It had taken me forever to tease my hair into a big bird's nest so the bow would stay. I wasn't going to go through that again. I reached my gloved hand over to turn up the volume and Dad grabbed it.

"Hey! Don't have a spaz attack. I was totally listening to that!"

Dad removed my hand, turned down the volume, and looked me in the eyes. "Someday, Maggie, God's going to bless you with a baby girl. And when he does, I pray she will be just like you. Then you won't know her language either."

Dad was right about the baby girl and he was right about the language barrier. He'd get a kick out of seeing me try to communicate with her.

"You hungry, Cat? You want a little Riceappladoash?"

She shakes her head in denial, over and over. "Ba, ba ba, ba, baaaaa!"

I giggle. If I didn't know better, I'd swear a bawking chicken had invaded my daughter's mind. "Just kidding honey. Just kidding. No more of that yucky Riceappladoash."

Well, one thing's for sure. There might be a language barrier but there's not an action barrier. Sometimes actions communicate better than words.

My child hates my food. Too bad she's not an accomplished liar like me.

Chapter Twenty-Eight

"Men are like fine wine – they all start out like grapes, nd it's our job to stomp on them and keep them in the dark until they mature into something we'd like to have dinner with."
—Anonymous

Twitter

Chef of Hearts
@PickinTomatoes

Protect your heart and your hands: wear protective gear. For tips, read *Pickin' Tomatoes*,
May issue of *Cooking and Women*. #Love hurts.

Facebook

The Chef of Hearts – Tasty Therapy

929 Likes • 33 Talking about this • 117 were
here

Only 929 people like me? Not a thousand yet? *Come on!*

When was the last time you said you're sorry?
Fight fair with Love Hurts Thai Beef Salad.
Pickin' Tomatoes, May issue, *Cooking and Wom-
en*.

There we go, a little social network marketing done. Now time to send
off my newest column.

From: Maggie Malone
To: Peter Rudolph
CC: Peg Winthrop
Subject: *Pickin' Tomatoes column*

Hi Peter,

Here's my column for the June issue. I'm really cookin' now!

Maggie

Pickin' Tomatoes

Dear Chef of Hearts,

I have a sneaky feeling my boyfriend takes me
for granted. He doesn't begin to understand
the amount of work I do around our apartment.
The laundry, the cleaning, the cooking, the
grocery shopping—all of it goes unnoticed. Unless, of course, I don't manage to get it all
done. Then he notices, that's for sure. Between my regular job and the chores, I'm ex-
hausted. And pissed off! Any advice?

Underappreciated Woman
Jacksonville, Florida

Dear Underappreciated Woman,

I feel your pain, sister, and you're right to
trust your sneaky feeling. You've got to trust
those gut feelings. If sneaky feelings played
by the rules, they'd be called reliable feelings.

The only solution to your dilemma, in my opinion, is war. Women like you around the world
are taken for granted every day. Well guess
what? I have three words to say to you: No
more under-appreciation! Women need to unite
and retaliate against the male sex. Together
we can achieve victory and serve some tasty
food too.

Operation Household Chaos

Stage one: Stop doing little things like putting dryer sheets in the dryer, cleaning the
windows, adding deodorizer to the carpet while
vacuuming, and cleaning out the refrigerator
every week. This will cause general confusion
in your household. Do this for precisely two
weeks.

Stage Two: Stop doing laundry. Wrinkled and
dirty shirts are serious weapons. Stop doing
dishes. Forcing men to wash their own dishes,
heaven forbid! Stop all sex. Be strong la-

dies, be strong. And finally, stop cooking—for him, that is. If the way to a man's heart is through his stomach, the way to his brain is to withhold his food. But don't deprive yourself or your friends. The aroma of food baking in the oven or simmering on the stove makes for great torture!

Stage Three: Continue Stage Two until you reaffirm your own self-worth and receive a full apology from your boyfriend.

Stage Four: Resume chores cheerfully and enjoy makeup sex! Good luck!

Torture Enchiladas

Preheat oven to 350° F.
Serves 6-8

Ingredients:

1 rotisserie chicken
1 can sliced black olives
1 clove garlic, minced
1 bunch green onions, sliced
2 (8-ounce) packages Mexican shredded cheese
2 (14-ounce) cans enchilada sauce, hot or mild
1 teaspoon cumin
1 package taco seasoning mix
1 teaspoon cocoa powder, mixed in 1 teaspoon cold water
1 package large flour tortillas

Debone and chop up chicken, put into large
bowl. Drain black olives, add to chicken. Add
garlic, green onions, and one bag of cheese.
Mix well. In a pan over medium heat, cook enchilada sauce, cumin, and taco mix until simmering. Add cocoa mixture, stirring well. Remove from heat. Add half of the sauce to the
chicken mixture, stirring to combine.

Heat frying pan to medium and cook tortillas
one minute per side. Do not use cooking spray!
A dry, hot pan is imperative for good tortillas, ladies! Fill each tortilla with chicken
mixture, roll, and place in greased casserole pan while the next tortilla is cooking.
Do this until all tortillas are used. Pour
remaining sauce over the rolled tortillas,
sprinkle remaining bag of cheese over top.
Cook for thirty-five minutes or until sauce
is bubbly. Eat while husband or boyfriend is
watching. *Bon appétit*!

Your sister in arms,
The Chef of Hearts

• • •

From: Peter Rudolph
To: Maggie Malone
CC: Peg Winthrop
Subject: PR blitz

Hi Maggie,

Got your "Underappreciated Woman" column. Wow, glad I'm not on your bad side. No, seriously, your fans will love the column. You are really cranking them out. I looked at Delta flights for the NY shoot and saw one for this Thursday at 8:43 a.m. Will that work? I thought we could fly back on the 7:30 flight that evening.

Also, I tentatively booked you for an appearance on Fish, 104. 7. If you don't listen to it, it's a contemporary Christian radio station that has an inspiring morning show. They love your *Pickin' Tomatoes* column and are trying to reach out to different listeners. So I was thinking maybe May 20th around 8:30 a.m.? They'll call you at your house to do the show. Then Q100, "The Bert Show," will call you around 9:30. I figured both radio shows would cover a broad spectrum of listeners.

Let me know what you think.

Peter

• • •

From: Maggie Malone
To: Peter Rudolph
CC: Peg Winthrop
Subject: *Pickin' Tomatoes column*

Hi Peter,

Sounds great! I'm looking forward to all of
it.

Maggie

Chapter Twenty-Nine

"If life gives you a lemon, make lemonade. However—if life gives you a pickle, you might as well give up, because pickle-ade is disgusting."
—*Clifton J. Gray*

"No, I'm good. Thank you." I turn away from the assistant hoping she will take the hint.

"But don't you want the stylist to touch up your hair again? Maybe spritz your makeup with Evian?"

"I'm fine. Really." *Go away and leave me alone. Go away…*

"But it's been twenty minutes since you last had it refreshed."

Good God, give it up! I walk away, hoping to get rid of Suzie, assistant to Satan. She darts ahead of me, her blond hair bouncing along in a high, perky ponytail.

"How about…"

I start to hum. "La, la, la." Maybe if I act like she's not here, she'll disappear. I do not need this hassle, not after everything I've gone through today to get to this photo shoot.

First there was Mrs. Maroni. She was delighted to take care of Cat for the day and agreed to get to the house no later than 6:30 this morning. Granted, that's quite early but I needed to get to the Atlanta airport by 7:30 to make it through the security check-in lines. So what did Mrs. Maroni do? She arrived at 6:40. Up rolled her big black car, out came the man in the dark suit, whipping the door open for her, and then finally Mrs. Maroni, slow as cold molasses and babbling in Italian. After five minutes of listening to what had to be a recitation of the Italian dictionary, I couldn't wait any longer. I grabbed my purse and was about to bolt when Cat, the human alarm clock, decided to go off on a full-blown hunger rage. I darted upstairs, cuddled her, comforted her, and told her goodbye. By that time, it was 6:50 and I was going to be late, I just knew it.

Then there was the problem with my car. When I turned the key, nothing happened. Old Bessie had finally kicked the bucket. I ran into the house, grabbed the phone, and called a cab. Cat was drinking her bottle, and when she saw me, she started crying. So I took her from Mrs. Maroni and proceeded to feed her, pacing around the room. *Crack-thump*! Half of the heel of my ten year old black pumps snapped off and only quick action on my part saved us from making a painful plummet to the floor. I handed Cat back to Mrs. Maroni, limped to the stairs, intent on changing my shoes. But by then, the cab was outside my house honking like a flock of Canadian geese flying south for the winter. What could I do? I didn't have time to change my shoes so I did what I always do in difficult situations. I grabbed my ever-present roll of heavy duty duct tape from the hallway table and taped the heel to my shoe. Not pretty, but functional.

And finally, the icing to top off this really dysfunctional cake of a day was the airport. When I made it to the security point, the TSA employee decided to give me a full pat-down instead of the usual scan. He checked me up and down, in all my nooks and crannies, and said, "Duct tape is allowed on commercial flights. You can proceed, ma'am." I thought I saw the hint of a smirk on his face but then the sound of Peter laughing distracted me. He was still laughing about it when we boarded the plane. I, on the other hand, did not find it all that amusing.

With such an inauspicious start to my New York trip, I just don't have the patience today for Suzie—devil spawn that she is. I spot her advancing towards me with a hair stylist in tow. *Uggh*. If my sanity is to survive, I'm going to have to outmaneuver her. Just like a skilled running back in the Super Bowl.

First I cut off her approach. "Um, Suzie?" In this game, it's much better to be on the offense than the defense. "Is it possible for me to get a…a…" I need an errand, something high maintenance to distract Suzie. I ease onto the field like I might blitz a linebacker, only I'm not, I'm catching the pass. "A decaf cappuccino with a shot of vanilla, heavy on the foam, a sprinkle of cinnamon, and some chocolate shavings?"

Right away, Suzie goes for the ball. "Oh, yes ma'am." she nods, pony-tail twitching and swishing. "No problem at all. We have a Starbucks just around the cor—"

"A Starbucks. Wonderful." I intercept the pass and I'm off and running towards the end zone. But I don't have the touchdown yet. She'll be back right away. "Do you have any other coffee places?"

"Well, there's a Caribou Coffee, but that's quite a few blocks."

Got ya! I head for the end zone and I score. *Touchdown! Touchdown!* "Caribou Coffee. That's what I need. A Caribou Coffee decaf cappuccino with a shot of vanilla, heavy on the foam, a sprinkle of cinnamon, and some chocolate shavings. Yup, Caribou, that's perfect. You are a saint. Thank you."

I give Suzie a gentle push towards the door and she is gone. The hair stylist, directionless without Suzie, wanders away. It was just a simple game of football. The Chef of Hearts is not only an award-winning journalist and famous chef, but also a champion running back.

"Miss Malone? We're ready for you on the set," a crew member calls.

I glance down at my new outfit. I've had to change clothes three times so far. The current outfit is an emerald green, slightly fitted, short silk dress, with chunky amethyst jewelry and trendy red platform stiletto shoes, sans duct tape of course. The stylist assured me it is in perfect keeping with the successful yet sexy image I am trying to portray.

I walk out onto the set feeling confident and successful. *Oh, there's Peter.* I raise my hand in greeting, smiling and happy that he had flown in with me for the shoot. As I'm watching and waving, my stilettos start wobbling and I trip over the lighting wires, crashing into the cameraman, who crashes into another cameraman, who takes out the hair stylist. We all fall down like human dominoes.

I untangle myself from the body limbs and chords and limp out onto the set with as much aplomb as I can muster. My Sarah Jessica Parker stilettos have broken a heel. What is it with heels and me today? "Does anyone have any duct tape?"

This day just gets better and better.

• • •

"You are a hoot, Maggie Malone." Peter breaks the silence, and I force my attention away from the back of the airplane seat.

"Excuse me?"

"You've got to be the spunkiest, most tenacious woman I know. You jump into everything—writing, photo shoots, PR events—with both pistols raised and firing. You seem to be fearless and yet, you're afraid of flying in an airplane. Why is that?"

"I am *not* afraid of flying." I wrinkle my brows in denial. The plane rises off the runway, bucks a little bit, and ascends steeply. I seize the armrest with both hands and suck in my breath. I'm horrified, petrified. *Oh my God, we're going to die. I feel nauseous. The Chef of Hearts cooked her last meal and tossed her cookies high above Manhattan...*

Peter laughs and tries to unclench my fingers from the armrest. He pries them loose one by one and smoothes them out straight. "Really?"

Breathe, Breathe. You can do this. I expel my breath with a loud whoosh. "Okay, so maybe I get a little nervous when I fly."

Peter's eyebrows arch to the overhead compartments.

"Alright, alright, so I get a lot nervous. I told you about my best friend, Justy, and some of our wacky stories from boarding school. Well, she lives in France and she and her parents invited me one summer, when I turned sixteen. It was the first time I had ever been on an airplane and the flight didn't go well at all. Ever since then, just the thought of flying makes me nervous."

I return my gaze to the back of the airplane seat and begin to count the number of blue zigs and red zags in the pattern. The only thing keeping me from a full-blown panic attack right now is focus. If I don't focus on something, anything, all those memories of that flight will come rushing back and I'm toast. The plane does a little hop forcing me to lose count of my zigs, and go back almost twenty-four years to that unforgettable plane ride.

"Ladies and gentleman, welcome aboard to American Airlines Flight 3021, flying nonstop to Paris, France. My name is Shannon and I will be your flight attendant today. If there is an emergency, you will locate your flotation device..."

Flotation device? Oh my God, do they think we're going to crash in the ocean? I cinched my seatbelt as tight as it would go. Not that I was chicken or anything but I was traveling on a plane for the first time. Besides that, I was traveling without Dad, a concept that had seemed so adult and appealing just yesterday but was currently freaking me out. How could Dad have allowed me to go to France for the whole summer? What kind of father does that? True, it was my birthday present. And I might have had a few crying tantrums about going. And there was the barrage of calls from Justy's mom, but still, it's like he wanted me to leave.

"…the oxygen masks will drop from the ceiling. Please secure one to your face, breathing deeply before you assist anyone else."

Oxygen mask? We need an oxygen mask? What'd I miss? What'd I miss? Are we going down now? Of course we aren't. We haven't even taken off yet. But it doesn't matter, I can't breathe. I tried to inhale and couldn't catch my breath.

"If you feel nauseous, there is a bag located in the seat pocket in front of you."

I frantically rifled through the seat pocket, came up with a dirty Kleenex—gross—a package of unopened gum—I pocketed that—and a flight magazine. No barf bag. Just the thought of not having that bag if I needed it made me nauseous. I felt a lump rising in my throat.

"Hold the bag directly over your face and…"

The lump launched itself and the lunch that seemed so good at the time, McDonald's, spewed forth from my mouth like a projectile missile. Big Mac, fries, apple turnover, milkshake—it all went airborne…

Get a grip! I make myself stop reliving that horrible flight and take a big gulp, hoping that it's air and not something else I'm pushing down. It's weird that something so long ago could still bother me so much. It's not like we crashed or that the flight was bad that day, but it sure did a number on me. After the flight attendant cleaned me, my seatmates, and five or six seats in front of us, she gave me the option of debarking the plane and calling my father. Just the thought of going home to Daddy, tail between my legs, gave me the courage to remain on the plane. Maybe I had embarrassed myself by throwing up, but I was going to France if it was the last thing I did. So I glued my eyes to the back of the seat in front of me and counted the circles in the pattern. By the end of the flight, I had calculated the exact number of circles in all the seats around me, had figured out how many people wore specific colors of clothing, and even counted all the number of various letters in the safety brochure. To this day, I still have the sheet of paper that holds this engrossing information. I just can't bring myself to throw it away because it's a record of the first time I remember being determined to do something and actually following through and doing it, despite the hardships.

I begin counting the red zigs again in the seat pattern—*four, five, six*—when I feel someone's touch. I twitch in surprise, look down, and see Peter's hand clasping my own.

Good God, is he hitting on me? I can't believe he took my hand. What's going through his mind? Do people hold hands if they're coworkers these days? Various scenarios wrestle and spar in my mind in their haste to be dominant and I'm just about ready to withdraw my hand when the plane banks sharply to the right,

Who cares what Peter is thinking, who cares what I'm thinking? I clutch his hand like it's my lifeline until I fall asleep.

Sometimes, it's just better to turn off the brain.

Chapter Thirty

"You know it's a good recipe if it starts with a stick of butter."
—Paula Deen

"I don't know. I just sort of make up the columns along the way." I trap the phone with my right ear and shoulder and attempt to hold the baby jar with my right hand. "Thanks Peter, that means a lot to me. I actually enjoy dishing out relationship advice…No—I don't think my ex reads my column. I'm not exactly friends with him. He's like—how do I put this delicately? A piece of stinky blue cheese."

I hold the receiver away from my ear as Peter whoops in laughter. "Well, he is…yes, I realize I'm an adult and I can cuss. But I'm trying to stop lately so I've come up with culinary cussing…that's a good one, son of a duck. I'll have to remember that one."

I put the spoon up to Cat's mouth and she clamps her lips shut tight. "Come on, Kitty Cat, in the mouth. In the mouth…What? Oh, yeah. I'm babysitting again for my sister's…I mean my aunt's daughter's baby and I'm feeding…" *Oh my gosh, whose baby is this?*

"I'm feeding her some baby food…I don't know, strained something…Yes, I have them on my calendar. Feb. 2, 8:30 a.m. for 104.7 The Fish, then Q100 at 9:30…Oh really? You got me an interview with *Fox 5 News Atlanta*? That's great!" I walk over to my calendar. "Nope. Nothing on that day…Yes, I'm penciling in 10 a.m. at their studio in downtown Atlanta…I know. It is exciting. It just seems to be taking off doesn't it? Am I sitting down? Why? No! She didn't! She reads my column?" I stomp my feet up and down in excitement. "She wants me to be on *Paula's Best Dishes*? I can't believe it."

I bolt out of my seat and begin to pace up and down the kitchen floor. I'm going to need new clothes. I'm going to need The Salon Doctor!

"What? Of course not. I'll tell you right now, I'm free. I don't mind it's this Monday. I'm just glad she had a cancellation…Yes, I'm penciling it in as we're talking, Mr. PR Coordinator."

I turn back to Cat and spoon out another bite of mushy food. "Here's the choo choo. Chug a chug a chug a! Into the mouth, woo woo! No really. It's all great…Yes, book me a flight to Savannah early Monday and e-mail me the reservations. And Peter? Thanks for everything…Yes, I will. Bye."

I sit down, dazed. I can't believe it. I'm going on her cooking show! I take a bite of food and start to gag. Cat's food. Good God. I study the jar. Prunes! What was I thinking when I bought this? This is way worse than Riceappladoash. But I can't focus on that right now. I'm going to be on Paula Deen's show on Monday!

An unwanted thought digs itself into my mind like a burrowing vole. *Won't Richard be impressed that I'm going to be on television?* Beef jerky! Why in the world would that pop into my consciousness? It's been over a year and still that man has so much control over me. Will things ever change?

"Richard, you'll never guess what," I bubbled the moment Richard came home. "I finished organizing your desk drawers, categorized and alphabetized your files and even came up with this neat system…"

"Margaret, can't it wait until I'm through the door? Just a moment, please."

"I'm sorry. I'm just so excited. I spent all day organizing and cleaning your office. I thought you'd…"

"No, that's the problem, you didn't think. This is exactly why you shouldn't work outside the home, Margaret. You can't handle more than one thing at a time, and our home life would suffer. You need to get your priorities straight." He poured himself some bourbon, threw in a few ice cubes, then sat in his leather reclining armchair and stretched out his legs. "Well? What? What did you want to tell me?"

For a moment, I was speechless, stung by his callousness. This demanding man was the man I married? My eyes pooled and panic began to take root. How could I have been so…

Richard groaned. "Come on, don't do that, my sweets." He reached out a hand and pulled me onto his lap. "Now, tell me about that wonderful organization system you've come up with."

Relief washed away the panic, and I began to tell him about all the work I had done. And as Richard stroked my hair and murmured compliments in my ear, I realized how important it was to me to please him.

Richard was right. I needed to get my priorities straight. Then we'd both be happy.

Well, guess what Richard? It may have taken me a while but I finally did get my priorities straight. And you're not one of them.

"See, honey? Mommy loves it." I coax Cat by eating a spoonful of jarred prunes in demonstration. The slime slides down my throat and I force myself not to gag.

Cat shakes her head and replies, "No, Mama."

I put down the jar, and clap my hands. My number one priority just spoke her first words!

• • •

I watch from the sidelines as Paula Deen fries up some shoe string potatoes, adds the finishing touch to a key lime pie, makes a tasty margarita, and entertains with her southern charm—all without breaking her stride. I'm amazed. Now here is a woman who knows how to multitask!

An assistant pops up beside me. "Ma'am you're on in thirty seconds."

Wow. That was quick. I flew in this morning and before I knew it, I was fluffed, puffed, and ready for taping. I had maybe two minutes to meet Paula during the commercial break. She's lovely, just lovely, and her accent is way more pronounced in real life. And now here I am.

"Hey y'all," Paula says. "Welcome back. I have a treat in store for you. Today I've got a guest who is becoming the queen of womanly advice. Her column, *Pickin' Tomatoes,* is taking America by storm. Maggie Malone, come on out. America wants to meet you!"

I take a step. I am proud. I am calm. I am a professional. *I am ready.* I glance toward the camera and freeze. The blinking little red light is mesmerizing, hypnotizing.

I feel a gentle push on my back and a whisper in my ear. "You're on, Ma'am."

I ignore it. I can't stop watching the flashing red light. I feel a harder nudge on my back. "Ma'am, time to go." I ignore it too. I'm paralyzed by that fudgin' light.

Someone body slams me from behind and I stumble into Paula's kitchen, breaking my eye contact with the camera's red light. Paula approaches, her smile warm and enveloping.

Hee hee ha. Hee hee ha. *I can do this. Just don't look at the red light.*

Paula takes me by the arm and we drift over to the counter and the multitude of cameras and lights. I feel like a bug under a magnifying glass. Everyone's watching my every move. Everyone, including millions of people on national TV. *Oh my God.*

Hee hee ha. Hee hee ha. I try to plaster on my P. B. C., but my face is frozen. My lips are so dry they get stuck to my teeth. Do I lick them on national television? I must look like a freak. I finally get up the nerve to lick my lips and they unglue from my teeth. I beam a thankful smile.

"It's so good to have you here, Maggie." Paula welcomes me in heavy southern drawl. She takes out an ice chest from beneath the counter.

What's in the box? The P.C.B. is plastered to my face.

"Well, what would we like to go with our shoestring potatoes and key lime pie?" She looks at the camera. "How 'bout a little butter, ya'll?" She breaks into laughter and gives my arm a gentle poke. "Just kiddin'. Jamie? You in the mood to help us girls grill some steak?"

Jamie drifts in from the sidelines, a big smile frosted on his face. "Now, Momma, you know I'm always in the mood for grilling some steak."

Paula's son, Jamie, is going to cook with us? She didn't tell me that. Hee hee ha. *I can do this. I can do steak.* Hee hee ha. *What's in the box?* I keep smiling.

"And of course, we can't have steak without a little… Darlin' give your mom a drum roll, please."

"Sure, Momma." Jamie takes two fingers and beats them against the counter.

"Lobster!" Paula announces, opening the Styrofoam box.

Oh my God. I stare in disbelief as Paula draws out not Sparky, the Sparkinator, but Sparky's father, Moby Dick. It's like a whale of a lobster, it's so big.

"I thought it would be fun today to cook a little steak and lobster. What 'cha think, honey?" Paula turns towards me. "Want ta do the honors and kill it?" She waives Moby Dick in my face.

I shrink back in horror, as my P. B. C. shrivels up like a prune.

Paula turns back to Jamie, gesturing towards him with Moby Dick. "I hear your wife, Brooke, likes to read *Pickin' Tomatoes*. Do you have any questions for Maggie from Brooke?"

"That's interesting you bring that up, Momma." He fills a large pot with water, sets it on the stove, and turns towards me, a smile stretching across his face. "Well, Chef—I can call you Chef, can't I?" He winks at me and continues. "I do have a few questions for you. Not from Brooke, though, from me. Ever since Brooke started reading that column of yours, I find magazine pictures of diamonds taped to the commode, chore charts posted on the refrigerator, and for some reason, I wake up a million times during the night with sore spots all over my chest."

"Oh, son, that's horrible. I didn't know." Paula puts the lobster down on the counter and it begins to crawl towards me. "Here, Jamie, have a bite of your Momma's key lime pie. It'll fix you right up." She digs a spoon into the fluffy meringue topped pie and pops it right into his mouth. "Is it good, son?"

He swallows, nodding his affirmation, and continues."What I want to ask is," he inhales a deep, shaky breath, "who the hell do you think you are, telling women to do that stuff?"

My eyes go wide, and my mouth drops open like one of those wooden dummy puppets ventriloquists use.

"Cut!" the director says, rising from his chair. "Jamie, tone it down a bit. You can't cuss on national TV."

"Son!" Paula stares at Jamie, her hand on her chest.

"Well, Momma, it's a valid question and you did say to ask her a question," Jamie replies, grinning at my obvious discomfort.

"Jamie, let's start back with 'What I want to ask'. But this time, play nice and no cussing," the director reminds. "And, action!"

Jamie turns to me and says, "What I want to ask is…"

Good God is he going to cuss again? I don't know if I can take this. Is that a pain in my chest or is it just the food I cooked this morning? I can see tomorrow's headlines: Burgeoning columnist, The Chef of Hearts, dishes it permanently on the set of *Paula's Best Dishes*.

"What is going through my wife's mind?" Jamie inquires.

The red light of the camera catches my eye and my mind goes blank. The foreboding, blinking red light, like the eyes of the lobster, Moby Dick…Moby Dick. I break free of the camera's power and glance towards the crawling crustacean on the counter. *Holy mackerel, that lobster is inching his way right towards me.*

At that moment, something inside of me snaps.

"Well, Jamie," I begin, "men and women are kind of like lobster and steak. They go nicely together but they have nothing in common. Men don't understand women and women don't understand men. So stop trying to figure out your wife and butter her up with a compliment once in a while. Plan a romantic dinner…buy her some flowers. Maybe then, your house will return to normal. After all," I beam a high wattage smile at Jamie, flash it at Paula, and power it up for the camera, ignoring that little, red blinking light, "everything's better with a little butter!" Then I grab Moby Dick from the counter and toss him into the pot of boiling water.

Paula hoots at my quip and claps her hands in glee. "You got that right, honey." She steps over and wraps her arm around me. "Now, what's your technique with steak? Do you like to rub it or marinate it?" She nudges me towards a huge, raw beef carcass lying on the counter and I don't even flinch. The Chef of Hearts is nothing, if not a professional.

My eyes zoom in on the oozy beef flesh, bacteria no doubt percolating away, and my breathing begins to quicken. Okay, maybe The Chef of Hearts is not that much of a professional. I whirl away from the salmonella spawn and face Paula. "Well, Paula, we could see my technique or we could see yours. Personally, I'd really love to see yours. I may be The Chef of Hearts, but you're The Queen of Hearts in the Kitchen."

Paula grins and faces Jamie. "Son, this here is a smart one. You better start reading her column. She certainly knows what she's talkin' about." She pivots and addresses the camera. You saw her here first, America, The Chef of Hearts. Therapy never tasted so yummy!"

Chapter Thirty-One

"Food is our common ground, a universal experience."
—*James Beard*

Twitter

Chef of Hearts
@PickinTomatoes

Make war not dinner. *Pickin' Tomatoes,* June issue, *Cooking and Women.*#No More under-appreciation.

Facebook

The Chef of Hearts – Tasty Therapy

989 Likes • 61 Talking about this • 22 were here

Are you taken for granted? Under appreciated? Retaliate with Torture Enchiladas. Sometimes you just can't fight fair. *Pickin' Tomatoes,* June issue of Cooking and Women.

I giggle at what I type. *I am so bad, and yet so good…*

Dear Chef of Hearts,

My husband has high cholesterol and refuses to
stop eating bacon. Can you e-mail him and tell
him to stop?

What am I, his mother?

Dear Chef of Hearts,

My lover is going back to his wife. Any advice
on how to keep him? Or better yet, hurt him? I
want to….

Feel your pain sister, but not going there.

Dear Chef of Hearts,

Do you have a good lawyer because you're going
to need it. My wife is leaving me. She says
you told her she's a person too. Where do you
get off telling her that? She's not a person,
she's my wife!

Okay, need to report that one to management—potential lawsuit, potential stalker too.

The phone rings and I reach for it. "Maggie Malone…Oh, yes, Mr. Andrews, good to hear from you…Oh, you got in touch with Richard's lawyer. That was quick…What? He's saying I lied about the affair? No, that's not the way it happened…Yes, I realize that…No, I don't want anything, I just want the marriage over…What? He's declaring I was a failure as a wife? I can't believe this."

How could Richard say such things? All those years of taking care of him, his needs, his wants. Did he really think I was a failure as a wife? That hurts. Almost more than the affair and the lies.

"Just push the divorce through…Yes, the records can state uncontested…No, I don't want a meeting with him and his lawyer. That's why I hired you. Just do the paperwork, send it to me and I'll sign it."

I disconnect, slam down the phone, and take a deep breath. I gaze out the living room window towards Dad's hydrangeas. They looked so depressing all winter—gray skeletons of faded beauty—but now, new green is sprouting forth. I guess that's the way of things. Out with the old, in with the new.

I turn back to my computer, which has slipped into sleep mode, and I'm struck by my gray reflection on the screen. I tighten the skin on my cheeks. How did I get to be middle-aged? Am I just a skeleton of faded beauty too? Is that why Richard had an affair with Celeste, because she was perennially young and beautiful? He never seemed to lack compliments to give her about her youth.

"Margaret! Celeste and Adam are here. The reservations are for 8:30!" Richard hollered from the hallway. "Do you think you can be ready some time tonight?"

I grabbed my purse, sprayed a little cologne behind my ears, and took one last gander in the mirror. Black pants and turtleneck for understated elegance. Hair expertly coiffed and makeup, well, it wasn't Christie Brinkley level, but it was the best I could do. I headed towards the bedroom door.

"Don't you look amazing, Celeste," I heard Richard comment as I started down the stairs. "How old are you, all of twenty-one?"

I strolled out just as Richard was clapping Adam on the back. "Adam, you're one lucky man. You must have married a child bride."

"Hey guys, sorry I…" I stared at Celeste's sapphire blue silk wrap dress and stopped mid sentence. The dress clung to her every curve, leaving nothing to the imagination. I turned to Richard and Adam and saw by the way they were ogling her, that it didn't stop them from trying to use their imaginations.

Why oh why didn't I wear a dress? Or better yet, nothing at all. Maybe then I'd get ogled too.

"What a pretty dress. You look great Celeste," I said, trying to give credit where credit was due, though my heart wasn't in it.

"Thanks Maggie," Celeste purred. There was an awkward silence and then Adam chimed in. "And Maggie, wow. You look…wow."

I waited for Richard to agree, but he was busy guiding Celeste out the door. I followed feeling like a third wheel.

No, technically, the fourth wheel. Adam was the third wheel and I was, I guess, the spare.

You know what I need? I need Justy. I need to borrow some of her greenery. She's got a lot sprouting right now. I pick up the phone and dial. "Just? How's it going? Really? You saw the ultrasound today?" I can't help but smile. Maybe I do have some greenery after all.

We're having a boy.

• • •

I pick up my coffee mug, eyes half closed, and take a sip, trying to force the caffeine to my eyelids. *Wake up. Wake up.* I start to think about the schedule for the day: *Take a shower…get dressed,* …and the phone rings. "Hello?"…*do radio interviews…bathe Cat…*

"Hey Maggie, it's Taylor from *Kevin and Taylor,* 104 the Fish in Atlanta. How's it going?"

I choke and spray coffee down the front of me. *Flippin' flapjacks!* What are they doing calling this early? It's not 8:30, it's…my eyes dart to the kitchen clock…it is 8:30. I'm still wearing my Winnie the Pooh jammies, not that they can see me, this is a phone interview, but still, it's the principle. A business suit or my chef whites would be much more appropriate.

"Uh, great. Just great. And you?" I reply, trying to sound normal and professional, all the while mopping up my coffee with one of Cat's binkies—sorry Cat. Good thing she's still asleep. It was a long night with lots of teething angst.

"This isn't too early to be calling you, is it?" Taylor asks.

"No, of course not. Been up hours. Working on a column, trying out new recipes. You know how it is."

"Well, Maggie," Kevin chimes in, "thanks for being on the show today. We're discussing happiness in jobs. Are you happy with your career choice of writing columns and counseling women?"

"Why, yes, Kevin. As a matter of fact, I love what I do. It's not just a job, it's my life." Okay, that sounds like an ad for the Army: It's not just a job, it's an adventure. *Hello, I'm Corporal Maggie Malone, proud to be an American...*

I'm getting punchy. I guzzle more coffee and start to feel a bit nauseous. Maybe all that caffeine needs some food to soak it up, so I reach into the freezer and pull out a breakfast meal.

"Man, that's great. Isn't that what we all want in life? To love what we do? What about you, Taylor? You love what you do?" Kevin inquires.

"Kev, you're bad," Taylor admonishes. "Of course I love what I do. I love being a radio host. Why else would I do it?"

"Lots of people settle for less, especially in today's economy. That's why you've got to stay strong in what you believe. Do you pray, Maggie?"

"I honestly can say I pray every day Kevin, every day. Dear Lord, help me not burn this food."

"Ah, come on. An amazing chef like The Chef of Hearts doesn't burn food, does she?" Taylor asks.

"You'd be surprised, Taylor, you'd be surprised. There are some days when I feel like I don't know how to cook at all."

"Ri-ight. Ha-ha. You obviously don't know the meaning of the words 'I don't know how to cook' like I do. The best I can do is heat up takeout and microwave frozen dinners for my husband. I bet you've never microwaved a frozen meal in your life."

"Ha! You've got me there." I try to rip off the plastic from my blueberry pancake and sausage on a stick without making a sound. Let's see: *Wrap in paper towel and microwave on high for one minute.* "I believe in wholesome, gourmet meals." The microwave dings and I pull out my breakfast on a stick. *Ah...*I dip it into a cup of maple syrup, swirl it around, and plunge it into my mouth, all the while clutching my coffee mug in the other hand and cradling the phone on my shoulder.

"So why don't you give us an example of a wholesome, gourmet meal. For example, what are you eating for breakfast this morning?" Kevin inquires.

"Kaahhkk... " I choke on a bite of my blueberry pancake sausage on a stick.

Is it possible to give yourself a Heimlich maneuver? I throw myself against the counter and all I manage to do is hurl my coffee all over the room and on the ceiling—note to myself: never attempt the Heimlich while drinking coffee—and the phone of course, goes airborne. I swallow repeatedly. Thank heavens the bite finally slides down while I'm skidding across the floor after my phone.

"Hello? Are you still there?" I hear Kevin say.

"Sorry about that, we must have a bad connection. Well, I like to start my day off with…" I grab the empty frozen breakfast box and study the front of it. "…a bowl of blueberries. They're high in antioxidants." *What else? what else? Think Maggie!* I flip the box over and quickly peruse the list of **Ingredients:** *salt, dextrose, leavening, dried egg yolk, artificial flavor…* "And then for protein, I usually have a couple of egg whites scrambled with a little…*soy lecithin.* "Soy lecithin."

"Excuse me?" Taylor says. "What did you say?"

Did I just read aloud soy lecithin? "Soy sausage. I meant to say soy sausage." *Culinary jargon…I need culinary jargon…* "And a few minced chives, diced tomatoes, and a sprinkling of shaved parmesan." *Wow. That sounds good.* Except for the soy sausage and scrambled egg whites. Who eats that fresh, healthy junk? I'd probably prefer soy lecithin, whatever that is. I heartily take another bite of my breakfast on a stick.

"Yum," Taylor replies.

"Okay one last question, Maggie. And this is for The Chef of Hearts," Kevin says. "If you had some advice for all the single women out there who are frustrated in their search for Mister Right, what would it be?"

I wrack my brain for something relevant, something clever, when I remember my "cheat sheets." Good thing I looked up a bunch of quotes from famous people last night and sticky taped them to the wall. "Well, one of my all-time role models, Audrey Hepburn, once said, 'Nothing is impossible; the word itself says I'm possible.' So, single women of America, Mister Right is possible. You can't just give up on looking or cooking. It really is true that one of the best ways to a man's heart is through his stomach."

"Well, you heard her here, America, live on Fish 104.7," Kevin says. "The Chef of Hearts—America's Cooking Therapist. Tune in later and we'll be chatting with a man who talks to God, via his mobile phone."

• • •

"You know, Maggie, I'm not so sure I buy into this whole Chef of Hearts thing. I mean what makes you the authority on relationships?" Bert asks. "And by your own admission, you're divorced. So I guess that means you couldn't find Mister Right. What makes you think you can help other women find Mister Right?"

I turn beet red. Never in a million years did I expect that the Q100 show would give me flack like this. I thought it'd be a no-brainer interview. They called on time, I was appropriately dressed and waiting by the phone. But no-o-o, they have to play hard ball. I glance at my cheat sheets, hoping to find a celebrity quote that'll save me from this debacle. Zip. Nada. Nothing. Nothing that applies to radio hosts being jerks. I flip my finger towards the phone. *There's something that applies.*

"Come on, Bert, don't rag on her. You'll piss off millions of women listeners. They love her advice. And I love her advice too," Jenn says. I decide right then, Jenn's my kind of girl. Now there's a good radio host, not Mr. Jerk over there.

"I'm not ragging on her. I'm just saying, what makes her think she can advise women on dating and relationships? I mean, I know the woman can cook, she's a chef. But does she have a degree in counseling or something?"

Okay. Now you're just being snarky. "Well, Bert, I don't have a degree in counseling. Never said I did. I'm just like everyone else, muddling my way through life the best I can. What's wrong with trying to use the knowledge I gained from making my own mistakes and help thousands of women come up with better choices? Just because I didn't find Mister Right, doesn't mean I can't try to help others on their journey. What about you? You have a degree or anything? What makes you qualified to spout off on unsuspecting guests you invite on the show? Do you have a degree in jerkism?"

There's dead, stagnant, embarrassed silence, and then Jenn begins giggling. Bert gives a snort of laughter. "Now that's what I call the real Chef of Hearts. Not afraid to speak her mind. This is real life on *The Bert Show,* Q100! We'll be back after a commercial break."

• • •

VININGS NEIGHBOR

Local woman goes gourmet with advice in her *Chef of Hearts* column in cooking and women magazine. See page 3 for details.

• • •

ACCESS ATLANTA
Top Entertainment News:
Chef of Hearts, **love guru, cooking up radio waves**

• • •

THE ATLANTA JOURNAL CONSTITUTION
Arts and Entertainment:
The *Chef of Hearts*, Atlanta's own cooking therapist. Appreciate her appetizing counsel, enjoy her entrée therapy, and savor her sweet success. This weekend at Atlanta's Food and Wine Festival

• • •

"This is Suzanne from *Good Morning Atlanta* and we've just been talking to The Chef of Hearts, *Cooking and Women* magazine's own Dr. Phil of phenomenal feasting. Stay tuned for weather and news on your favorite Atlanta News station, WPBD."

Chapter Thirty-Two

"You can't get ice cream out of shit... I don't care how much you stir."
—*Unknown*

The pounding at my door increases in volume and tempo and I cinch my robe tighter around me. What idiot is at the door at nine o'clock on Friday night? Nine o'clock on a rainy night? It's coming down cats and dogs out there. I peek through the spy hole of the front door and jump back. Richard.

A million thoughts and images burst through my consciousness, tangling in their greed to be on the forefront, and I fling open the door. "What do you want, Richard? You have some nerve showing up here!"

"Hello, Marga-rita," he slurs, his dark business suit dripping wet. The stench of alcohol barrels towards me like an eighteen wheeler.

"Are you drunk?"

"Of course I'm drunk, that's why I drank!" Richard laughs at his own ridiculous joke. "Seriously. Margaret, use your head," he says, weaving back and forth. "You know, it occurred to me, you had it good in marriage. Nice clothes. Nice house. But you sure messed it up. Nag, nag, nag. Where was I? When was I coming home? I want a career. I want a life. Blah, blah, blah."

I try to shut the door but he jams his foot in the opening. "It was always about you, you, you. Margaret Malone. Never Margaret Thompson, was it? So I screwed around a teensy bit. What man doesn't? But now, Maggie Waggie wants a divorce. Well, guess what? So. Do. I. But a funny thing happened last week. I was working my eighty, maybe hundred hours— I'm a hard worker, ya know—and I turned on the TV. Guess what I saw?"

I push hard against the door, hoping to force his foot out of the opening but I can't budge it. "Some cooking channel, with this Southern lady, Paula somebody. And who do I see with her? You guessed it! Margaret! So I think, who is this woman? Certainly not the sniveling, pathetic wife I've known for the past seventeen years. Looking pretty good, too, with red hair. And I think, maybe I want some of that. I mean, you're still my wife, right?"

Richard slams his body against the door, but he's weaving so much, he just kind of bounces off the door frame. He rubs his arm like he has a boo-boo and whimpers.

Is this is the same controlling man I married seventeen years ago? A giggle rises like a bubble in my throat. And another one. Until they're bubbling over the edge and I explode with laughter. What a reject. He's not my Mister Right. Never was. How could I have thought he was? A couple of outdoor lights flick on across the street and I realize we're making a scene.

"Good God, Richard, you're pathetic. Come on in while I call you another cab." I open the door and Richard stumbles in.

"Like what you've done with the house, Marrrge," he comments, bumping into the furniture. I push him towards a chair and he collapses into it.

"Stay," I command, hurrying into the kitchen to call a cab. I don't want Richard here any longer than necessary. What if he notices the baby stuff? Or wakes up Cat? I start dialing as fast as I can when I feel hot breath on my ear, and jump. Son of a bacon burger! I put the phone down and turn around. Richard may be drunk but he sure moved fast.

"Richard, why don't you go back to the chair while I call the cab?"

He reaches out a hand and strokes my hair. "Margaret, it can still work. We can still work. I miss you. Come home."

For one lone moment, I feel longing. Longing for that life too. It could work. There were times when it did work. I loved Richard. Maybe, I still do.

"The Chef of Hearts got any advice for her husband, Magpie? Or maybe she'd rather cook up a little something spicy for him," he says, grabbing me and forcing a kiss on me.

I don't know if it was the kiss or the fact Richard used my father's pet name for me that did it, but it was like a cold water reality shower. Anger builds up deep inside of me. *I am so over this. So over Richard. He is not going to control me. I will not be his Margaret ever again.*

Struggling in his embrace is getting me nowhere. I fumble behind me and feel the cold iron of my frying pan. I grasp it, prepared to clock Richard over the head, impervious to the fact that I might kill him. I don't care—in fact I want to kill him. But then he just kind of sags against me, his whole weight collapsing on me, and I fall back against the counter.

Confusion tempers my anger and I put down the frying pan. "Richard?"

"*ZZZ-Zzz-ZZzzz-hckGGuggh-Ppbhwoo…*"

I poke him and nothing. I hit him on the shoulder and nothing. The man has passed out and he's snoring. What am I going to do with him now?

• • •

The mature thing would have been to call a cab. In retrospect, I wish I had. It would have defined Maggie Malone as evolved, But alas, no. I chose a different action that defined me even more. I managed somehow to get my semi-unconscious soon-to-be ex-husband to my car and deposited him in the passenger seat. Then I ran upstairs, got my sleeping daughter, strapped her in the car seat, and we all went for a ride. And that is how we ended up at the Atlanta bus station.

I look around to see if anyone's watching or listening. The only person here is the ticket man, glued to the TV. Richard, Cat, and I shuffle over to the wooden bench. Let me just say, it's almost impossible to lug a baby's car carrier while balancing a drunken man on your shoulder. It requires quite a bit of patience, hard work, and some, uh, choice culinary motivational words.

We make it to the bench where I dump Richard like a sack of potatoes. "Richard?" I poke his shoulder to see his reaction. He begins to snore again and slumps over on his side like a homeless person. Still not convinced Richard is asleep, I take a finger and flick his cheek. He continues to snore and lets rip an extremely loud bodily function.

Yup, definitely out cold. He'd never do that awake. *What to do, what to do…*I mull over the possibilities, then slide my hand inside his jacket, pull out his wallet, and extract a big wad of money.

"Don't you know it's dangerous to have this much cash on you, Richard? You could get mugged." I pocket the money and am about to leave when I have an epiphany. I stare at the nasty linoleum floor. Is that dried vomit? If there is one thing I can praise about Richard, it's his impeccable appearance. Never a hair out of place. Never a wrinkle in his shirt or a spot on his tie. And though he called me a germaphobe, he had it over me in spades in that area. Like the flip-flops in the shower – our shower.

"Richard, why are you wearing flip flops to take a shower?" I asked as I watched my husband stride across the bathroom carpet to the shower. He was buck naked except for a pair of black flip flops.

Richard opened the glass shower door and turned to look at me, one eyebrow raised. "Margaret, the world is full of germs. You never know where one might be hiding."

"But, Richard, seriously, I just scrubbed that shower stall today. There can't be a germ left alive in there."

"Are you prepared to swear to that on the stand?" Richard put his hands on his hips, a Greek god in all his glory, wearing flip flops.

I giggled and saw him frown. He couldn't be serious. I knew we were newly married but really? The giggles continued and Richard stood there glaring at me. That dried up my amusement real fast. I did not want to have our first fight.

"No, counselor, I'm not. Therefore, I conclude it's prudent you wear flip flops in our shower." I sidled up to him, dropping clothing tidbits as I went. "Perhaps I'll invest in a pair of flip flops too."

"Astute conclusion, Mrs. Thompson. Astute conclusion."

I pull off Richard's shoes, yank off his socks, and stuff them deep into the trash. My, aren't we the epitome of sartorial elegance? Let's see how you like those germs, counselor.

Minutes later, Cat and I are back in the car. I am just about to exit the parking lot when I see a homeless elderly woman pushing a shopping cart. I fumble in my pocket, roll down the window an inch, and poke Richard's wad of cash towards her. She approaches the car and grabs the money, her ruddy face crumpling into a cackle.

There. Richard has been taught his lesson and he has also made a contribution to society. Payback is so cathartic.

Chapter Thirty-Three

"Life is half delicious yogurt, half crap, and your job is to keep the plastic spoon in the yogurt."
—*Scott Adams*

```
Dear Chef of Hearts,


My whole life is one big lie. I'm involved
with two men and in love with them both. I
spend my weekdays living with man number one
in his apartment, and then under the guise of
traveling for work, spend the weekends liv-
ing with man number two in his house. How do
I straighten our my messy life and come clean
about the lies? And what if neither man wants
me once I confess?


Living a Lie
Miami, Florida
```

My eyes widen. This letter hits a little too close to home. It's one thing living your own lies and dealing with those consequences. It's a whole 'nother ballgame reading about someone else in a similar situation. And having them ask you for advice. How ironic is that? Maybe this is *my* payback. For all the lies I've told.

I flip closed my computer screen, and plunk my chin upon it, stewing about both her situation and mine. Then, as if my stew is not rich enough, I throw in some more ingredients. Richard. How could I have left him passed out on a bench at the bus station? What kind of a woman am I? He may be a philandering pile of putrefied prunes—I giggle at that thought. *Good one, Maggie.* But seriously, did he deserve that? Okay, maybe he did, but I'm working on that whole evolved image thing. And what about Cat? She deserves to know her father, even if he is spoiled, dried-up fruit. I massage my temples with my fists, caught in limbo land between guilt and desire. I never should have done what I did, but man oh man, I really wanted to. Maybe guilt's meant to be my payback. Mama Beignet always did say guilt was the best punishment.

"Oui, Mama, we are fatigued. We shall go to bed early," Justy said at dinner. She gave a fake yawn to prove her point.

Everybody stopped talking and stared at Justy and me. Papa Beignet raised one of his bushy caterpillar eyebrows. Uh-oh. I knew they wouldn't go for the tired line on a Friday night. I coughed a little. Maybe the sick line? "And, I'm not feeling that well either," I replied, a hand against my forehead. "I have a killer headache." I gave the eye to Justy and she coughed too.

"Oui, Mama, moi aussi."

Bingo. Mama Beignet leaped out of her chair. "Oh, ma petite chou, why did you not tell Mamma Beignet? You shall go to bed right now." She pulled on my arm, trying to lead me away from the table.

"But, but, it's only polite that I stay at the table at least until dessert," I replied, glancing at the chocolate ganache cake that was perched on a pedestal in the middle of the table, like a queen holding court. I had to look away before I started drooling. It looked so good.

"Non, I would not think of it. You are sick, ma Cherie, and need rest. And, Justy, you are sick too. To bed, both of you."

She grabbed Justy by the other arm, led us down the hall, and into Justy's bedroom. After helping us change into our bedclothes and tucking us into the twin beds, she kissed us both on the forehead. "Now you go right to sleep and Mama Beignet will check on you. Bonne nuit," she called out as she closed the door.

Justy and I looked at each other and giggled. We set our alarm clocks and went to sleep. At midnight, we leapt out of bed, tore off our jammies, and put on the hip clothes we had saved up for and purchased in secret—miniskirts, fishnet stockings, high heels. It was party time. Paris here we come.

But the whole night was a failure. When I tried to climb out Justy's window, I slipped and fell right in the rain soaked soil, ripping my stockings and getting muddy sludge all over me. We had to climb back in the window so I could change and as Justy was going through, her heel caught on the windowsill. When she yanked it, it rebounded right into the glass, breaking it into smithereens. We spent the rest of the evening cleaning up the glass and trying to devise a story to explain the broken window. We finally fell asleep in the early morning, with no plausible explanation.

When Mama Beignet woke us at ten, with trays of croissants, hot chocolate, and soothing motherly words, the guilt started eating me alive. And when she suggested we stay in bed to rest, I couldn't take it anymore. Sniffling, I walked over to the window blind, intent on pulling it up to show her the broken window. But when I got there, she wouldn't let me do it. Then when Justy tried to explain what happened, she wouldn't let her. Mama Beignet said she didn't want to know. She said it was enough that we knew what we had done, and guilt would be our punishment and our companion. We had to stay in bed that whole day, without any TV or books. All we had was each other and a broken window for company.

Guilt. Who wants it as a companion? Maybe I should just come clean with Peter, Peg, even Richard. I'll confess—that's what I'll do. It's not like I committed some horrible crime. I just told a few lies. A woman's got to do what a woman's got to do sometimes. Everyone will understand. It's human nature to sympathize. I flip open my computer, feeling less guilty by the minute. I'll start with Peter. I'll invite him over for dinner tomorrow and have a heart to heart. It'll be the perfect opportunity.

A musical clanging begins and I smile. The other day I was cooking and Cat needed entertainment. "Try these, sweetie," I said piling some of my pans around her and handing her a wooden spoon. Since then it seems she can't get enough of playing the pots and pans. I look at my baby sitting in her exersaucer, tapping each pan and experimenting with tones and rhythm and know, just know, she's going to be a famous performer one day. I feel so proud. *Maybe she'll play the violin, join a symphony and…*

The musical clanging segues into a riotous banging and I cringe in horror. What if she joins one of those heavy metal bands? Dyes her hair green, paints her nails black, and wears a silver studded dog collar ? I rush over and attempt to grab the pans and wooden spoon. Cat turns a bright tomato shade, and I look around the room for a new source of entertainment. Something educational, classical, quiet. I'm in a quandary about what to do while Cat looks like the blueberry girl from *Willy Wonka and The Chocolate Factory,* about to explode at any moment.

Motherhood. I guess you need to pick and choose your battles. I hand her back her instruments, resigned to love my heavy kettle performer. Maybe she'll still visit while she's touring the country with her band.

• • •

From: Maggie Malone
To: Peter Rudolph
CC: Peg Winthrop
Subject: Dinner and column

Hi Peter,

I was wondering if you'd like to have dinner
with me.

I can't start the e-mail like that. That'll make him think I'm asking him out. Which I am. But I don't need to advertise it. I need to be truthful but not too truthful. I backspace and begin again.

Hi Peter,

I was wondering if you'd like to have…

Mind altering sex. Now there's a thought. Not the right one, but still. Focus!

```
Hi Peter,


I was going over some logistic reports and
also studying the stock fluctuations…
```

The Chef of Hearts at her best. The Purveyor of Prevarication. My backspace finger is beginning to get a cramp. You'd think I'd have some muscles built up in it by now…

```
Hi Peter,


Would you like to come over for dinner tomor-
row night? We could work on the next column.


Maggie
```

Perfect. Short and sweet. Honest but not too revealing. Let's see what you do with that, Peter. I glue myself to the computer, determined to wait for an answer. Even if it takes hours and hours and I have to deprive myself of food and sleep. Okay, maybe not food. I unwrap and cram a whole candy bar into my mouth. It's important to have small protein snacks throughout the day.

```
From: Peter Rudolph
To: Maggie Malone
CC: Peg Winthrop
Subject: Dinner and column


Hi Maggie,


Great idea, I'd love to. What time?


Peter
```

    Wow. That was prompt. A time…A time…*How about coming over
right now?* This whole truth thing is like a disease.

```
From: Maggie Malone
To: Peter Rudolph
CC: Peg Winthrop
Subject: Dinner and column


What about six o'clock tomorrow?


Maggie

From: Peter Rudolph
To: Maggie Malone
CC: Peg Winthrop
Subject: Dinner and column


Sounds fine, I'll bring some wine. Where do you
live?


Peter
```

    Fine? He wrote it sounds fine? I hate the word fine. Fine means non-
committal. You don't care one way or another. If you did, you'd say it
sounds amazing. Spectacular. Stupendous. Great, he thinks it sounds fine.

```
From: Maggie Malone
To: Peter Rudolph
CC: Peg Winthrop
Subject: Dinner and Column


I live at 4100 Brookview Drive NW 30339. Look
forward to seeing you.

Maggie
```

I'm just about to log off when another e-mail from Peter pops up.

```
From: Peter Rudolph
To: Maggie Malone
CC: Peg Winthrop
Subject: Dinner and column


I'm kicking myself because I slipped up and
used the word fine in the last e-mail. I guess
I just typed it automatically. My ex-wife hat-
ed that word. Are you offended that I used the
word fine?


Peter
```

I giggle. The word fine must be universally offensive to women.

```
From: Maggie Malone
To: Peter Rudolph
CC: Peg Winthrop
Subject: Dinner and Column


Of course not. Fine is a perfectly accept-
able word in the English language if you are
writing a poem and need a word to rhyme with
spine. See you tomorrow night.


Maggie
```

There, done. Now for Richard. I pick up the phone and dial his cell. *Don't be there. Don't be there. Don't be...* "This is Richard. I'm not here at the moment, but leave a message and I'll return your call as soon as possible."

"Richard, this is Maggie, uh, Marga, I mean, Maggie. I just wanted to make sure you're okay. I don't know if you remember but last night you came to my house drunk. And you insisted on going to the bus station. Okay, that's not true. I dropped you off at the bus station and…alright, I'm just babbling now. If you have a moment and feel like calling, call and we'll talk. There are some things we need to say to each other and there's someone you should meet."

I hang up and sag in my chair. Good God, honesty is stressful. Maybe I should warn that "Living a Lie" lady to take a valium before coming clean about her lies.

Now last on my list, Peg. But, do I really want to tackle that problem? I think of all the possible horrible scenarios and realize, hey, I need to take a shower. Plus, some laundry could use folding and Cat needs to wake up too. Procrastination is a wonderful thing. After all, Rome wasn't built in a day, was it? Besides, if Peter is coming over tomorrow, I'll need to go to the grocery store.

Tomorrow's kind of like the final exam for The Chef of Hearts. Can she dice, slice, sauté, broil, bake, tell the truth, and find Mister Right? I start getting one of those riotous feelings in the pit of my stomach. The kind where nerves are battling common sense and logic and the nerves are winning. I've never done well on final exams. I solemnly tape up the June cover of *Cooking and Women,* feeling like I'm going to get a big, fat F tomorrow.

Chapter Thirty-Four

"We're as good as our last meal."
—Chef Ramsay

"Hello? Maggie? You in here?" Peter pokes his head through the back door. "I rang the front doorbell but I guess you didn't hear it."

"Hey, Peter, sorry 'bout that. The bell's been dead for a few months. Come on in, I'm in the kitchen."

"Something smells good." He sniffs the air and drifts over to the stove. "What's for dinner?" he asks, lifting a lid off a pot.

I smack his hand with a wooden spoon. "Hands off, it's a surprise."

He chuckles and reaches for the folded apron lying on the counter. "Do you need me to chop anything? You know my skills as a master chopper." He pulls the apron over his head, tying it in the back, and turning around for my inspection. "What do you think? Is it me?"

I dissolve into giggles. Somehow, an apron with the caption, I'm Still Hot, It Just Comes in Flashes, doesn't really suit him. "You want another apron? I've got more."

"What, you saying I'm not hot?"

I throw my hands in the air. "I'm not saying anything, just trying to be helpful." I reach in a drawer and pull out another apron without looking at the front of it. "You know what would be a really big help? Would you mind taking out this trash?"

"No problem, I need to get the wine from the car anyway. Where's the trash can?"

"Just go out the front door and it's to the left of the driveway. And the bar's to your right when you come back in. I'd kill for a glass of Merlot right now."

"Your wish is my command," he declares, giving me a little bow, and exits the kitchen.

Okay, everything's coming together. I rub my hands and pace, the stress of the evening threatening to overwhelm me. Technically, tonight should go without a hitch. I'll start the evening off with a few of my Right Stuff Mushrooms, progress to a little beef wellington, scalloped potatoes, and conclude with some chocolate heart volcano. Peter will be in such a state of orgasmic culinary throes, he'll be putty in my hands. Then I'll mention in casual conversation that I have a baby. And, by the way, I've never been a chef. And, oh yes, I'm not divorced yet.

What am I thinking? Tonight'll never go off without a hitch. What if I my mushrooms become the wrong stuff mushrooms? Or worse, what if I kill my meal? I think I've retired from being a meal assassin but still, things happen. And why would Peter understand all those lies? I don't know if I would.

I hear Peter rummaging in the bar and the microwave beeps. It's show time. I don my oven mitts like a boxer preparing for a fight in the ring. I can do this, I know I can. The evening will come together and Peter will understand. One of those celebrity quotes from my interview cheat sheets pops into my head. Muhammad Ali used to say, "Float like a butterfly, sting like a bee." Well, that's what I'll do.

I bounce back and forth a bit, punching at the air with my mitts, and open the microwave door. Bring it on, I can take it. A knock at the back door startles me and I jump at least twenty feet in the air, maybe even twenty-five feet. I shut the microwave and open the door. My mouth gapes open so wide I could fit an orange in it. Richard has just entered the boxing ring, his face pale, dark baggy circles beneath his eyes, and he's clutching a bouquet of red roses.

"I got these," he says, stating the obvious. I just stand there in the doorway, mouth still a cavernous hole.

He thrusts the roses at me and a thorn stabs me as I take them. Typical. Are these supposed to be a peace offering? More like a Trojan Horse, I'd say. I wouldn't be surprised if there were spy autobots lurking in those petals. I walk over to the counter, sucking my finger as I go, and toss the roses on it.

"What?" I face Richard with my arms folded and crossed.

"I know you said to call, that we need to talk. But I wanted to apologize in person."

Good Lord, he's apologizing. I can't say anything. It's as if I'm deaf, dumb, and paralyzed. Maggie is being held hostage by Margaret.

"I don't know what happened the other night. I guess I was upset about the divorce papers. I always thought, in the back of my mind, that you'd come home. And when the papers came from my attorney, all rational thought left me. I hopped on a plane and drank all the way to Atlanta. Before I knew it, there I was on your doorstep. Drunk. When I woke up in the bus station, it all came rushing back."

Mushrooms. My mushrooms are ready. I wander over to the microwave, open the door, and retrieve my mushrooms. It's important to serve food when it's warm. "Stuffed mushroom?" I present my dish to him. I've gone into my boxing corner on timeout. If I don't acknowledge what's happening, it'll just go away. La, la, la…

Richard picks up a mushroom with two fingers, sniffs it, and, nibbles at the edge of it as if it might be poison. His face registers surprise and he pops the whole thing, kit and caboodle, into his mouth. "That's actually good, Margaret."

The name Margaret clocks me in the head like a right hook. I emerge from my corner, swinging a punch. "My name's Maggie, Richard. All these years I've been Maggie and yet you persist in calling me Margaret." Anger is building, strengthening my punches.

"I thought you liked the name Marg—"

"No, I never liked it. You did," I retort, removing my appetizer dish from his presence. He doesn't deserve The Right Stuff Mushrooms, slimy fungus that he is.

"Well, regardless, Margaret, excuse me, Maggie, that stuffed mushroom is excellent. Congratulations. I guess you really can cook now."

For a moment I hesitate. A compliment. How do I respond to that?

"It's a shame you never tried to cook when we were together."

What? My mitts go back up. "What do you mean by that? You come in here, under the guise of apologizing, and then you get snarky with me?"

"I'm not getting, what did you call it? Snarky. I was just reflecting on our marriage. But if we're going to get personal here, then why the hell did you leave me in the bus station? Without any shoes. What kind of a woman does that?"

"The real kind, that's who! You were drunk. What was I supposed to do? What do you want, Richard? I don't have time for this. I have company." I yank off my oven mitts and stand, hands on hips.

"You have company?"

"Yes, Richard, I do. I have friends. I have a life. Surprising, isn't it? Call me and we'll talk but you need to go. Now." My anger erupts. "Better yet, don't call, and we won't talk. There's nothing you can say that I would ever want to hear."

Richard narrows his eyes. I know that calculated look. There's the man I was married to. He never lost a fight. With me or in the courtroom. I start to push him towards the back door.

"You know, I think I'd like to meet your company," he announces, shrugging me away. He strides towards the living room.

"Richard, that's none of your business. Just take your flowers an—"

"Maggie, did you say you wanted a glass of Merlot?" Peter calls out from the living room.

"Peter, I'll be there in just a…"

"Hello," Peter says from the doorway.

I look from Peter to Richard and then back to Peter again. This can't be good. A new fighter has just entered the ring.

"Uh, Peter, this is Richard. My soon-to-be ex-husband, who's just leaving," I explain, in a valiant attempt to get to my timeout corner in the ring. "Mushroom?" I thrust the dish in Peter's face, trying to block out Richard.

Peter's eyes grow into huge saucers. "Oh…I didn't realize you were still married. It's, um, nice to meet you, Richard," he responds, ignoring my food offering. Instead, he reaches around me and presents his hand to Richard.

Richard ignores his hand, sizing him up and down and pursing his lips. I plop down my dish, grab Richard's arm, and try to propel him towards the door. "Richard, I'll call you and we can…"

"Margaret, stop it." Richard wrinkles his nose. "What is that smell?"

A strong and familiar odor wafts towards me. I turn my head and see smoke pouring out of the oven. My Chocolate Heart Volcano. I run

over to turn off the oven and the smoke detector blares like a foghorn…
EEEEEEE…

Cat! It'll wake up Cat!

I leap towards the broom closet, intent on whacking the smoke detector so it'll go off. But just as I grab the broom, I hear Cat's cries ring out on the baby monitor, which is hidden behind a vase on the counter. "Wouaaa wouaaa wu wu wouaaaaaaaaaa…"

Both Richard and Peter look stunned, glancing back and forth between the vase from where Cat's cries appear to be coming and me. The cacophony of cries from Cat upstairs and the blasting from the smoke detector is deafening.

"Hello. Am I too late for dinner? It sounds like you might have started without me. Eww…is that dinner I smell?"

The three of us turn in unison towards the back door.

Peg is standing there, wearing a black and white spotted skin tight dress and her signature mile-high stilettos. With her is a man carrying a video camera. My boxing ring has now become a circus ring, complete with cast, crew, and clowns, and The Chef of Hearts, balancing on a high wire.

In a bold, offensive move, I attack and disable the smoke detector with my broom. Cat quiets down and we are left in silence. For a moment.

"Nice apron, Maggie," Peg comments and I look down. I don't even know what apron I'm wearing. I read the caption upside down: Dinner is Ready When the Smoke Detector Goes Off. Of all the aprons to grab, I grab this?

"You know, Maggie, it was so thoughtful of you to invite me to dinner tonight," Peg remarks.

Peter turns towards me, a confused look on his face, and I shrug my shoulders. "I didn't invite her," I mouth.

"These last few days, as I've been reading the drivel e-mails you send Peter—by the way, I really do appreciate you copying me on all of them—I've been getting a nagging feeling that something's not right about your past, Maggie. I took the liberty of hiring a private detective to do a little digging. And sure enough, he hit pay dirt. So I brought along Bob, here, to film a little exposé. Thought we might post it on YouTube. You know, a little publicity for the magazine."

I'm going to vomit. I glance at Richard and he smirks at me.

"Peg, what are you talking about?" Peter asks, shaking his head.

"Oh, that's right Peter," Peg responds, "you don't know, do you?"

Peter throws his hands up in the air. "Am I the only one here who doesn't understand what's going on?"

Peg gestures towards the cameraman and he begins filming.

"I'm Peg Winthrop, an editor with Cooking and Women magazine. We're here today at the home of The Chef of Hearts, America's Ann Landers of Appetite. Tell me, Chef—oh, but I can't really call you that, can I? You've never attended a culinary school, or even worked in a restaurant. Tell me, Maggie Malone, how is single life treating you? Whoops, my mistake again. You're not single, you're married. Lots of lies here to keep track of. Tell me, Maggie Thompson, how's your baby doing? You know, the one you haven't told America about? In fact, maybe America should just call you, 'The Chef of Lies' from now on." She throws back her head and laughs,"Mwua haha."

I sag onto a wooden chair, defeated. There is no beating Cruella de Vil. Peg has lost it. Strike that, I've lost it. The game, the show, the final exam—whatever you want to call it. The Chef of Hearts has failed.

Chapter Thirty-Five

"A bad review is like baking a cake with all the best ingredients and having someone sit on it."
—Danielle Steel

How could I ever have wanted a perfect recipe for life? Cooking with a recipe is not foolproof, nor is doing all the right things in life. Neither one guarantees success. I lean my forehead against the glass of the airplane window, and study the droplets of rain pinging against it.

Raindrops…I read somewhere they are too light to fall from clouds. They first start out as tiny particles that water vapor wraps itself around, then they bump into one another and merge into bigger droplets. Only then, are they heavy enough to fall from a cloud and come to us as rain.

In a way, that's like me. I was just going through life as a baby raindrop when I decided I didn't like my middle-aged housewife cloud anymore. I left my husband, had a baby and before I knew it, I was cloudless. A few lies, columns, recipes…bingo, a new cloud was formed. My raindrop got bigger and bigger, and before I knew it, I was falling.

Damn, that's eloquent. I should include this in one of my columns.

Columns. What columns? I'm not The Chef of Hearts anymore. I was fired. After Peg finished her little speech about me being The Chef of Lies, the situation really heated up. Peter left, speechless, Peg and her cameraman left, not so speechless. And Richard? Well, Richard put two and two together and figured out he had a daughter. He stormed off, threatening to sue for custody. Then early Monday morning, I got an e-mail termination notice from Peter. Impersonal and brief. Due to extenuating circumstances—blah, blah, blah—Cooking and Women has decided to terminate—blah, blah, blah.

I watch a woman across the aisle reading one of those gossip magazines and she looks up at me, does a double take, and flips through the magazine to the front cover. There I am, gracing her trashy magazine in all my glory, in my kitchen, cowering in a chair, looking like a deer in headlights. No matter what I do, I can't seem to escape the publicity, the notoriety of it all. My face is plastered on every single trashy tabloid, the whole fiasco is smeared all over the Web, and tweets are zinging about The Chef of Crock.

Well, at least I can flee to France. People haven't heard about The Chef of Hearts over there. Or if they have, they won't care. I'm just some American. When Justy called last week—right after I was fired—and told me she almost had a miscarriage, I jumped at the chance to go to France. She's done so much for me. The least I can do is help take care of her. I already had a passport for Cat and me because we were going to have her baptism in France. Granted, the visit's a little earlier than I expected, but it's good timing, actually. Mama and Papa Beignet will be there. They've been helping out with Justy's bed rest. And Cat's first birthday is next week. We can have the baptismal ceremony right at the house and a party after. Justy won't have to leave her bed.

The plane begins to accelerate for takeoff and that familiar thread of fear winds itself around my heart. I grasp the seat in front of me, place the other hand protectively on Cat's carrier —she's sleeping soundly, lucky little devil—and think of a way to distract my mind from panic or worse. Can I count zigzags? There's no pattern on the seat cushion in front of me, it's just a tired looking blue fabric. A lump rises in my throat and my mind searches for distraction. A game, a game…the alphabet car game! A…there's an A on that man's ball cap. B… bathroom sign…It's not until I reach R that the word Richard pops into my mind.

Richard. Well, there's a distraction. Yesterday's conversation is definitely food for thought.

"Hello?" I answered, wishing for the umpteenth time I had caller ID. If I weren't so worried about Justy, I'd never answer the phone. But if it was Access Hollywood calling again, I was going to scream. I hated their TV show, I hated them, I hated their mommas. Okay, that was just plain mean…

"Margaret, I mean Maggie?"

Could life get any better? "What Richard?" *There was no way I was go-ing to have small talk with this man. He had nothing to say that was of the slightest interest to me.*

"How's she doing?"

"Excuse me?" *I replied, stalling for time. He had the nerve to ask me about Cat?*

"Catherine. How is she doing?"

"She's fine. She's well. She's good. There, satisfied? Tell your lawyer I am keeping you in the loop about our daughter. Now, goodbye." *I was getting ready to disconnect when he spoke up again.*

"Wait! Maggie, don't be like that. I'm not suing you for custody. I know I said I was but I was angry. I've had some time to think things over and really take a look at my life. I've made some mistakes, you've made mistakes. We've hurt each other. But Maggie…I have a daughter, we have a daughter. Can't you tell me something, anything, about her?

His voice cracked and it threw me for a loop. Startled me actually. Richard never got emotional. He had nerves of steel. Could the man actually be sorry? "Um, well, she's beginning to talk."

"Really?"

The sound of genuine interest peppered his voice and I continued. I could stop at any time. I was just throwing him some bones. "Yeah, it took her for-ever. We couldn't seem to get past ba ba."

"I was the same way. Mother used to say I had a whole language built around different intonations of the word ba-ba. She called it the Ba-Ba lan-guage."

For a moment, it was like I was talking to the Richard I married. The Richard I loved.

I forged ahead, feeling alternately disoriented and buoyed by this new territory of camaraderie. "You want to know what she said a couple of days ago?"

"What?"

"I was in the checkout line at the grocery store and she was talking to her-self. Her word of the week is duck. Duck this, duck that. She points and says duck to everything. So, as I was unloading the cart, she said duck, duck…You know where this is going—she of course said the f word. I was so flabbergasted that I reacted before I could think it through. I immediately said, 'No, Cat, we don't say the f word. That is a bad word.' But, being the stubborn girl she *is—like her father I might add, and Richard laughed at that—she latched onto the word. So now the favorite word of the week, which she must say at least a hundred times a day, is the f word."*

"She doesn't."

"Yup, she does. Ou..." I tripped over the r in our and caught myself just in time. Richard had not earned the right to be part of our. "My baby cusses like a sailor."

"You used to say a few choice cuss words if I remember correctly."

"Well, I'm a mother now. I may utter a few culinary cuss words from time to time but..."

"Culinary cuss words?"

"You know, fudgin', holy Twinkie..."

Richard groaned. "You do not say holy Twinkie. I can't believe a wife of mine says—"

Cold silence stretched across the phone line, effectively amputating any feeling of camaraderie we had.

"I am not your wife anymore," I state, voicing what we were both thinking but hadn't uttered.

"I know. I just forgot for a moment.. Would you mind if I called you again? Maybe to schedule a day I can spend some time with Catherine?"

Richard spending time with Cat? What if he took her away from me? What if... What if nothing. Cat deserved a father, good or bad.

I force myself to reply. "That's fine Richard. We'll be out of town for a couple of weeks but then maybe the three of us can get together. And Richard?"

"Yes?"

"Her name is Cat. I call her Cat."

I look out the window and see that we are flying high in the sky. I begin my alphabet game once more. A...all, B...baby, C...Cat...

What is the real purpose of tears? Moisture? Relief? Pain? I ought to google that to use in a column. I wipe my eyes with the corner of my sleeve.

D...damn....I still wish there were a recipe for success in life.

Chapter Thirty-Six

"Homegrown tomatoes, homegrown tomatoes
What would life be like without homegrown tomatoes?
Only two things that money can't buy
That's true love and home grown tomatoes."
—*Guy Clark*

"How ya doing, Kit Cat?" I call out from the kitchen.

She doesn't answer me because she's mesmerized by the motion of her electric swing. I walk over, squat down beside her, and repeat, "How you doing?"

"Good! Good!" she replies. "Fast! Fast! Fast! Fast!"

I laugh. Everything my daughter says these days is followed by an exclamation mark. At least we made it past the f word, long forgotten in her expanded vocabulary.

Feeling hungry, I walk back into the kitchen, pull out a fresh tomato, and slice it with my paring knife. A little crust of French bread, some olive oil, a few leaves of basil, and it'll be like I never left France. Ho hum…a woman can dream.

There's nothing quite like homegrown tomatoes. Most people in their entire lives will never experience what a real tomato tastes like. Mass produced supermarket tomatoes are nothing like homegrown tomatoes. They've been artificially turned red with ethylene gas and chemically ripened. Yes, they're beautiful—evenly colored, symmetrical, perfect—but their taste never matured, just their color. Those tomatoes are a shadow of their real potential. So way back in the winter, I decided to revive Dad's tradition of having our very own home-grown tomatoes. I bought a small greenhouse with a paraffin heater, courtesy of my prize money from the

Cooking and Women writing competition. And now, I have beautiful, homegrown tomatoes. Orangey yellow, lumpy in shape, but juicy and sweet…Perfection.

I take a bite of a tomato slice, and begin singing aloud to Cat. "Do you know the muffin man, the muffin man, the muffin man. Do you know—" I take another bite of tomato.

"…the muffin man who lives on Drury Lane," a masculine voice chimes in.

"Ack…" I choke on my tomato bite and whirl around. There, in the kitchen doorway, is Peter. The silence is so palpable, I could slice it with my paring knife.

I manage to swallow my bite and clear my voice. "Ahem…Uh, hello." I look down at my feet, not knowing what to say or do. Hmm, I never noticed how big my feet look in fuzzy slippers. Fuzzy white and black spotted slippers with a cow head on each. Embarrassing. The only thing worse is the fact that I am also in my jammies. Cat and I are, at this moment, sporting matching cow jammies. What can I say? Target had a sale and I was sick of my old ones. There's nothing like a little retail therapy.

"Nice cover wall," Peter comments, as if nothing at all has happened the past few weeks.

I raise my head and wince. I meant to take down all those *Cooking and Women* covers.

"You know, you're missing July," he comments, studying the collage.

"Uh, yeah, I know. I was fired, remember? Didn't really want to put up…um, Peter, what are you doing here? You have to admit you've been pretty cold to me this past month."

Now isn't that an understatement? I tried over and over to apologize via e-mails but he wouldn't respond. And then, while I was in France, Justy convinced me to call him. When I say convinced I really mean coerced. The woman is relentless when she gets it in her mind to do something. And she had it in her mind that I needed to call Peter.

"Mon dieu, Maggie. Give the man a call. Maybe he lost your e-mails." She raised her head from her mound of pillows.

I snorted."Get it straight, Just. E-mails don't get lost. They're not like regular mail. Maybe they don't go through, bad internet connection, I don't know. But they don't get lost."

"D'accord. They are not lost. So give the man a call for me and the bebe, petit Jean Paul." She patted her huge, rotund stomach, and I rolled my eyes.

"That is so low. Using you and the baby to coerce me."

Justy gasped, her hand clutching her stomach, and I rushed to her side. Good God, I made her go into premature labor. I dropped to my knees beside her. "Just! Are you okay? Are you in labor?"

"Maggie, please. Hee hee ha, hee hee ha." She grabbed my hand. " I cannot take this. Je vous en prie!"

"Do you want me to call Jean Paul? The hospital? What? Tell me what to do!"

"Non. Hee hee ha, hee hee ha." She shook her head. "The pains are getting better. I am okay. Call Peter. That's what I want."

Good Lord, I was selfish. Here was my best friend, who always came to my rescue. How could I not do what she asked?

And so I called. And called. And called. Pouring my heart out over the answering machine. Leaving detailed messages about my return flight and arrival. Peter didn't pick up on a single phone call, but Justy made me do it over and over again, each time experiencing labor pains. It wasn't until the fourth time, after leaving one more message for Peter and going to the grocery store to get Justy some chilled water—sparkling not fresh—that I caught on to the scam. As I opened the front door, juggling three massive bottles of Perrier, I overheard her talking to Jean Paul.

"Oui, oui, she is getting me Perrier. Non, I will make her call Peter one more time. I think I feel more pains coming. Oui, je t'aime aussi, Jean Paul."

I had been had by my best friend. If we didn't have a baby to deliver, I would have delivered her a piece of my mind.

But a week later, holding little Jean Paul and seeing tears run down my friend's face and her husband's, I realized I didn't care. Life was all about family, even if they messed with you sometimes.

"Um, listen, can we start over?" Peter asked.

I blink and blink again. "I thought you said you were disappointed in me, in all the lies, and there wasn't anything between us after all."

"I know what I said, but maybe I was wrong. People can be wrong, can't they?"

"Of course they can. I should know. I seem to be wrong all the time lately. But, Peter, maybe it's best if we…"

"If we what?" He edges towards me and I back up until I'm pressed against the counter. "If we don't pursue this? That's a possibility. But aren't you always going to wonder what would have happened?" he asks, leaning towards me. "Aren't you curious to see if there is something between us?"

"But you didn't answer any of my phone calls. You didn't even call me back." I poke him in the chest with a finger and back him away from me. Two can play this game. I am so over not having any power in a relationship.

"You're right, I didn't and I'm sorry about that."

He looks so sincere and endearing that I lose all feeling of empowerment and I panic. *What am I doing?* My hand fumbles on the counter and I feel around for something, anything. I grasp it and thrust it between the two of us. "Tomato?"

Peter looks surprised and begins to laugh, a big belly laugh.

I begin to giggle too. I can't help it. But my giggles vanish all too soon and there's that expectant silence again. Prodding me, poking me to take charge. *I can do this. I can do this...* I take a deep breath. "Alright, I'll start. My name's Maggie. Maggie Malone," I lay down the tomato and extend my hand. "I'm forty, almost divorced, a mother, and currently jobless."

Peter grins, shakes my hand, and then pulls me into a hug.

Startled feelings bombard me like little meteors of emotion. Confusion. Guilt. Worry. I stand there, arms at my side. But as I smell his cologne, a combination of soapy clean and citrusy fresh, I ignore all those little meteors, and my arms reach up and wrap around him.

All too soon, he steps away. "Uh, well, actually, I need to bring up that jobless thing. A lot has been happening at *Cooking and Women*. For starters, Peg's been fired. Corporate didn't like how she garnered all that negative publicity. On top of that, The Chef of Hearts has received hundreds and hundreds of e-mails from people, celebrities, you name it, all expressing their support for you. They don't care about your cooking background, your ex or soon-to-be ex-husband, or the fact you have a baby. They want The Chef of Hearts back. The *real* Chef of Hearts. And Corporate is offering you a new contract."

I'm stunned. Amazed. *Cooking and Women* wants *me* back? Maggie Malone? What should I cook next? Maybe I should take cooking lessons in France with Justy's husband Jean Paul. Or maybe I should expand my audience and counsel women, men, and kids. I could write a column called *Cooking and Family.* Ooh, ooh! No! I could start my own cooking show! The Chef of Hearts…

"So what do you say? Will you come back to *Cooking and Women?* We miss you. *Hell,* I miss you," Peter says.

I put my finger to his mouth, and correct him. "Not hell, holy hominy." I gesture at Cat and whisper, "There's a *baby* listening to us. She already knows the f word."

Peter laughs and tugs me back into his embrace. I'm just beginning to enjoy the moment when a thought disturbs my mood. A really important thought. Life threatening actually.

I have *got* to go to the Salon Doctor. My roots are showing.

My hands fumble behind me for my ever present pencil and note pad but Peter swats them away, winding them around his neck.

There are times you shouldn't multitask. Kissing's one of those times.

• • •

COOKING AND FAMILY

Relationship questions?
Kid questions?
The *Chef of Hearts* is back!
Chopping up problems
and serving them up for dinner
Therapy's never tasted so good
p.91

Dear Chef of Hearts,

I am a divorced woman with four teenage boys, and recently my boyfriend has asked me to marry him. He also has children, four teenage girls. Is it a mistake to combine two families? We would have eight children. It'd be like the Brady Bunch! Is it possible for this to work out? How do you know what's the right thing to do?

Carol Brady
Denver, Colorado

Dear Carol Brady,

Erma Bombeck once said, "The family. We were
a strange little band of characters trudging
through life sharing diseases and toothpaste,
coveting one another's desserts, hiding sham-
poo, borrowing money, locking each other out
of our rooms, inflicting pain and kissing to
heal it in the same instant, loving, laughing,
defending, and trying to figure out the common
thread that bound us all together."

To me, that sounds pretty good. What better
way to grow up than with a bunch of siblings?
Life should be about families and figuring out
the common threads that bind us. As far as the
right thing to do—does anyone ever really know
what the right thing is? There are no sure
things in life, no success recipes. Sometimes
you've just got to cook and hope you don't
burn anything.

So my advice to you is seize the moment and
go for it. You'll make it work. And in the
process, have a lot of laughing, loving, and
loads of laundry.

Wise Chili

Serves 8

Ingredients:

Olive oil
1 pound ground chicken or ground turkey
Cooking spray
1 1/2 pounds ground sweet Italian sausage
2 tablespoons corn starch
8 ounces diced red onions
8 ounces diced celery
8 ounces diced peppers
3 garlic cloves, minced
3/4 cup vermouth
2 ears of corn, corn taken off cob
3 (16 ounce) cans of navy beans (reserve the
liquid)
1 can Rotel mild diced tomatoes with lime and
cilantro (reserve the liquid)
36 ounces chicken broth
1 teaspoon smoked paprika
1 teaspoon chipotle chile pepper spice
2 tablespoons cumin
1/4 teaspoon ground Annato Achiote
1 1/2 teaspoons dried oregano
Salt and pepper to taste
A few cilantro sprigs
Tortilla chips
Sour cream
Lime, cut up in quarters

In a large soup pan, sauté chicken or turkey
in olive oil until cooked, drain liquid and
set aside meat. Spray pan with cooking spray
and sauté sausage. Drain fat from sausage,
stir in cornstarch, mixing well and cook a
minute. Add sausage to set aside meat. Drizzle a little olive oil in the pan, add onions

and celery, and cook on low five minutes. Add the peppers and corn, sautéing three minutes, and pour in the vermouth, scraping up the yummy bits of flavor. Return the meat mixture to the pan, add the beans, tomatoes, chicken broth, and spices. Bring to a boil, then simmer for one hour. Season with salt and pepper to taste. Serve with a dollop of sour cream, crunched up tortilla chips, cilantro sprig, and a lime wedge.

Ladies, try making this soup the day before—it tastes even better the next day. Some food, like fine wine and people, is better as it ages.

Here's to large families!
—The Chef of Hearts

Twitter

Chef of Hearts
@PickinTomatoes

Combo family? Supersize your meal with Wise Chili. *Pickin' Tomatoes,* September issue, Cooking and Women.#Life.

Facebook

The Chef of Hearts – Tasty Therapy

2400 Likes • 321 Talking about this • 98 were here

Life is like a bowl of chili, full of flavor
and full of beans. Share some with your family. Read *Pickin' Tomatoes*, September issue of
Cooking and Women.

Recipes

Mr. Right Salsa

Ingredients:

1 (16-ounce) can diced tomatoes with basil and oregano

1/2 bunch cilantro, chopped

1 small Vidalia onion, chopped

1/2 jalapeno pepper, seeded and chopped

2 teaspoons lime juice

Garlic salt, to taste

Combine and serve with chips.

Sweet Dreams Chicken

Serves 4

Ingredients:

8 boneless, skinless chicken thighs

Salt and pepper to taste

2 handfuls of flour

8 slices bacon, cut into pieces

2 tablespoons butter

1 tablespoon olive oil

1 (10-ounce) package precut mushrooms

1 (10-ounce) package precut carrots

1 (10-ounce) package precut onions

2 teaspoons minced garlic

1/4 cup chicken broth

1/4 cup beef broth

2 ounces tomato paste

1 1/2 cups Burgundy wine

1/4 cup Cognac

1 teaspoon thyme

1 teaspoon marjoram

1 teaspoon parsley

Season chicken with salt and pepper, then coat with flour and set aside. Heat frying pan over medium heat. Add bacon and cook until golden brown and crispy. Drain fat and set bacon aside. Melt butter, add chicken, and carefully monitor color. Ladies, you want lovely brown chicken, not black. Cooking is all about the details! Set chicken aside.

Pour the olive oil into the same pan then add mushrooms, carrots, onions, and garlic, cooking until tender. Put everything, including chicken, into a slow cooker. Add remaining ingredients and cook on low heat for six and a half hours.

Adam's Ribs

Preheat oven to 325° F

Serves 4

Ingredients:

2 racks pork baby back ribs

McCormick Grill Mates Barbecue seasoning

1 bottle Sweet Baby Ray's Hickory barbecue sauce

Foil

Rub ribs liberally with Grill Mates, front and back, and let sit on counter while oven is Preheating. Place ribs on one long sheet of foil, turning up the edges of the foil to keep in juices. Add another sheet of foil to top ribs, forming a sealed package. Be careful to roll the edges to seal well, otherwise juices can leak out! Put package on a cookie sheet and place in the oven. Cook for three hours. Let rest for thirty minutes. Remove and discard foil. Using pastry brush, add sauce to ribs. Place ribs on hot grill for fifteen minutes to crisp them up, turning once.

Apple of My Eye Pie

Preheat oven to 425° F

Ingredients:

1/2 cup raisins

3/4 cup bourbon

6 to 7 cups or 9 medium cooking apples

3/4 cup sugar

2 tablespoons all purpose flour

1 teaspoon cinnamon

1/8 teaspoon salt

1/8 teaspoon nutmeg

1/8 teaspoon allspice

1/2 cup caramel sauce

2 tablespoons unsalted butter, cut up in pieces

2 (9-inch) refrigerated pie crusts

2 teaspoons apricot preserves melted

1 tablespoon buttermilk

cinnamon sugar to sprinkle

Combine raisins with bourbon in a medium sized bowl and soak overnight. The next day, set out refrigerated pie dough for twenty to thirty
minutes to soften. Peel apples and cut into half-inch slices. Ladies—you
can cook these apples over a double boiler but why make more work for
yourself? Cook them in a microwave in a dish for five to ten minutes or

until tender. That's why we have a microwave. So use it!

Combine 3/4 cup sugar with flour, cinnamon, salt, nutmeg, and allspice. Drain raisins, reserving 1/2 cup of bourbon, and add to flour mixture. Pour caramel sauce and reserved bourbon into mixture, add apples and stir. Fit one refrigerator piecrust into 9 inch pie pan. Brush preserves over crust, spoon apple mixture onto crust and dot pieces of butter on top. Here's the fun part. Roll out remaining pie crust and using tip of knife, cut out decorative shapes. Thanksgiving is coming up, so be creative and cut out festive leaves for the holiday!

Arrange dough shapes over apple mixture, and brush them with buttermilk. Sprinkle with some cinnamon sugar. Bake at 425? F on middle rack of oven for ten to fifteen minutes or until brown. Shield edges of pie with foil. Bake at 350? F for thirty minutes or until bubbly . Serve warm with vanilla ice cream.

The Right Stuff Mushrooms

Preheat oven to 400° F

Serves 8-10

Ingredients:

28 extra large, cleaned white mushrooms

1/2 cup Italian bread crumbs

1/2 cup already cooked breakfast sausage, chopped (follow instructions on package)

2 green onions, minced (white and green parts)

2 garlic cloves, minced

1/2 cup grated Parmesan cheese

8 ounces mozzarella shredded cheese

1 tablespoon olive oil

4 tablespoons minced parsley

1 teaspoon Italian seasoning

Salt and pepper to taste

Cut off stems of mushrooms, carving out cavity in mushroom top. Put tops in microwavable dish, cover loosely and heat on high for three to four minutes. Turn mushroom caps upside down to drain on paper towel and set aside Mince remaining mushroom parts and put in bowl. Add garlic. Microwave on high for three minutes, draining well when finished. Mix in remaining ingredients with minced mushroom pieces. Ladies—you can use Italian sausage. Just remove it from its casing and cook it. But if you want to save time, use already cooked breakfast sausage. Tasty and easy!

Combine well. Add filling to mushroom tops. Place on cookie sheet. Drizzle olive oil over mushrooms and sprinkle mozzarella cheese over each of them. Bake until cheese is melted, about five minutes.

Filet and Hearts

Serves 2

Ingredients:

1 can of artichoke hearts in water

2 filet mignons

1/2 tablespoon butter

1/2 tablespoon olive oil

1/4 cup Madeira or dry white wine

1/4 cup beef stock

1 package prepared Béarnaise Sauce

Prepare Béarnaise according to package. Drain artichoke hearts. Add hearts to Béarnaise sauce. Set aside. Put butter and olive oil into skillet and heat on medium high. Add steaks, sautéing three to four minutes per side until desired temperature. Remove steaks and wrap in foil to keep warm. Add Madeira and beef stock to pan, stirring well to scrape up the bits of flavor. Simmer for a few minutes. Place steaks on plate, spoon wine sauce over them. Top with artichoke and Béarnaise Sauce.

Fish and Crab in Harmony

Preheat oven to 400° F.

Serves 4

Ingredients:

2 pounds Orange Roughy fillets

1/2 teaspoon lemon juice, plus 1 lemon

1/4 teaspoon Chesapeake Bay Seasoning

1 (8-ounce) lump crab meat (ready to eat)

1/2 cup Duke's mayonnaise

1 tablespoon fresh chopped dill

1/2 cup panko bread crumbs

1/2 cup shredded Swiss cheese

Salt and pepper

Spray casserole dish with cooking spray. Set aside. Squeeze juice of one lemon over fish, top and bottom. Season both sides of fish lightly with salt and pepper. Combine crab meat, mayonnaise, dill, Old Bay, and 1/2 teaspoon lemon juice in small bowl. Using knife, spread crab mixture over top of fish. Roll up fish (with crab inside) and set, seam down, in casserole dish. The dish should fit snugly around the fish. Bake for twenty minutes.

True to You Shrimp Kabobs

Serves 4

Ingredients:

1/3 cup honey

1 teaspoon grated fresh ginger

4 teaspoons fresh lime juice

1/8 teaspoon Old Bay seasoning plus extra for shrimp

1/2 teaspoon hot sauce

4 bamboo skewers

8 slices bacon

16 medium peeled and deveined shrimp

2/3 cup teriyaki sauce

Combine honey, ginger, lime juice, 1/8 teaspoon Old Bay, and hot sauce. Divide into two separate bowls and let sit at room temperature for thirty minutes. Soak bamboo skewers in water to prevent burning while grilling. Microwave bacon four minutes and cut each slice into half. Season shrimp liberally with Old Bay and wrap bacon around shrimp. Brush shrimp and bacon skewers with teriyaki mixture from one bowl, discarding any remaining sauce from bowl. Grill shrimp three to four minutes or until no longer pink. Serve with extra sauce for dipping.

Love Hurts Thai Beef Salad

Serves 4–5

Ingredients:

3 tablespoons minced garlic

2 teaspoons red pepper flakes

1/3 cup fresh lime juice

1 tablespoon water

1/3 cup soy sauce

1/4 cup teriyaki sauce

1/4 cup olive oil-extra virgin

2 tablespoons brown sugar

2 tablespoons ginger puree

1 cup bean sprouts

4 cups salad mix

1/2 cup shredded carrots

1/2 cup basil leaves, torn

1/2 cup mint, torn

1/2 cup cilantro leaves

1 flat iron steak (flank steak)

Olive oil

Grill Mates

Combine garlic, pepper flakes, lime juice, water, soy sauce, teriyaki sauce, olive oil, brown sugar, and ginger in bowl. Mix well. Let sit for at least an hour. Combine sprouts, salad mix, carrots, basil, mint and cilantro and spread on platter. Drizzle olive oil and liberally apply Grill Mates to meat and let sit thirty minutes on counter. Grill meat five minutes on one side and four minutes on the other or until desired doneness. Lightly cover with foil and let sit for ten minutes. Cut against the grain into strips. Arrange meat over salad mixture and pour dressing over top. Serve immediately.

Torture Enchiladas

Preheat oven to 350° F.

Serves 6-8

Ingredients:

1 rotisserie chicken

1 can sliced black olives

1 clove garlic, minced

1 bunch green onions, sliced

2 (8-ounce) packages Mexican shredded cheese

2 (14-ounce) cans enchilada sauce, hot or mild

1 teaspoon cumin

1 package taco seasoning mix

1 teaspoon cocoa powder, mixed in 1 teaspoon cold water

1 package large flour tortillas

Debone and chop up chicken, put into large bowl. Drain black olives, add to chicken. Add garlic, green onions, and one bag of cheese. Mix well. In a pan over medium heat, cook enchilada sauce, cumin, and taco mix until simmering. Add cocoa mixture, stirring well. Remove from heat. Add half of the sauce to the chicken mixture, stirring to combine.

Heat frying pan to medium and cook tortillas one minute per side. Do not use cooking spray! A dry, hot pan is imperative for good tortillas, ladies! Fill each tortilla with chicken mixture, roll, and place in greased casserole pan while the next tortilla is cooking. Do this until all tortillas are used. Pour remaining sauce over the rolled tortillas, sprinkle remaining bag of cheese over top. Cook for thirty-five minutes or until sauce is bubbly. Eat while husband or boyfriend is watching. *Bon appétit*!

Wise Chili

Serves 8

Ingredients:

Olive oil

1 pound ground chicken or ground turkey

Cooking spray

1 1/2 pounds ground sweet Italian sausage

2 tablespoons corn starch

8 ounces diced red onions

8 ounces diced celery

8 ounces diced peppers

3 garlic cloves, minced

3/4 cup vermouth

2 ears of corn, corn taken off cob

3 (16-ounce) cans of navy beans (reserve the liquid)

1 can Rotel mild diced tomatoes with lime and cilantro (reserve the liquid)

3/4 cup vermouth

36 ounces chicken broth

1 teaspoon smoked paprika

1 teaspoon chipotle chile pepper spice

2 tablespoons cumin

1/4 teaspoon ground Annato Achiote

1 1/2 teaspoons dried oregano

Salt and pepper to taste

A few cilantro sprigs

Tortilla chips

Sour cream

Lime, cut up in quarters

In a large soup pan, sauté chicken or turkey in olive oil until cooked, drain liquid and set aside meat. Spray pan with cooking spray and sauté sausage. Drain fat from sausage, stir in cornstarch, mixing well and cook a minute. Add sausage to set aside meat. Drizzle a little olive oil in the pan, add onions and celery, and cook on low five minutes. Add the peppers and corn, sautéing three minutes, and pour in the vermouth, scraping up the yummy bits of flavor. Return the meat mixture to the pan, add the beans, tomatoes, chicken broth, and spices. Bring to a boil, then simmer for one hour. Season with salt and pepper to taste. Serve with a dollop of sour cream, crunched up tortilla chips, cilantro sprig, and a lime wedge.

Ladies, try making this soup the day before—it tastes even better the next day. Some food, like fine wine and people, is better as it ages.

About the Author

J. W. Bull lives in Atlanta, Georgia with her husband and two sons. She has worked as a sous chef for Lavande Restaurant, and is currently a private violin teacher and a member of The Georgia Symphony. Her next book, MUSICAL CHAIRS, is a mystery involving Maggie's cousin, Molly Malone—plucky part-time symphony player and fulltime Irish fiddler.